ESCAPE TO

Falmouth

LENA JOY ROSE

Publisher: Minna Press

www.minnapress.com

Cover illustration and layout by Aeron Cargill.

ISBN: 0982963009
ISBN-13: 9780982963005

To my mother, Hermine Rose

PROLOGUE

The Cherokee Nation, North Georgia, 1738

"Our bird soars no more. The wings are clipped forever... forever more," moaned old Paco, dragging out the words in halting Cherokee. He emerged from his vision in a swirl of smoke. The acrid smelling *kanikanik* leaves smoldered in his pipe, permeating the air. His eyes, holding unfathomable secrets, refocused on the silent breech cloth clad warriors. They sat cross-legged, their heads shaved clean and shiny except for the narrow ponytail dangling down their backs.

The warriors' olive skins, taut over prominent cheekbones, glowed from sunlight filtering through the hut's tiny window. Even though they had a new shaman, out of respect they still listened to Paco's ramblings. After a while, the men rose to their feet, giving each other sidelong glances, convinced the shaman had finally lost his mind.

"We have better things to do than to listen to this *u-lv-no-ti-s-gi* . . . old man," said Flying Heart setting his lips in a grim, flat line.

"Crazy old man," Grey Beard repeated in rapid Cherokee. "We wasted our time. We wanted to know when the rains would come or when the Creeks would attack." He curled his lips in a sneer, and reached for his tomahawk and bow and arrows. Nodding for the others to follow, they filed out of the hut.

Bracing on his walking stick, old Paco struggled to his feet on wobbly legs. The vision had sapped his strength. He knew down to his gut such a revelation should not be dismissed lightly. He must convince them. His people must be warned.

"Opah . . . Grey Beard . . . White Clouds . . . wait!" his thin voice sounded plaintive even to his own ears. He hobbled from the hut after the warriors. "Listen . . . the golden lion raised his head, the ugliest head you want to see from over there, over there," he wielded his stick vaguely in the direction of the Smoky Mountains. None of them even bothered to glance back at him.

By this time, a crowd of curious onlookers gathered shaking their heads sadly at poor old Paco. Unable to follow the Braves, he fell to his knees in the dirt between the huts. "The golden lion, he came out of the mountains, I tell you . . . and the white men made him their God!" He babbled to no one in particular.

He drew two swift breaths, raised his head and looked a young lad dead in the eye. "Thousands followed him. Hundreds rode on its mighty golden back. They marched into our village and drove us . . . into the wilderness, like beasts," Paco said, his voice drifting and falling like a feather. He made one last ditch effort to stand. But his knees buckled and he crumpled to the ground.

"They are leaving a trail of flowers, beautiful white flowers . . . all the way across the mountains." His voice trailed into nothingness. With his last shuddering breath he remembered to tell them about the eagle, but it was too late.

A whippoorwill sang its nocturnal tune and dusk settled on the village. Way off in the distance, faint, ominous beats of African talking drums echoed through the mountains beating out rhythmic, mysterious messages.

"My friends, circumstances render it impossible that you can flourish in the midst of a civilized community. You have but one remedy within your reach, and that is to remove to the West."
- President Andrew Jackson

CHAPTER 1

Cherokee Nation, 1838

At first Awanessa felt a silent, watchful presence. She opened her eyes and saw the *Anitsasgili* crouched in the darkened corner of her sleeping area. She rose from the narrow cot to rest on her elbows, craning her neck for a better look. The eerie form lurked in the shadows, his face a blur. She knew him.

Awanessa bolted to a sitting position.

"Etu?" she asked the *Anitsasgili*, her breath rushing out on a high squeak. Shards of light streamed through the window of her log cabin creeping over the washstand, across the spinning loom to dance in the corner. Before her eyes, the *Anitsasgili* inched back and drifted into the thick logs of her cabin's wall.

Awanessa stared at the now brightly lit corner, shaking her head. She swung her feet over the side of the bed, toes curling into the straw floor mat. The sooty smell from the cabin's fireplace lingered in the morning air. She sat clutching an indigo-dyed shawl across her shoulders, kneading the frayed threads to her chest, soothing the ache of losing her brother.

According to Cherokee legend, her brother's soul will not leave this earth until the next of kin avenge his death. Her father was dead. She had no other sibling. And poor Gentle Dove, her mother, was out of the question.

Small keening sounds escaped Awanessa's lips, obliterating the faint din of villagers going about morning chores. Dread roiled in the pit of her stomach. It was up to her to avenge Etu's death, but a big problem loomed. It was against Cherokee law to seek blood revenge.

Thoughts of Etu's restless soul kept her fingers twirling the fringes on her shawl. One fuzzy thread loosened and absently she pulled. Her mind stretched back to the day her tribesmen brought in her brother's battered body on a litter.

She had swallowed the lump growing in her throat. The cabin had instantly become a flurry of activity with villagers swarming around to help.

"Catch her—catch her," someone had shouted just in time as Gentle Dove fainted at the sight of her son.

All through the long night Etu's family and the clan prayed, wept and sent offerings to the Great Spirit for Etu's recovery.

"Don't go, Etu—please, just hold on," Awanessa whispered in his ear, holding his limp hand, infusing her own warmth into his. He turned his head and milked-over eyes fixated on her face. Haltingly he spilled out his story and last wishes in Cherokee, but only Awanessa could hear his words.

Despite all their best efforts, at daylight he had whispered one word, *aduyastodi?* She pumped his limp hand and whispered back, "yes, I promise." His hand fell to his side and he passed into the spirit world.

Awanessa made a final pull on the loose thread puckering the garment around its diameter and looked down at her shawl in dismay. In case her mother should walk in, she decided to stuff it in the bottom drawer of her chifforobe.

Tears streamed down her face. Etu had teased mercilessly about finding her another husband. He would choose the most unlikely man in the tribe, Silent Oahnu or Smiling Moon who couldn't even lace his moccasins.

More sunlight burst through the window of Awanessa's cabin. It dawned on her: Etu had returned to remind her of the promise she made to him at his bedside.

She wouldn't tell anyone about his *Anitsasgili* visiting her this morning. This was between her and Etu. She would be branded as loony as her ancestor who had false visions.

Earlier last night, before Etu appeared in the corner of her room, she walked a path with him. It wasn't a dream; it was more like a vision.

"Where are you taking me Etu?" she had asked.

"Just follow me," he said, looking impatient. All the time he stayed a step ahead, pointing down the path and repeating directions.

Awanessa felt resolved, fated almost, in what she had to do. Before he died, Etu had managed to give descriptions of the men who murdered him. They had wanted him to show them where gold was located in the Smoky Mountains. When he refused, they had beaten him and left him for dead.

She sprang to her feet pacing the worn-out puncheon floor, her eyes searching for items she could stash for the vengeance trip. She had no clue, but following instinct or guidance from the Great Spirit, she started to collect what she needed.

For a few minutes she rummaged through an old trunk. A fetid smell rushed up her nostrils and nestled deep. It was a medicine pouch stashed with steeped juniper leaves and a mess of unrecognizable medicinal barks. She tore rags from the petticoat of an old dress and set them aside.

Was it a good thing to do what Etu wanted or ignore it? She asked these questions over and over in her head, glad no one could see her mumbling, like Enola, the oldest woman in the village. But again, Etu's face floated in front of her and the doubt disappeared. She had to do it.

Even though hardly anyone in her clan used bows and arrows these days she didn't have much choice, she did not know how to use a rifle. She checked her bows and quivers, giving a quick tap on the leather-bound flask to make sure it was filled to the brim with water. Later she would wrap a piece of Gentle Dove's chestnut loaf bread in tobacco leaves along with some dried persimmons. She hid the bag under her bed. She would wait until it was time.

* * *

The full moon receded behind the clouds and the Smoky Mountains merged as one with the sky. A screech owl hooted in the thin morning air. Howling dogs in the distance added a solemn note. Crickets chirped incessantly and the fading light of the fireflies flickered on and off in a weak attempt to outshine the new day. Like a nocturnal animal at prey, Jeremiah

Browne skulked in the forest. He felt safe for now, shrouded beneath a canopy of trees.

Unknown creatures skittered through the underbrush out of his path. An inhuman shriek followed flapping wings, high up in the trees, while the forest buzzed and hissed around him. But he felt safe with the wild creatures of the night, until he heard those god-awful howls.

High-pitched howls merged into one shrill sound hanging in the air like the long discordant note Massa George's wife always played on her pianoforte after supper. Fear stroked Jeremiah's breast and he broke into another run, skidding on layers of damp oak leaves in his path. Fleetingly, he wished this relentless chase would end now. But he'd come too far; he couldn't give up. Not now. Not ever.

Those hounds stuck to his trail, like "white on cotton," as Massa George's slaves would mutter whenever a runaway returned to the plantation with a body part or two missing. The thought fired Jeremiah's blood pushing him on. He could hear the hounds getting louder but still off in the distance.

He barreled his way through the forest, parting tangled vines while skeletal trees swayed in on him. Before he could duck his head, a talon-like branch dipped and clawed his cheek. His breath swooshed through cracked lips, in a dry spurt, like sawdust flying from his woodshop. He tasted blood tinged with briny sweat.

From a distance, howling echoed through the mountains bouncing off tree trunks. He didn't even know if he was going in the right direction. He forgot to check the North Star hours ago when he first heard the bloodhounds. One minute they sounded close, the next minute an echo. He could see them circling, pawing the air and jumping him like they did his father.

His heart thudded erratic as he skirted tree stumps and boulders. Drawing on his last bit of strength, he lengthened his strides, hoping to outrun them or at least throw them off.

A log loomed in his path and he tumbled headfirst into a shallow ravine of water and gravel. Sprawled flat on his belly, he scooped water with his hands and drank. He submerged his gashed cheek, instinctively closing his eyes. For a brief, blessed moment all was silent. If only he could stay like this for a while longer.

No. He could not set foot on Massa George's plantation again or on any other, he thought. Sniffing free air like this was no good; he wanted to take deep gulps. He must find a way.

As if looking for guidance, he glanced up into the luminescent moon sneaking behind the clouds. The North Star had disappeared. It was an omen, his time had run out.

He shuddered. His mind said 'move' but his body quivered with the idea of resting for a few more minutes. He must keep moving or else he'd be crows' meat by daybreak.

He slithered on his belly, like a snake, through dew-covered grass until he reached the thicket. Once he felt sheltered, he stood and listened. Somewhere an owl hooted again the ominous signal to keep going.

He caught the unmistakable sounds of thundering feet crashing through the thicket mixing with excited yelps.

Daring to glance behind into the deep shadows, he at once realized his mistake in stopping at the ravine. The trackers and bloodhounds had picked up his trail.

His legs flew beneath him.

He ran until his body slowed of its own volition. Not even the relentless barking, now louder than ever, could make him run any faster. He zigzagged around trees that jumped out in front, daring him to pass. Thorns and sharp stones jabbed through the sole of his worn-out brogans, shooting shards of pain to his ankles. Still, his body lumbered forward. By some undivine conspiracy, the woods opened up into a wide clearing.

The chilly morning air slapped his face. His eyes darted left and right like the rabbit he and Massa George's son, Devlin, had cornered when they were young boys.

Jeremiah glanced behind him again only to see the hounds, led by men brandishing rifles over their heads, charging through the thicket. He had nowhere to hide.

All he could do now was to make one last-ditch run across the open field. But his body refused to comply.

"Sic em Puck, sic em Bo," the trackers yelled, their voices high-pitched with excitement.

They came at him, wielding their rifles in the air, like vultures circling their carcass.

Jeremiah's heart flipped and plummeted when the dogs' hot breath fanned his heels.

"Hell!" he exclaimed, lashing out with his foot.

"That's where you going boy."

Jeremiah blocked out the maniacal laughter from the men and mustered one last spurt of energy to get away, but the abandoned army stockade loomed in his path.

With a sick feeling in his stomach, he knew his time had run out. The trackers would let the dogs take him down first before they finish him. Like a flash of lightning, his father's tortured features streaked across his mind and he knew this was also his end.

He wished he had a stick to beat the hounds off but he kicked and fought instead, stalling their advances for a split second.

The dog dropped its jaw, baring fang-like teeth and drooled yellowish skeins of saliva.

Jeremiah balanced on his left leg, while two others yapped like mongrels at his flying right foot.

When they finally caught his leg, their sharp canine teeth gored and yanked the flesh. Another dog held the tattered remains of his pants between its teeth and sat back on its haunches as if waiting for a command.

"Josh, come on over here, we got him," one of the men shouted to the other lagging behind.

Pain anchored Jeremiah's leg to the ground. He tried to run again but couldn't. The need to survive hummed through his body.

His attackers pounced.

The blows came quick, hard and loud. Jeremiah snarled and fought with every bit of strength left in his body.

Blood spewed from his mouth, his nose and trickled down his chest. He staggered; his fists flailed in the air but didn't connect.

A rifle butt crashed in the back of his head, the thundering roared to a crescendo, sending white streaks across his eyes. Without even a groan, his body fell and thrashed the ground.

"There ain't nothin' sweeter to beat than a cuffee or injun, huh Phil?" Josh said on a panting breath, looking over his shoulder, proud of his conquest.

Jeremiah's fingers groped the dirt and fisted on a nearby tuft of grass, his back slightly arched.

"Been trackin' you for days now, boy." Jeremiah's brain registered the words but couldn't figure out who said them.

"Son-of-a-bitch can sure run. Reckon he'll make us some pretty shiners though when we deliver him to—."

Whoosh, whoosh, the sound of arrows sailed into the melee and gurgled cries erupted from both men and dogs.

"Injun attack!" They shouted as they rushed away.

Silence.

Jeremiah's back straightened and flattened on the ground. He tried to turn his head but couldn't. He tried to at least force his eyes open but they were swollen shut.

He thought he died so he stiffened his bleeding, battered body into a rigor-mortis-like state.

The deathly silence stretched on. After an eternity, small, gentle hands held his head while his body dragged along the ground. All the time, a soft ethereal voice whispered as if through a wispy cloud, *mitakuye oyasin, mitakuye oyasin*—just like a lullaby, he thought.

Yes, he decided, he had to be on his way to heaven. He felt sorry for the poor angel God gave this job. His bloody mess of a body must be staining her white gown. She staggered so with his weight.

He fleetingly remembered a painting of heaven, and angels with huge white wings he saw in Massa George's study.

Why the hell didn't this angel just fly, instead of dragging him through the dirt?

Irritated with his less than ceremonious entrance into heaven, he let go and his mind fell into blackness.

* * *

Awanessa looked down at the unconscious runaway, his head lolled over her aching arm. She rested for a minute. What was she going to do with this huge brute of a man? Fie on her impulses to rescue everything needing help. She had no choice; he was the spoils from her victory. And now she was saddled with him.

She had to get him to safety fast or he'd probably die out here in the clearing. She had wounded the two trackers and they escaped into the woods with their dogs. The third man must have run off before the others. She had no doubt about their identity. Her brother Etu had described them before he died.

They had hunted down and killed Etu because he had refused to lead them to the rumored gold in the mountains. The other two men, even though wounded, had escaped. But they may come back. She decided not to take any chances. It made sense to leave this place in a hurry.

Strands of clouds undulated across an indigo sky. Birds squawked in the thicket as if being roused from their fitful sleep. She laid the runaway under a scaly-barked, maple tree and examined the extent of his injuries. She rinsed his wounds with water from her flask.

Awanessa was still a little bit awed by the vision. It commanded her here, directing her to bring along the medicine pouch stashed with steeped juniper leaves and other medicinal barks. It was providence she had thrown in a half flask of whisky, once belonging to her father.

The runaway winced when she dribbled the whiskey into his open wounds. They didn't have time to do real damage, she thought. She cradled the man's head and looked up into the morning sky. Crows circled overhead, their wings gliding smooth and silent.

Saving a runaway slave was not the right thing to do. Unlike some of the other tribes, her people were law-abiding. Many of the richer Cherokees even had slaves working their plantations. They turned in runaways, not aid them. Squashing her misgivings she told herself, she had to follow her vision. The thought eased her conscience.

She lowered his head to the grass and fashioned a tourniquet from the rags she carried in her satchel. She should not tarry, she thought. She had done what she set out to do, avenge her brother's murder. But the runaway, outnumbered, had fought like a magnificent warrior. With reluctance she realized she did not have it in her heart to leave him for the vultures.

Sorrow mixed with impotent rage swelled her chest. It wasn't only because of the runaway's plight but the turmoil of her people weighed heavy on her heart.

Removal they called it—like her people were offending warts. Tears stung her eyes. She hunched her shoulders. No one had the right to force her people from their lands and send them away to parts unknown.

The quick flight of a dozen grosbeaks from their perches followed by rustling in the underbrush made her pause. Without looking up, she sensed a difference in the air. A sudden silence.

Her spine stiffened. The hair underneath her fat braid rose from the nape of her neck down to the small of her back. She felt a presence.

They were back too soon.

Shifting onto her haunches, she turned inch-by-inch on her moccasin-clad feet, all the while her nimble fingers kept busy.

Swoosh! She sent an arrow flying in the direction of the thicket. She was about to send another one when a tall figure strode into the clearing.

"Oh, *Osiyo,* Rides-With-Wind," Awanessa said in relief, greeting her tribesman. She peered behind him to see if others followed. "I could have killed you."

"So I see," he said, nodding his turbaned head.

Even though many of the younger people spoke English nowadays, Rides-With-Wind refused to speak anything but Cherokee. He approached wearing buckskin breeches, the color of parched Carolina dirt, cracked in places yet smooth in some. He sauntered up to her, his butternut-colored, long-sleeved calico shirt billowing in the early morning breeze.

"What do we have here?" He stooped with hands on his bended knees.

"Well, as you can see, it's a man, she pointed to the runaway breathing rhythmically on the ground. "They hunted and beat him down with more mercy given to a four-legged, *ganatlai.*"

"No need to ask who did this to him," he said, raising one eyebrow. He barely glanced at the runaway and his gaze swept over her face silently asking the question.

She avoided his eyes and ripped the hem of her chemise to fashion another tourniquet. All the rags she had brought were already soaked with the runaway's blood.

"Two slave catchers they—," she pointed with her chin in the direction of where the men escaped. "They hunted him down just like—."

"Why are you out here at this ungodly hour at this place?" He cut her off in a demanding, rough voice. He rose and grabbed her shoulders, turning her around to face him. "Why are you protecting him?" He glanced down at the runaway with distaste.

She jutted her chin out in defiance and faced him. "This," she said, pointing to the wounded man, "is for Etu." Those same bastards killed my brother for gold and now vengeance is done. Etu came to me in a vision, telling me to do this." She splayed her hands out as if she had no choice in the matter.

He continued to stare at her slack-jawed.

"I couldn't very well leave him for the vultures to devour now, could I?" Her voice rose in defiance.

"Yes you could. What are you doing interfering with things that don't concern you?"

"I'm tired of all your questions—why this? Why that?" Awanessa strode back to the runaway, tossing the other man an irritated glance over her shoulder. He was more concerned with her rescuing the runaway than her motives.

Rides-With-Wind stroked his chin, his mouth turned down at the corners. He tried again. "You know many moons ago our people abolished the ancient law of blood revenge. Killing those men who took Etu's life is against our laws."

"Fie on laws!"

"Not to mention the plantation owner who hired these men to hunt down this wretch," Rides-With-Wind continued in a morose tone.

"But who would avenge my brother?" She turned away from the runaway's body and stalked closer to Rides-With-Wind, "and have his restless spirit roam this earth forever?" Her voice rose and trailed off.

"One of our clansmen would have done it."

"You don't even make sense. If blood revenge is outlawed then who would do it?"

"Then why did you do it?

She fixed him a hard stare, "I had to."

She turned her back and knelt to clean the man's wounds. She decided to ignore Rides-With-Wind for now. She breathed in deep and muttered under her breath, "*mitakuye oyasin . . . vengeance is done, vengeance is done.*"

Rides-With-Wind strode away to the clearing and stood still. "Did you know you killed one of them?"

A jolt of shock rushed through her body. "But—"

He wiped his face with his hand and cupped his chin, a baffled expression on his face. He inspected her arrows and looked back at the dead man.

"Those arrows are mismatched you know? They're not yours." He shouted over his shoulders. What he said didn't make any sense. In a daze she focused on her charge. She had inflicted wounds on two of the three men. How could she have killed the other one? All of a sudden she felt dizzy. She had only meant to wound, not kill.

Rides-With-Wind ambled back to her side, rubbing his hands together as if washing his hands of the situation. He sighed, looking up to the mountain peak, deep in thought. Then he spoke.

"Our entire nation is living in fear right now; no one is thinking about anything else, so you may get away with it—especially if this is our own little secret." He gave her a sidelong glance.

She didn't have to wonder at his meaning. He had been trailing her since the last Green Corn Dance, asking her to marry him at every turn. She hoped she didn't have to do it in order to keep him quiet about her breaking the law.

"Well, the deed is done. Tell me though, how did you know to come here, and at this time?"

"Etu sent me," she repeated, folding her arms tight across her chests. She knew he didn't understand. Most of her people wouldn't understand either. They had adapted so much of the United States' lifestyle—their clothing, religion and even patterned their government after the United States constitution. The Cherokees were losing the old ways and didn't mind. But her grandfather had instilled those ways in her, to believe in her visions. Believe in honor. Believe in their traditions.

Awanessa stood and drifted a few yards, gazing at the mountain peak. The heavy mist lifted a layer of its blue veil and rose to meet the new sun. "Etu's soul will now cross over to the other side," she murmured into the passing breeze.

Rides-With-Wind stroked his chin. "So, you had a vision? Our elders will not like this." He set his mouth in disapproval and stooped for a closer look at the runaway, noting his coffee-toned skin, noble features, strong capable hands and his warrior's body. A scowl flashed across Rides-With-Wind's face as if what he saw hit a discordant note deep inside.

CHAPTER 2

By late morning they arrived in the Cherokee village, the runaway draped across Rides-With-Wind's sway-backed mule. Barely conscious, the runaway clutched the bridle to stay on. Awanessa thought of the difficult time she had convincing Rides-With-Wind to help her with the unfortunate man but he had grudgingly relented.

The sun rose high in the sky. Already the children's faces shone with sweat. Their innocent laughter rippled through the air while they played. Women beat rugs on the side of their small log cabins giving curious looks at the approaching group. Others, oblivious, sauntered down to the stream, chatting and hugging loads of laundry close to their hips.

Several men ran to help when the little party arrived. The men froze in mid-strides; they looked down at the cargo with incredulous expressions.

Awanessa's heart thudded inside her chest. Maybe she should have listened to Rides-With-Winds when he argued her people would be angry for bringing the runaway in their midst. How naïve she was not to listen. She might now be putting him in worse danger.

She spread her palms up in an unconscious gesture. Three of the men planted their feet apart; arms folded in front of their chests and glowered. She let her hands drop to her sides.

She peeked at Rides-With-Winds—no help there. His face smirked with a "told-you-so" expression.

A crowd gathered around. Farmers leaned on their hoes; women hoisted toddlers on their hips. At first glance, they didn't look much different from the white settlers in the valley. Up close, the Cherokee men wore turbans and the women had long braids. Most wore serviceable, calico dresses and shirts dyed in different hues. Unlike the settlers, Cherokees mostly wore moccasins.

The runaway groaned in pain, breaking the silence. The sound galvanized Awanessa to turn and look at her peoples' stern faces. The thought flew in her head to appeal to their familial instincts first. She rubbed her hands together: "You know how close I was to Etu. *Du-yu-godv?*" She glanced at them for confirmation and continued. "Before he died he told me what happened to him." Her eyes filled with tears. "Last night I had a vision. I saw him." Some of them involuntarily stepped back, superstition embedded in their bones.

"He directed me to the clearing where I would find the men who had slain him." She rushed on while she was ahead. "I—I got rid of them—drove them off. They had beaten this runaway almost to death and I had to save him."

One of the elders stepped forward, shaking his head. "You are a willful girl." He pursed his lips in disapproval, his eyes hard. "This is how you avenge

Etu's murder?" His lips curled and he glanced at the runaway.

"Enola," he bellowed to the crouched form of an old woman who limped forward when she heard her name. "Get your salves and attend to this runaway." He turned to Awanessa. "As soon as he's recovered we'll return him to his master and the Council will collect the reward. You're fortunate they are all away in Washington now. Take him to her cabin," he ordered the men. "Someone will have to stand guard outside your cabin and you cannot stay inside there with him." He stalked off, holding his hands behind his back.

Awanessa felt duly chastised.

Her best friend, Tyanita, petite and lithe, ran toward her. Awanessa's mother, Gentle Dove, followed close behind. They grabbed her arms, eyes full of concern. "Are you hurt?" Gentle Dove asked.

"No ... but he is." She pointed to the man lying still on the litter the men had brought for him. The crowd scattered, mumbling amongst themselves, shooting wary glances at the runaway. Two burly men brushed her aside and took command. The runaway's head lolled at an odd angle. His arms dangled and dragged the ground while they carried him down the tree-lined path to her cabin.

"Where do you want us to put this brute?" asked Rides-With-Wind, a sullen expression on his face. "Don't you think Old Enola could help him better than you?"

Without acknowledging Rides-With-Wind, Awanessa pointed to Etu's old bedroll next to the hearth. Gentle Dove unfurled it over the worn puncheon floor. "Lay him gently now," Awanessa said.

Awanessa turned to the two men. They looked from the man on the bedroll and back to her with wide questioning eyes. But they didn't say anything. She thanked them and they backed out, their faces expressionless.

In the meantime, Gentle Dove rallied the women to fetch gourds of water. Old Enola shuffled in. Her stooped posture made her look up at everyone with raised eyebrows. She paused in mid-stride when she saw the runaway lying on the pallet. She set to work cleansing the man's wounds, her lips clamped in disapproval.

Awanessa expertly applied a poultice over areas of the man's body—the strong smell of sage and comfrey mixed with other herbs burned her nostrils. Her eyes watered.

She helped the women clean-up and returned to the runaway's side. One by one they left. She sat for awhile wondering about the consequences of her impulsive actions. Unease swept through her. She had to get him away but for now she was so tired.

She dozed and woke to find the cabin empty except for the two men out front, guarding at the stoop. She felt eyes on her and turned to see the runaway studying her through coin-slit eyes.

"Where's–this?" he said, trying to raise his body and grimacing with the effort.

Awanessa leaned over and pressed his head back on the pillow. "You're safe," she said. He closed his puffy eyelids in a long blink, and opened them again.

"What's your name?" she asked. He stared at her face, unblinking, until she thought he wasn't going to reply.

His lips moved. "Jeremiah," he said low but clear.

His eyes were the color of midnight. And when they glittered at their depths she thought of a starry night. They glittered on, probing hers for a long minute, speaking without words, compelling her to say, "Awanessa."

A glimmer of a smile tugged at one corner of his lips and disappeared. His eyes closed, his entire body relaxed.

She watched him for a few seconds and edged away from the pallet to leave. He sensed her withdrawal. Without opening his eyes, his fingers splayed out and latched on to hers the way he had held on tight to the tuft of grass when she found him. "Don't go," he said in a whisper.

She leaned against the wall and stretched her legs out. He breathed in a steady rhythm but still held on to her fingers. She slowly extricated them, stood, and quietly left the cabin.

Outside, the men glanced at each other in surprise when she passed. Apparently they thought she had already left with the other women. She didn't meet anyone on the way to her mother's except for children playing a game of *Anejodi,* stick ball.

Late in the evening she awoke in Gentle Dove's roomy cabin. Tyanita and Enola were talking low to Gentle Dove.

"You're awake, finally," Tyanita said.

"That's what happens when you leave your bed early to pick up strays." Old Enola said. Her face looked as if she had swallowed some of her own concoctions. She had gone to Awanessa's cabin to check on the runaway again as he slept. "It's not nearly as bad as it looks. The worst were those dog bites on his leg."

"He's going to be in a lot of pain though," Awanessa said trying to hide her concern.

"Give him some of this to drink, if he starts to cough up blood." Old Enola shoved a tin can filled with syrupy liquid across the table. She shuffled to the door. As an afterthought, she said over her shoulder, "if he doesn't go mad in a week, he'll be alright."

"Mad?" the other three women cried in unison.

"Yes, remember when the coyote bit Dakota's boy while he hunted? Nothing I could do for him—poor lad went mad and took his own life." Enola cast a knowing glance toward Awanessa and closed the door behind her.

"I'd better go with you Awanessa when you go back there," said Gentle Dove. She wrung her hands as if squeezing water from her turban. "He's not one of us; we don't know anything about him and what if he goes mad on you?"

"I agree," said Tyanita. Her eyes fixated on the spinning loom in the corner as if seeing it for the first time.

"Fine. Do it then, if it makes you feel better."

Tyanita's face broke out into a relieved smile. Her voice turned cheerful. "Send Little Salali to get me if you need any help." She walked back to Awanessa's side and bent to brush a light kiss on her cheek. "Don't forget now."

"Go, go." Awanessa waved her on. "See you tomorrow."

Awanessa's stomach rumbled with hunger. It would be odd to sleep in Gentle Dove's cabin again. She had lived alone since Tallulah, her husband, died of the fever so many moons ago. She felt not one twinge of regret. He was a cold, mean-spirited man. She had always resented the elders for suggesting the marriage. She never had any love for him.

She thought of Jeremiah's massive frame lying on her cabin floor. She had no doubt he was a runaway slave. He wasn't free like some of her Negro friends in the valley. His back had old scars as if he had a severe beating in the past. Even his neck had an old welt— from the sides to the back. She wondered if he had escaped a hanging. Regardless, he must be the finest specimen of his race she thought.

She leaned back on to the wall. Killing one of the trackers, even though they were all evil, still didn't feel right with her. It didn't matter those were the same men who beat Etu to death. She knew in her heart the Council would not be happy with her actions when they returned from Washington.

She didn't trust Rides-With-Wind. She knew he wanted her but she had no feeling for him. Nothing mattered to her but the heart of a person. So many times he had been in Council for one thing or another. The latest was blackmailing another clansman. She wondered if he was on his way to alert Jeremiah's master.

Three days later, Jeremiah was on the mend. Someone always guarded him so he would not be alone with Awanessa. Around twilight she decided to take him a little supper of cured ham and corn cakes. Before she could leave her mother's cabin, Tyanita rushed back through the doorway. She stopped a few feet away, her breathing short and rapid. Her lips trembled.

"What is it?" Alarm spread through Awanessa's body and she turned to greet her friend.

Tyanita's hand covered her mouth, holding back the words. "The Council—the delegation—" she choked. Taking a deep breath she started again, tears welling in her huge brown eyes.

"Sit, sit down and tell me," Awanessa pulled out a stool. "What happened with the delegation?" Already she knew it was not good news.

"They returned from the hearing in Washington. It's final."

Awanessa clenched her teeth and looked beyond Tyanita's shoulder. The words she didn't want to hear rippled through her mind, coming through ribbons of fog.

"They failed. It's only a matter of time—."

CHAPTER 3

After Tyanita left, Awanessa rushed back to her own cabin with dread and anticipation. In the furor sweeping through the village, the guards had left their posts outside her cabin door.

Thank goodness Jeremiah was much better now, but he had to leave the village immediately. She knew just the right place to hide him.

Jeremiah had been up and about for most of the day tilling her vegetable garden, and caring for her livestock. His silhouette loomed large in the shadows, taller than the hutch where she stored her clay pots and pans. "Awanessa?" he whispered.

"It's me! You must go now." She grabbed food supplies, a pan for cooking and a blanket, stuffing them all down in a deep satchel. He moved quickly, not asking any questions and she led him out into the cool night air.

* * *

Two days later and the villagers went about their normal activities. The pretense unnerved Awanessa. The look on everyone's faces had changed. Their eyes shone like doe hearing the first round of a rifle, not knowing from which direction it came, or when the sound would go off again. She too pretended everything was the same as she performed her daily routine.

She worried how Jeremiah fared by himself in her hiding place and if the food had lasted. The next afternoon she stole off to visit him. The hiding place was not far from the village. She had discovered it by accident a few months ago when she fell from picking herbs on the ridge. After tumbling into a bed of vines, her feet had dangled into nothingness. Jumping down to investigate she had found a cavernous hole. It was big enough for two people to stand and walk around in. She doubted whether anyone else knew it existed. It wasn't a cave, as it had two entrances, but it was the safest hiding place for Jeremiah.

The vines parted when she stepped gingerly through, and she carefully covered up the entrance. The village was so close, she could still hear people bustling about. Her eyes slowly adjusted to the dim cavern and she made out his silhouette. He was stretched out in the far corner, daylight flickering on his face from the other opening at the opposite end.

"Are you well?" she asked. She approached him and removed the satchel of food from her shoulder.

A slight smile tugged at the corner of his mouth. The swelling was gone from his face, revealing chiseled features.

"Doing just fine. Glad you came, was just waiting for the dark to light out." Jeremiah rose from the pallet to his elbow. Awanessa handed him a bowl of hominy and scanned his face for any signs of madness. He smelled like the sweetgrass and sage soap she gave him to wash with in the nearby secluded pond. The wounds on his body were healing. She looked into his black almond shaped eyes and smiled. Even though he had a twinkle in them he did not smile.

"I think you need to spend a few more days here to get better for your journey."

"Weren't for you," he said with a sigh, "wouldn't be alive today—but can't stay much longer." He searched her face. "Why'd you do it?"

"It's a long story, here, take this," she said, and sat down next to him. They never really had a chance to have a conversation.

He spooned down several mouthfuls of hominy before he shoved away the bowl. Placing both hands under the back of his head, he laid on the pallet, indicating he had nothing but time. With legs tucked beneath her, she gave a shortened version of how their paths crossed. He pursed his lips, a soft whistle escaped. "Some dream. You gifted with the sight?"

She chuckled. "No, no. I had a clear vision of my brother, Etu, who told me where to go."

He whistled again under his breath, his eyes wide. "You get them overly much—these visions?"

"This was my first powerful one. But I know one when I get one."

"Lucky for me too," he said. His eyes roamed his hideaway like a cornered rabbit. "Can't stay here much longer you know—can't let them find me." He flexed his leg and winced.

She pushed him back. "Rest easy—you can't leave until you're much better. Promise me you won't leave yet."

He didn't answer, but peered through the vines at the villagers running back and forth. "Looks like something's a cooking out there."

"Tomorrow night is the Eagle Dance. Our people are worried and need some cheering," she said, her voice strained.

"How come? Everyone looks kind of peaceful and happy to me. This place is like heaven."

"Oh, it would seem so to you," she said, a little unnerved. "My entire tribe is being forced to move far away from our homeland." Her eyes pooled with tears.

Jeremiah turned to her and clasped her small hand, entwining their fingers. His easy familiarity sent little pulses of shock up her arm followed by a feeling of warm honey, spreading throughout her body.

Oblivious to her reaction, his brows furrowed. "Actually," he said. "Last month, some gentry folk came into my woodshop to buy furniture from Massa George, talking about finding gold in these here Smoky Mountains and these being 'prime passels of land Americans need'..."

The setting sun had now spread an orange-colored hue through the dense leaves on to the ground. She relaxed even more while he continued to talk, listening to the easy cadence of his voice. So, he wasn't a regular slave; he was a skilled furniture maker. She wondered at the kinship she felt with this man. Maybe it was her keen protective instincts for the downtrodden.

Awanessa shook her head. "We're supposed to move way out West to a land we know nothing about—Oklahoma." She clung to his fingers, relishing their bulk against hers.

"But heaps of other Indians—Creeks, Chickasaws, and some Cherokees in other villages down in Georgia been moving out there for a while now, so, why not just go?"

"They didn't move; they were forced. We're not going anywhere" she said, a mutinous expression on her face.

"Know how you feel." He said, giving her hand a gentle pat. "Too many though—y'all can't fight them."

"I worry about our future."

"Can't do anything about the future . . . or the past." He reached back and parted the wall of vines to peer at two unsuspecting children playing behind the corn crib. "All we have is now."

"Tell me about it . . . tell me about what happened to you Jeremiah," she gave an urgent tug at his hand. She would do anything to rid her thoughts of the impending disaster facing her people.

Jeremiah stroked the back of her hand. "First of all, Jeremiah is the white man's name they gave me. Naming me after the prophet in the Bible is funny."

"How so?"

"Well, from reading the—"

"You can read?" she interrupted, surprise broke over her face. "No wonder you sound so—"

He threw his head back and laughed with exhilaration. "Yeah, read better than most white men. No one knows, but that's another story. How about you speaking English so good and proper yourself?"

"They sent me away for years to the Baptist Mission School in Valley Town." She tapped the back of his hand, "but I wasn't talking about me. I'm curious about why you think the name Jeremiah is funny?"

He rubbed the raised scar on the back of his neck. "Cause, I reckon God chose Jeremiah to be a prophet and he didn't have any say-so in being one. In the same way, I didn't have a say-so either when my given name was taken away."

So, your birth name is?

"Husani."

The silence stretched on for a couple seconds while she absorbed the palpable emotion laced behind the name. "Husani—it's such a beautiful name," she whispered. "Does it have a meaning?"

"Yes, it means . . ." he inspected his other hand and his face took on the countenance of a blush, "handsome." His lips parted into a rare, brilliant smile.

"Oh," she said, clutching the base of her throat. "It's so perfect!"

"But that's gone now; I can never be Husani again." He sighed, his smile fading as quick as it came.

"Yes you can," she said in a quiet tone, not seeing how he could, but believing it all the same. It was her turn to part the vines and stare out on to the land she loved so much, taking in the meandering secluded path interspersed with magnolias and hemlock trees. The white magnolia blossoms, not yet in full bloom, peeked out from the dense, green leaves reminding her of white doves.

She wanted to rest her head on his shoulder but didn't. His presence mixed with the fragrance of sage, sweetgrass and the new magnolia blossoms felt intoxicating.

Wondering how this could be happening to her, she met his eyes and found his gaze tender and filled with longing. She knew he felt exactly as she did.

For a long minute they stared at each other, their hearts speaking with no words. At last, he raised her chin and his head came down. They shared a gentle, comforting kiss. His hands tightened their grasp and his right hand came up stroking her hair, smoothing it down her back. Her heart pounded, warmth suffused her body. She clung to him. The kiss deepened and his body tensed. He extricated himself from their embrace. He rubbed the back of his neck and turned away, avoiding her eyes.

Awanessa felt bereft. But when he faced her again the moment was lost. She turned away to hide her confusion and peeked through the vined wall. She sprang back in alarm: two white men approached the Council house.

* * *

Awanessa left Jeremiah in a hurry telling him to lie low while she investigated. She stayed close to the bushes, eavesdropping on their conversation.

"Let us go, you hear me Injun?" the barrel-chested white man protested. He shrugged off the Cherokee who escorted them. "I'm getting paid some pretty shiners to find that there runaway you're hiding, you hear?"

"I tell you, there's no runaway." The Cherokee said, pushing the two men further down the path toward the Council House.

The men's faces looked rough and rugged. One of them short and squat, the other rail thin and gaunt. They looked familiar—like the men who had escaped when she found Jeremiah. Awanessa's heart lurched. She swallowed hard and edged closer behind the huckleberry bush and heard enough to confirm her fears but the men disappeared from Awanessa's sight.

Rides-With-Wind cast a furtive glance from side-to-side and darted after the men. "Two-timing fox," she muttered in anger.

After waiting for an interminable length of time, finally two Cherokee men escorted the white men from the village. The villagers thought Jeremiah had escaped the village so they were no help to the white men. She felt relieved. Her chest felt heavy; she had to warn Jeremiah. But she had to stay away for now. She could not arouse suspicion.

Late in the evening, after all the chores were finished, the drums started to beat a rhythmic sound. The men's boisterous shouts echoed throughout the village. Dancers entered the circle in single file singing and chanting.

Awanessa cast a veiled glance in the direction of Jeremiah's hiding place. She had to find the right time to warn him about the trackers searching for him.

Red, blue and multi-colored costumes swirled around in frenzy. Each dancer wore an eagle mask. The leader of the dance swooped like an eagle with huge feathers of the Golden Eagle. Whenever the wings swooped downward barely an inch from the floor, the spectators applauded. The dancing went on until late in the night. Women passed around plates piled with wild turkey, corn cakes, and yams.

Awanessa wondered if her people would ever dance again. They were trying to hold onto their ways despite the looming threat of unrest. Her body sagged, her face pensive in thought.

Just thinking about Jeremiah right now made her feel a longing which she found inexplicable. She couldn't understand why she felt so safe and comforted in his arms. Logic told her it was an illusion. For how could a runaway slave offer comfort when it was impossible for him to secure the same for himself?

Awanessa hugged the fringed shawl around her shoulders, seeking comfort. Her simple calico skirt swirled around her legs as she stood and wandered amongst the trees. The shouts and singing followed her down the path. Even the festivities were an illusion. The future was so uncertain, she sighed. She sat on the fat stump of a felled oak tree—her favorite spot.

She decided to reign in her thoughts and have faith they'll remain on their land. After all, if it weren't for their Chief Janaluski coming to the aid of President Andrew Jackson in the war, Jackson wouldn't be alive today. She had felt certain Andrew Jackson would remember the good deed done by her people and let them remain in their homeland. But Jackson retired from the presidency, and this new man, Van Buren was just as blind to the Cherokee plight.

A shadow in the dark came upon her with stark white eyes. The strong scent of sage and sweetgrass soap gave away Jeremiah's presence. He hulked down beside her on the stump, not saying a word.

"What are you doing out here?"

"It's dark; everyone's busy. I'm careful."

They listened for a while to the singing.

"Your people are amazing," he said. "In a way they are much like mine."

Awanessa stiffened. She didn't see how he could make such an observation, but she kept silent.

He took her silence as objection to his comment and went on to explain. "Your people don't know what the future holds, but you still go on and enjoy your merry-making. My people sing and beat the drums too—with the customs they brought from the Mother country. Sure helps to lift the weight off our shoulders and easier to face the next day."

"I see," muttered Awanessa. She didn't like the comparisons.

The whoops of the warriors filled the night air. Jeremiah talked in dulcet tones. "The Cherokees near Athens when they came on to the plantation, they talked of their Eagle Dance but it was close to winter, how come they're doing it now—in April?"

Awanessa tilted her head to peer through the darkness into his face. Everyday his intelligence and his keen sense of observation surprised her. "The Eagle Dance is a special dance for our people. We have all kinds of dance and there is a reason for each one."

When Jeremiah remained quiet, she continued in a musing tone. "My favorite though is the green corn dance." She smiled in reflection.

"For what . . . more corn?"

"No," she laughed. "It's a way for all the clans throughout the valley to get together with their families. I get to see people who I haven't seen in a long time."

"So—you just eat and drink and dance?"

"Oh, it's much more. It's so beautiful. When we get together for the green corn dance, we douse all the fires in the village." Her voice turned wistful and carefree the more she talked. "It's pitch dark, then Etu and his friends would try to scare me and Tyanita to death." I'd be so relieved when our medicine man, Black Hawk, would start a new fire from which all the clans' fires are rekindled. Then Black Hawk would sacrifice seven ears of corn, one for each clan in the sacred fire."

"For blessings?" He prodded.

"Well, it's sort of a purification ritual for our clans and then we give gifts and the feasting begins." Her voice returned to its normal tone. She bit her lip and grew quiet.

"So, the Eagle Dance then . . ." Jeremiah prompted.

She closed her eyes as if saying a quick prayer. "It's for victory," she muttered in a tight voice . . . "and for peace, It's our wish."

"Wondering when will this end—huh?"

"Yes . . . oh yes," she whispered.

"Ah girl," he said. She could make out his head moving from side to side. "Just do the best you can today. Don't you go worrying about what's gonna happen."

Her hand inched across the space between them and snaked down his elbow, nestling in his palm. He closed his fist. As if in one accord, they walked silently back to his hideaway. The villagers had continued singing after the dancers filed out. The plaintive sounds of a flute wafted down the path behind them.

Awanessa couldn't put her finger on it, but the night held a certain urgency. She inhaled deep gusts of air and leaned into Jeremiah, resting her head on his shoulder.

They parted the vines from his hideaway. As if in a trance they glided inside. She floated. He tilted her chin and gazed into her eyes. Without a word, their lips met, and they clung to each other. Alarm bells went off in her head but she could no more control herself than she could control the moon shining outside.

He whispered her name; she didn't answer. She did not know when or how he removed their clothing. He eased down behind her on the cushy bed of leaves he had made for himself. He stretched out his big frame. She could feel the heat emanating from his bare skin.

He snuggled up to her spoon style and she felt the hard angles of his body. Her heart almost jumped through her chest much like when she slid off a ridge trying to reach the dandelions in the wild fields, her feet dangling over the thorny thistles.

"Nessa," he whispered on a long drawn-out breath.

She groaned a response and inched closer to his solid bulk. He remained still for a moment and his fingers unthreaded the long braid down the middle of her back, playing the harpsichord along the length of her spine. He plucked with one finger, then two, up and down, round and round, setting a rhythm, causing her nerves to hum in anticipation. When he thought her well tuned, he turned her over to face him, placing feather-like kisses on her eyelids, the tip of her nose and traced the cupid's bow of her lips. With each touch her body spasmed. He soothed her with tender strokes of his hands, his thick, rough palms in stark contrast with her fine smooth skin. He parted her now loose flowing hair and pressed a warm kiss at the base of her throat. She sighed. He groaned. She felt weightless, his lips traveling along the arc of her neck. And when his tongue licked her earlobe, she felt her body leaving the ground, gliding through the air. His hands cupped her breasts and she swooped and glided higher. She met his lips.

As the kiss deepened, bees swarmed and resumed their humming throughout every nerve of her body. She searched; he found. He searched; she found and when they discovered the nectar, their bodies became one in the age old mating game, timeless as earth. Like eagles, they soared through the wide open sky, cavorting, circling, and flying in unison over the ocean with its ebb and flow, up, higher and higher until they reached the misty mountain peak.

As they descended into the valley, he held her to his chest and she felt the constant rhythm of his heart as they drifted into sleep.

She did not know how long she slept but slowly woke to an empty feeling. "Jeremiah . . . where are you?" Awanessa jumped up with a start—something was amiss. Her hand groped and patted the empty space beside her. He was gone.

CHAPTER 4

Jeremiah knew he was on dangerous ground again. He moved at a stealthy pace. He feared walking alongside the road; he must stay hidden. Thank Massa George's God or the Cherokee's Great Spirit, for the darkness. No chance of detection right now. But he had to find a safe haven before daylight.

After he saw those white men in the village, he knew they had come for him. His mind focused on only one thing. Survival. He could not face his mixed up feelings and distract himself anymore from his purpose.

He heard the distinct sounds of wild animals all around him, but felt safer with them than with people.

For some reason, he could not locate the North Star. Maybe because he didn't stay still long enough.

The more distance he placed between himself and people, the better off he felt. After trudging on for hours, the night sky bled into dawn. If he sat down to rest he knew he would fall asleep and be done for. So he kept moving forward. When he couldn't go any further, he climbed an embankment so he could sleep undetected.

Jeremiah approached the embankment, which to his relief opened into a small cave. He crawled inside, and thus hidden, his mind relaxed. He tried to block the images giving him no peace, but allowed memories of the Cherokee children's laughter when they played stickball. He allowed one other memory, of Awanessa's soft voice. And the haunting sound of the flute. He allowed only those memories to wash over him as he drifted into sleep.

* * *

"Tyanita, slow down," begged Awanessa.

"Oh, Awanessa, he's despicable!" Tyanita looked at her friend's puzzled expression. "That white soldier boy, Devlin," she explained, spitting on the ground. "How I detest him."

Awanessa chuckled, which she hadn't done in days. "Is he still after you, trying to kiss you?"

Tyanita wiped her mouth several times with the back of her hand. "This time he succeeded. He has a lot of gumption to think I'd have anything to do with him after what his kind is doing to my people."

"What's he doing here anyway?" asked Awanessa, glancing over her shoulder. She looked up the path. The lanky, blue-eyed stranger leaning against a tree stared right back at her. He worked his bottom lip as if pondering a problem. He had the audacity to tip his fingers to his forehead in a mock salute. He had been ensconced in the village for days now with the Council. Awanessa did not pay much attention. But she recalled this Devlin spent a lot of time chasing after Tyanita.

"Claims he's trying to show our elders there is no hope. We must leave our home peacefully right now."

"Seems he's doing more kissing than talking," said Awanessa with a sidelong glance.

Tyanita wrinkled her nose and sniffed the air with disdain. "I have to go and help my mother with the laundry," she said, stalking off with her head held high. Awanessa watched Devlin's eyes follow Tyanita to the stream.

Awanessa walked back to her cabin at a slow pace. A subdued air hung over the little village. Some of the women talked low amongst themselves while they focused on their basket weaving or pottery making. Even the children clinked their marbles with a soft touch. Most of the men were out in the fields tilling their crops. She smiled without mirth. Her people acted as if they were going to be here to harvest those crops later in the year.

Her mind flitted to Jeremiah. The full impact of his leaving stayed with her for a long time. It was simple, she reasoned, he didn't want her. Yet she wondered, where did he go? Even though anger rose in her chest when she thought of him, she didn't want him to be recaptured. Her uneasiness intensified at her own fate, the fate of her people.

She spotted Gentle Dove bent over a mortar. Awanessa sat next to her mother and added more corn to the mortar. They sat in companionable silence for most of the morning, adding corn and pounding it to a fine dust.

Awanessa didn't want to voice her fears. Afraid if she did, the wind would multiply their worries. Maybe going about their simple day-to-day activities will bring peace, at least in their minds, she thought.

* * *

Jeremiah awoke to a tight pain in his head. His lips felt stiff and dry, his tongue stuck to the roof of his mouth. He rose to his elbows, his stomach rumbled with hunger. He must have slept the sleep of the dead, he thought, peering out of the shadowy place where he rested unto the brilliant day. He wondered how he would manage until nightfall without water or food. He didn't dare risk hunting for food now.

A bat flapped by his ear, and Jeremiah remembered where he was. Dried leaves crackled in the cave. He hoped a possum or rabbit rustled by. The tightness in his head eased and his eyes grew accustomed to the darkness. After a few seconds, he could clearly see a man's silhouette only a few yards away. A voice shattered the dimness.

"You ought to be sleeping Sonny. Gots to save your strength for your journey tonight," the man said, in an amiable voice. He sat cross-legged regarding Jeremiah with steady eyes.

"Who are you?" Jeremiah asked, his skin growing clammy with fear. He didn't trust black, white, or Indian, man, woman or child. His only instinct—to survive and be free. Jeremiah started to drag his body backwards, along the leaves on the ground, in the direction of the cave's entrance.

"No fear Sonny, I in the same boat like you." When Jeremiah didn't reply, he continued, "what kind of runaway you be anyway with no provision?"

"Didn't have time," Jeremiah said, throwing him a long, speculative glance. He could see the other man clearly now. His coarse, calico shirt billowed over hemp-cloth breeches. His coal black face stood out in stark contrast to his iron-gray, peppercorn hair.

"Name's Absalom. Reckon I share some of my water and vittles. Ain't much for a strapping youngster like you though."

"Much obliged, Absalom," Jeremiah said, taking the proffered tin cup. He couldn't believe his luck. He'd never had any. But now his luck seemed to be changing. He took it as a sign he was on the right path in trying to change his circumstances.

"Ain't never hear no slave talking like you. Where you come from talking so uppity?" Absalom asked in an amused tone.

The sun's rays sent down uneven streaks of sunbeams at the cave's entrance. Jeremiah drank, careful not to deplete the supply. He took a mouthful of salt pork, savoring the taste before he answered. "From down yonder. By Athens."

Absalom whistled. "That's way down yonder." He scratched his chin. "You no cotton picking slave though, I knows it."

Jeremiah met Absalom's warm gaze. "Just make furniture that's all."

Absalom made a slow, low grunt of respect. "You know them white folks gots to be looking for your hide. You is valuable property. Betcha can read and write too?"

"Much good it will do me though," Jeremiah sighed, his chest constricting.

"Sho it can!" Absalom nodded his head back and forth. "Sho it can," he said in a softer, more contemplative tone. They sat in companionable silence for a while. Jeremiah told him his story and how he got to be here.

By late evening they had become firm friends. Jeremiah listened to him spoon out advice all day long.

"You gots to run with some sense though Sonny. Can't just get up and run."

"Didn't have time."

Absalom chuckled. "You ain't got time? Then you wait for the right time. Pose I didn't happen along?" Absalom didn't wait for a response, he started to whistle and pull the string from the old pillow case he fashioned into a knapsack. Absalom rifled through his possessions to find an old Bible, held together with twine.

"No I can't read Sonny," Absalom answered the question in Jeremiah's eyes. "But I carry this here good book for protection from evil." He shoved the Bible toward Jeremiah. "The white reverend talk bout going to hell—let me tell you, hell's right here."

"And heaven's here too—I just have to find it," said Jeremiah on a wistful note.

Absalom's lips turned down in a wry smile, "ain't in these parts for sure."

Jeremiah opened the Bible and turned one page at a time. The inside cover had an inscription, *Miss Julie Springs, Arcadia, North Carolina – 1777.* He fingered the yellowed pages, some were thick. Jeremiah tried to separate them but they were stuck together from water seeping into Absalom's makeshift knapsack. "How did you come by this Bible?"

"Done stole it after Miss Julie went to meet her maker. The old biddy won't be missing it." He chuckled at his own joke.

Absalom inched closer to Jeremiah and took the Bible. He flipped to the back. The inside back cover had a flap with folded papers.

Jeremiah's eyes sharpened with interest. He reached over, took out the papers and laid them out on his lap. He trembled with excitement at what he saw.

"For all that's holy, Absalom!"

Absalom grew pensive, and his eyes clouded over. "I tell you how this come to be: Every week the ole biddy would call me to her bedside and hold up this here Bible. Her mouth going in an out lack some little tweety bird, tempting me you know?" He pointed to the papers in Jeremiah's lap, "Just a tempting me."

Jeremiah swallowed and tried to be patient.

Absalom continued as if the younger man wasn't there. "The lady knows she warn't long for this world but I been with her since before the War. And when them Creeks get old Massa Rob, her husband you know?" Absalom slapped his chest. "Me! I brought his dead body home to bury. I went back out in the heavy rain to find young Massa Robby. When I finds him, he was just a blubbering. So I threw him over my shoulder and told him to close his eyes and play possum. Then I meet up on three more Creeks and I started to bawl and beg them. 'I'se just wanting to bury my master.' They let me go."

"You're a better man than me." Jeremiah rested his hand on the older man's shoulder and prodded, "the Bible?"

"Oh yes, yes. That there Bible," he said on a sighing breath. "The old biddy promised me she'd sign my free papers as reward. She show me the papers all the time. The war been 1812, and it now 1838! When she get sick down real bad – she call me to her bedside and tell me she waiting for young Massa Robby to come back from Boston. "Boat's coming soon Absalom and I give you your papers—you so deserve it." Absalom recounted in a high wobbled voice. "Then she'd rest her bony fingers over mine."

"So what happened?" Jeremiah said, trying not to sound impatient.

"Well, I knows she warn't gonna last till morning. And I make up my mind right there and then, I warn't going to be too far away from her. I don't trust no providence. So I went to the doorway and tells her daughter, 'Miss Julie want me to stay outside her door.'"

"And she let you stay?"

"Oh yeah. She be glad. In the wee hours I hear when Miss Julie struggle for her last breath. I snuck up by her bed, took the Bible, and search the drawer for her quill and bottle of ink. I put them in my waistcoat and buttoned it tight."

Jeremiah laughed. "What if it spilled?"

Absalom chuckled too. "No, I got soot. All I got to do is mix it with a little water." He tapped the powder in the inkwell to settle it. "Anyway, back to what I was telling you. I go back out in the hall holding my chest where the Bible was and put on such a caterwauling, that 'po Miss Julie gone. The whole house wake up and come running. They didn't pay me no mind and I just walked lackadaisic-like back to my cabin."

"So the son came soon after?"

"By evening Massa Robby come. I took the wagon down to the pier to meet him. 'Absalom boy, here's my trunks, load them in the wagon.' He turned and talked to a young woman who looked just like Miss Julie. When I loaded all the trunks, Reverend Goodfellow come up to him. It's then I know the woman's Massa Robby's wife. Then some other planters join him saying, 'sorry to hear about the loss of Miss Julie. What are you going to do now son?'"

"I know you snuck up to hear more, didn't you?" Jeremiah said.

"Right then and there, I decide it's time to inspect the horse leg."

Jeremiah chuckled without mirth.

"They saw me and hush them voice but I hear one word that make my head feel like a bale of cotton. I hear the word, *Sell!* I knows what it means. I think of Ole Matty, Pigeon Toe, Vera, and all the people what been family for nearly 30 years. I tell you Sonny, I don't know how I drive the carriage back home."

"So you took the Bible and ran?" Jeremiah prodded.

"No, no, you think I run hot-head like you?" Absalom softened the remark by giving Jeremiah a mock punch.

"I knows it warn't going to happen right away. These things take days. I warn't a field hand you know? I drive Massa Robby all 'bout the place and him, and him sisters, and him aunties, they all trust me," Absalom continued.

"So did you hear when they were going to have the auction?" Jeremiah asked.

"I didn't have to hear. I knows the day come when Massa Robby, he couldn't look me in the eye. I knows it was time."

"So you ran that night?" Jeremiah asked, riveted by the story despite himself.

"Nah. I made sure to put my plans in motion."

"What plans?" Jeremiah asked with brows furrowed.

"For one who run with only the clothes on his back you're asking 'bout my plans?" Absalom couldn't resist the good-natured jibe. He sobered. "I been busy. I plan my journey. I hoard supplies. And I snuck down to see Ma Timble down by the *Righteous Home* plantation. Ma Timble gots connection with free slaves and abolitionist from up North. This here cave is one of the places to hide on the journey."

Jeremiah's nostrils flared, he sucked in his breath and held it to steady his nerves. He couldn't contain his excitement. He straightened out the papers and positioned them on the warped Bible cover. Absalom fished out the quill and mixed the soot with a few drops of water.

"What's the last name?" Jeremiah asked.

Absalom peered closer, "Sign Massa Robby's name." He grabbed Jeremiah's arm, his cat-like eyes wild like a tiger poised for the kill.

"Don't you go put 'Massa' on the paper though."

Jeremiah squeezed back the smile and repeated, "the name?"

"Oh, it's Robert Archibald Wilberforce."

"So I'll write, *'I, Robert Archibald Wilberforce grant my slave Absalom Wilberforce his freedom. In the year of our Lord 1838.'*"

Absalom bobbed his head many times while staring at the paper. "Mighty official, it is, yes, mighty official."

Jeremiah stretched out the manumission paper and wrote the full name, dotted the two 'I's' and made a flourish at the end. He recalled the way he saw the gentry sign the receipts. Massa George always had them handy for the furniture Jeremiah made.

"Aha! Aha!" Absalom took the paper with both hands, holding it outstretched from his body, flapping it up and down in gentle motions to dry the ink. "Free as Jack Rabbit." He laughed out loud. He crouched in a corner of the cave laying it to dry.

He returned to Jeremiah's side beaming. He slapped Jeremiah on the back several times. His face a wreath of smiles, his eyes moist.

"Alright, it's now your turn. Miss Julie had these papers to free Vera and her daughter too but I knows she warn't going to do it—out of spite. You know why?"

"No," Jeremiah whispered. He knew Absalom had to milk this for all its worth. So he wouldn't spoil the older man's mood.

"Before the war, Ole Massa Rob used to leave his bed and visit Vera at night. Almost every night. I'd see Miss Julie standing at the window watching him. She'd be clutching her night rail round her body. I used to feel sorry for her. No mo though, no mo." He nodded several times in affirmation.

Jeremiah sensed another story. He decided he had to get to the other paper or he'd burst. "So you took all the papers?"

"Yeah, much good it will do Vera and her daughter. They probably on their way to Alabama or somewhere in the Deep South. No help for it. Everyman for himself. God bless the day you walked in this cave." He looked up to the ceiling. "Yes, God Bless the day Sonny."

In the meantime, Jeremiah straightened the other papers to sign Massa George's name. He dipped the quill into the inkwell and with the utmost care filled in the blanks:

I, George Sylvester Browne of Athens, Georgia, free my slave Jeremiah Browne on this date of April 20, In the Year of our Lord, Eighteen Hundred and Thirty Eight. Witnessed by Reverend Erasmus Kensington on April 20, 1838.

The two men stared at the paper while the ink dried. Absalom whistled low.

"Is a work of art I tell you."

Jeremiah knew in his gut this may help him, but it wasn't the solution. He had seen free black people taken captive by unscrupulous captors and sold into the Deep South. Plus, Massa George would lose too much money without him there to make his special designs so he would search the earth for Jeremiah. He got up and walked to where Absalom had laid out his paper to dry and laid his beside it.

"With this here paper Sonny, I'm heading as far as possible where Massa Robby can never ever find me and no one will know me. Think I'll shoot for Indiana or Illinois. I hear no slavery there—but they be sending back anyone who not free." He slapped Jeremiah on the back. "Might as well hitch a ride on my wagon Sonny boy," he said, rubbing his hands in glee.

"So, what do we do now?" Jeremiah asked.

"We stay right here, we takes a nap but as soon as it get dark we has to be ready."

"Ready for what?"

"Wha? Oh, the sound of the tom-tom, Sonny . . . is the ole message we bring cross the waters from Africa. I been waiting for days for it. But I feel it in my old bones we's hearing it tonight."

* * *

Dark, puffy clouds hovered overhead and the sky remained a flat, slate grey throughout the morning. Small trees, no bigger than shrubs, swayed in the gentle breeze. Awanessa gathered her skirts, making her way back to the village. She was done tending the livestock. She remembered the wounded bird she had placed in safety. She must stop to see whether it lived.

She found the little wren, taking care not to touch the spindly bandaged leg. She had found the poor little critter, a few days ago, separated from its mother and trapped in the wood shed. It was waiting for her, its little beak wide open for food.

Awanessa searched in her satchel for the tiny worms she had wrapped in a leaf—the leaves folded tight to protect her gift. She laughed when the hungry bird pecked at her arm. She dropped a worm in its open mouth and another, which it gulped down whole.

Dropping the last one in the baby bird's mouth, she froze. Sharp screams and shouts rented the morning air. Awanessa carefully returned the bird to its nest, picked up her satchel and sprinted toward the village.

As she got closer to the village she could see what was happening. Men lie bleeding on the ground; crying children ran helter-skelter, their hands in the air, while soldiers rounded up the entire village.

"Oh my God, they've come. Oh, my God, they're forcing us out," she whispered out loud. An aching burn spread throughout her chest.

A bayonet poked into her side. "Time to go, Squaw," a voice said behind her.

"My mother—" Awanessa jerked her head to look at the soldier behind her with fear-stricken eyes. But she could only move forward as the bayonet prodded her along.

"Go collect your things, squaw. You're marching outta here today. Glory be," he said, and grinned showing teeth like roasted corn kernels.

Awanessa marched at the point of the soldier's bayonet to her cabin. Old Enola struggled with a soldier to get back into her own cabin. He butted her with the back of his rifle and she crumpled to the ground. He stepped over her body and grabbed Little Flying Doe as she ran past him to get to her own family.

When the shots rang out around her, Awanessa shut her eyes tight for a brief moment. She stumbled when the soldier grabbed her by the neck and snarled. "Don't you try no funny business here Injun, I'm trying to be decent. Now hurry up and get your belongings." He gave her a shove and she stumbled into her cabin.

Awanessa hoped her mother had come looking for her. She screamed Gentle Dove's name, but no answer. Blood trickled in the floor crevice before she got there. "The bastards," she whispered. She ran through the cabin, tears streaming in rivulets down her face. She stashed all the medicinal supplies she could find. She also tied some gold coins in a handkerchief and dropped it into her bosom just before the soldier came in to get her.

The shouting and screams intensified while the soldiers ransacked and looted the cabins throughout the village. They clobbered men, women, and children. A few ran into the barns and corn cribs to hide. Some of the Cherokee men out in the fields heard the commotion. They rushed back but met the same fate.

Awanessa's eyes frantic, roved the area for Gentle Dove and Tyanita but no sign of them.

Led by the soldier's bayonet, Awanessa ended up in the center of the village. Hundreds of Cherokees stood battered and slumped over in despair. The soldiers rounded them up like cows in a pen. She joined the line with her people, eyes glazed over with terror and loss. They trudged out of the village. She never looked back.

* * *

On their slow march toward the stockade, multitudes of riff-raff moved into their village. Some rode stony faced in their wagons, not looking left or right. Crude chairs, tables, clothing, pots and pans piled high in the wagons. The younger men brandished their rifles in the air with jubilation. They jumped around in a jig, singing taunting songs:

"All I want in this creation
Is a pretty little wife and a big plantation
Away up yonder in the Cherokee Nation."

After a full day's journey on the Unicoi Turnpike, Awanessa glanced up from the red clay soil, her entire sphere of vision since she left her village. Her blistered feet lagged and her back ached from carrying her belongings. People thronged as far back as she could see. Most hung their heads in despair while some had glazed, confused looks in their eyes. The old and the very young rode on horses or in covered wagons. Overhead, a whippoorwill flapped its wings in swift motions and let out a keening sound, bidding the Cherokee nation goodbye.

It wasn't until late evening when they reached Fort Butler. Soldiers shoved them at bayonet point inside the cramped lodges. Awanessa's body ached, her mind numbed. More than anything she wanted answers. Did Gentle Dove and Tyanita die—like so many others whose blood now taint the ground? Would she see Jeremiah again? A hazy fog of despair enveloped her. She groped to find the solid wall behind her. Inch-by-inch, her back slid down the wall and she slumped to the ground.

CHAPTER 5

Over the next few days, Awanessa took stock of her people's situation.

They divided Camp into several lodges. She overheard the soldiers say they were meeting Cherokees from different villages throughout North Georgia when they get to Fort Cass, in Tennessee. Awanessa knew it would take another week and a half to get to Murphy. She had ridden in a wagon with Etu, Gentle Dove, and her father a long time ago. If she could not make one day's journey, she didn't know how she or anyone else could survive a 1200 mile journey on foot to this place called Oklahoma.

Not one to languish in self-pity, Awanessa decided to make the best of her situation and keep busy. She walked around comforting the old and helping the wounded. After many inquiries and pleas to anyone she recognized, someone mentioned they thought they saw Gentle Dove.

She searched row by row through the camp with hunger gnawing. She finally found her mother.

"Oh, *me-tsi, me-tsi, me-tsi,*" Awanessa wailed at the sight of Gentle Dove's pallor, then gasped over a gaping wound.

Gentle Dove placed her forefinger over her mouth, "*ahlawe'hi,* you must be quiet love. We don't want to make it worse for ourselves." Her small face crumbled into itself. "Thank the Great Spirit you're alive," she whispered. Her eyes devoured her daughter.

"But, you're hurt; let me see." Awanessa said, ready to take charge.

"The hurt's on the inside, child. It can never be healed," she sighed and gave herself over to Awanessa's administrations. Gentle Dove got weaker and drifted off. Awanessa didn't know whether her mother had fallen asleep. She thanked the Great Spirit she had the foresight to grab her medicine pouch before she left home.

Nevertheless, Awanessa's deft fingers sewed up the gaping wound on Gentle Dove's neck. Her mother whimpered as if the pain came from a hazy distance.

Awanessa tried to focus on Gentle Dove, but couldn't ignore the chaos around her—the moaning, the crying. Some had stoic looks on their faces. The children wailed from hunger while their mothers comforted them as best they could.

Yesterday, she saw Rides-With-Wind and her past anger melted with the tragedy in her Nation. Some of the men had escaped, but most of them were captured. Tsali, one of the Cherokee men, had escaped with his family into the Smoky Mountains. But the soldiers hunted them down and killed Tsali when he tried to protect his family. The army also captured Rides-With-Wind along with five other men hiding out in the mountains.

* * *

They had been in Tennessee, in another temporary stockade, for a week now. Awanessa sickened at the conditions, watched helpless. Scores died from all kinds of infectious diseases, malnutrition, dysentery and more. She couldn't even help her own mother.

Awanessa learned about an alternate, faster route to the territory which was easier than the land route. Maybe Gentle Dove could get better medical attention. She could only hope.

This morning she had managed to find Chief John Ross, petitioning him to ship Gentle Dove by boat to the new Indian Territory out West. Ross, part Cherokee and part Scottish, had been principal chief all of Awanessa's life. His hair was grayer than she remembered. His once full, rounded face had taken on a gaunt look. He peered at her with dull eyes. "My dear, I'm doing all I can to petition for better conditions."

"But my mother is dying. She can't last another week," Awanessa said, a sob caught in her throat.

"I'll try to get her on the next boat. In the meantime, give her as much comfort as you can—so many have already passed on. The suffering is unbearable. I know—". He opened his palm in a 'what more can I do' gesture. "I'm in negotiations now with the US army so I can take over the 'removal' of our own people," he continued with a little more hope in his voice.

"Yes, that would be much better." Her shoulders slumped in defeat. She wanted a commitment and couldn't get one. She turned toward the door.

Other people waited to speak, so she bade him goodbye.

Making her way back to Gentle Dove, soldiers stared at her without expression—their bayonets ready. Heat seeped through the thin soles of her moccasins and she dodged the diagonal cracks in the red clay ground. The dried-up looking landscape and bleached red soil gave mute testimony to the altered conditions of her people. Once, the Cherokees were a thriving group of people who had advanced more than any other Indian tribe in the nation. Now, they were reduced to living like sub-humans. Awanessa tried to lighten her mood before she returned to Gentle Dove's side.

Gentle Dove turned glassy eyes toward Awanessa's face. "You were successful?" Gentle Dove asked. Her voice even fainter and she tried to raise one arm but couldn't.

"Yes," Awanessa lied. "You have to get some nourishment so you can make the journey." Awanessa forced a bright smile while she raised her mother up for some of the leftover broth.

"I won't make it, dear... but thank the Great Spirit you will," Gentle Dove whispered. Awanessa scooped the precious broth trickling down her mother's chin and prodded her lips open to accept another spoonful.

"No, no more. Can't take anymore." Her head sank back into the rolled up skirt for a pillow.

Gentle Dove turned her head to the side in defeat. Her eyes landed on Ayati's sick son, Salali, nearby. He laid flat on his back.

A fresh wave of sadness rippled through Awanessa when she saw Little Salali like this, "little squirrel," Tyanita used to call him.

Gentle Dove's eyes followed the rhythm of the boy's protruding stomach with fascination. It inflated in and out in rapid motions. Her body reclined stiff on the pallet but ever so often, like a reflex action, her left fist would open and close.

Awanessa stroked her mother's hand in an effort to get the blood moving again. She continued the massage and in a quiet voice sang the songs Gentle Dove had crooned to her as a little girl. She paused her singing when she heard an imperceptible gasp. In an instant, everything and everyone around Awanessa blurred; no one moved, time stopped.

Gentle Dove's trance like state had ended; her gaze fixed and unseeing. She didn't even have the strength to struggle for her last breath.

Awanessa held the limp hand for a long moment; the activity in the stockade resumed. Mosquitoes she had been swatting all evening droned loud in her ear again. A child in the far corner made fretful cries and an old man moaned. Awanessa wiped the sweat from her forehead with the hem of her dress.

Shaping Gentle Dove's hands into a clasp, Awanessa rested them back on her mother's chest. She leaned closer and kissed Gentle Dove's cheek. With trembling fingers, Awanessa closed her mother's eyes. Ayati watched it all. She bit her lower lip, avoiding Awanessa's eyes, and hung her chin to her chest cradling her son's head. Salali's stomach still pumped.

Awanessa pulled the covers and huddled close to Gentle Dove's still warm body. She had no more tears left to cry.

* * *

Jeremiah and Absalom avoided the revealing slants of moonlight shining through the trees. Crouching from one tree to the next, they stopped and listened for the tom-tom drums to draw them closer.

Throughout most of the night they trudged on, their senses alert. Absalom's breath sounded shorter and louder than ever. Jeremiah tugged his arm to stop and rest a bit longer by the trunk of the live oak tree.

"Gots to keep going, Sonny," Absalom rasped between even shorter breaths. He put his hands on his thighs and sank with a grateful sigh on the dried leaves. He sidled his back up against the tree trunk and pulled out a flask of water from his knapsack. He gulped a mouthful of water and passed the flask to Jeremiah.

"How much further?" Jeremiah whispered between gulps. He wanted to keep going, but knew the older man had to regain his strength and get his bearings.

"We gots to head a little ways further," Absalom whispered back, his chest heaving. "Until we come to the river, then we wait."

Jeremiah decided the decision was good enough for him. He wasn't going to ask any more questions. Nevertheless, his heart pounded with excitement in his chest. He did not know who beat those drums, sending such clear signals, but Absalom had just called it the 'freedom line.'

He patted the paper tucked secure in the band at his waist. The paper felt reassuring against his bare flesh. He had heard of men who had free papers and who were sold right back into slavery. But Jeremiah decided he would take one day at a time and not think overly much on what's ahead. He knew one thing for sure though. Absalom felt content to pass as free when they get to Kentucky. But he didn't. He would get to Ohio, and make his way out of these United States into

Canada forever. He fixed the vision in his mind and left it there. First, they had to get to the river.

After a few minutes rest, they started their journey again. Absalom, fortified and more surefooted, made spry steps. They talked no more, using only hand gestures. Absalom forged ahead while Jeremiah scanned the landscape and listened for anything suspicious.

Absalom cocked his ear and tugged Jeremiah's fingers. Jeremiah listened and heard the distinct sounds of water. His excitement grew and Absalom's eyes bulged.

There amongst sinewy grass, sprouting from the river, a small boat nestled. Absalom stepped out into the moonlight and flayed his arms above his head. Jeremiah sucked in his breath when a stocky white man, wearing a black tricorn hat, waved wild hands in the air. Jeremiah hesitated, his face breaking out into a cold sweat.

Absalom took a few steps and grabbed him by the arm shoving him forward. Chills raced up Jeremiah's spine. It wasn't just the idea of trusting the white man as Absalom so obviously did. Jeremiah never liked large bodies of water, ever since he had almost drowned in one previous escape attempt. He shook his head to avoid the memory and forged behind Absalom.

"Git in, git in," their unlikely rescuer said. He all but pushed them in the boat. A white woman in a black bonnet sat at the front but she never glanced at them. "Y'all ready, Hank?" she asked in a low, husky voice.

Hank lifted some planks off the bottom of the boat and to Jeremiah's amazed eyes, it revealed a false bottom.

"Git in, git in, hurry," Hank said, poking him in the side.

Absalom slipped in the opening and disappeared. Jeremiah stuffed and curled his body like the letter 'C.' He curved around Absalom who had crouched, head between his knees, like a newborn babe. Not a word passed on the top or the lower levels—only the sound of swishing oars gliding through the water.

Jeremiah wondered if the white couple did this often and how many runaways suffocated. Jeremiah mirrored Absalom's breathing pattern so he wouldn't breathe in stale air. He listened to their breathing for a long while. The breath left Absalom's body when loud voices penetrated their hiding place. Jeremiah stopped breathing too.

"Kind a late for you to be out curing the sick, Doc Hank," a rough voice shouted to the couple.

"Yes, mighty late. My missus here and I are nigh dead on our feet."

"Well, we didn't hear of anyone so badly sick in these here parts that you couldn't have gone home earlier. Who called you out down river?" Another suspicious sounding voice asked.

"Oh my fine fellows, the army commissioned me and the missus to the stockades to lend our doctoring skills to help those poor sick Indians on the march. They've run out of medicine—we can't help anymore. Hundreds of them are dying," Doc Hank continued.

Jeremiah couldn't hear the response. But Doc's wife spoke. "As doc said, we're nigh dead on our feet; we've traveled all night and just want to get back to see our own little bairns."

"Don't know why they bothering to spare the expense to move them Injuns out West. Most of them half-dead already, anyway," the voice said.

"You mean them Cherokees who dress up like white people and think they is good Christian folk?" the first voice said, while the other one hooted.

"Go home doc and get yourself cleaned up—don't want no 'fectious diseases round here."

Silence. The boat glided on.

Jeremiah's heart slammed in his rib cage. "Nessa." He didn't realize he breathed her name. He swallowed and listened to the logical voice inside his head. According to the way of things, he couldn't afford to love. He'd seen how love destroyed. And it could only destroy them.

What of Nessa?

Didn't you decide to forget about her? Shucks, love only destroys.

A man in bondage cannot think about love—only to be free.

Jeremiah knew he should listen to his sensible, practical voice. The voice he always followed is calculating, self-preserving and looked for opportunities anywhere. It tells him when to bide his time and when to run. It has never failed him. However, of late, a more insidious voice lurked deep into the recesses of his mind.

Ever since his stay in the Cherokee village, he cannot rid himself of Awanessa. She stays in his thoughts, forming tentacles around his heart and gripping him at the oddest moments.

At last, the boat slowed to a complete stop, hitting the embankment with a soft thud. He could hear furtive voices, quick and low, footsteps and swishing of the underbrush. Jeremiah didn't even feel curious.

He reclined in the bottom of the boat and it swayed from side-to-side. He even closed his eyes so as not to see the image of her brown eyes turned up to his and the trusting smile. He even smelled the faint twinge of jasmine, always surrounding her. What she had feared for her people had come to pass. Jeremiah swallowed to soothe his dry throat. He didn't even have space to reach for Absalom's water flask. Thinking she may be in harm's way doubled-up like fists in his innards. Was she even alive?

The slats moved above his head and he peered up in Doc Hank's face, blanched in the moonlight. Absalom had already started to reach for the hands coming through the opening. Doc's hands returned for Jeremiah.

Jeremiah twisted his bulky frame from side to side, trying to free his body from the narrow opening. It struck him as he left the bottom of this boat as if being born again, this time a free man.

He almost chuckled with delight. He tried to do a full stretch and gulp in some of the fresh morning.

"Git down, git down."

Jeremiah and Absalom crouched low at the command, dragging their feet through shallow water. They made their way toward a dim lantern hidden among the tall, swampy grass. Doc turned to them, the moonlight bouncing off his pearly, blue-veined face.

"When the Missus and me go into that house over there, watch for the signal and git down to the cellar."

Before Jeremiah could say, "what signal?" Doc Hank and his wife were gone. She wiped her hands on her apron as she walked. He swung his black medicine bag with his left hand while he kept his right hand on the pointy end of his tricorn hat.

Jeremiah and Absalom kneeled in the shallow water to watch and wait.

Overhead, the black-crowned, night herons swooped when they spotted their prey. The murky water reflected only shadows of the birds' flight. Jeremiah's stomach growled and Absalom suppressed a grin.

They didn't speak but developed an entire non-verbal language of their own. Absalom pointed his chin toward the nondescript clapboard house, and Jeremiah kept his eyes glued for the sign.

In the meantime, he heard Absalom rummaging in his knapsack. He placed a piece of salt pork in Jeremiah's palm. In one fluid motion, Jeremiah curled his fingers around it.

Absalom patted his chest in several places and smiled when he heard the rustle of the free paper. Jeremiah followed suit and used his elbow to slap the reassuring free paper tucked in his waistband.

Dawn broke; the sky had taken on a new bluer shade with no memory of the night's former color. Jeremiah's eyes felt heavy, but he forced himself to stare at the old, weather-beaten house with a huge magnolia tree looming dark and dense behind it. As Jeremiah wondered which was older, the tree or the house, the signal came.

A guttural squawk rose and fell, like a lament, similar to the herons' cry.

Jeremiah's ears perked. When he heard it again, he knew this time it was no heron. Jeremiah gulped air; he nudged Absalom and they sprinted in a stealthy, zigzag fashion toward the cellar under the house.

They climbed down the short flight of stairs to a small opening with stone-lined walls and dirt floor. The cool air caressed his face. Jeremiah's eyes adjusted to light flickering from a lantern in the corner. Even in the dim light, Jeremiah could make out two, three-legged stools. Absalom plopped his weary body down and heaved a sigh of relief. His lips moved as if in prayer.

Standing next to him, Jeremiah reached for the other stool and straddled it. He ran his hand down the legs and grimaced when he felt the roughness of the crude stool.

They sat for a while—two souls communicating without sound. Each man knew how the other felt. Absalom rested his elbow on his thigh, his chin in his palm, and allowed his features to relax.

Jeremiah looked hard in the corner and rubbed his eyes to make sure he saw right. He spotted two stacks of hay and walked trance-like toward it, already feeling the softness.

He remembered putting one knee on the stack of hay to climb up. When his head hit the hay, the scent of jasmine filled his nostrils, silky hair caressed his cheek and, far off in the misty mountains a sultry laugh spiraled through the caverns of his brain. He knew without a doubt he must see her again. But how?

CHAPTER 6

Muffled, furtive sounds filtered into the camp from the makeshift outhouse. Awanessa's neighbor, Ayati, was gone. It did not bode well. Under these conditions, each person had to watch the other one's back.

More footsteps shuffling and a low wailing. Awanessa jumped to her feet to investigate. Ayati stumbled from the outhouse like a drunken sot, her footsteps criss-crossing the ground. She clutched the remnants of her torn chemise to cover her exposed breasts. Stumbling and falling, she covered her nipples so they wouldn't skid on the gravel-covered ground. A woman rushed from the opposite direction to cover her with a tattered blanket.

"I saw them," another woman said, her voice tinged with reproach, face tight as a mask.

"Who—what happened to her?" Awanessa's voice bordered on hysteria and she rushed to wrap her arms around Ayati.

"Over there," the tight-faced woman used her chin to gesture. In horror, Awanessa counted two, three, four soldiers emerging from the outhouse. One notched his pants at the waist while others buttoned their breeches, all the while joking and laughing with each other.

Awanessa led Ayati inside to her bedroll. She returned the tattered blanket and thanked the women for their help. All around the camp, little girls' eyes were wizened beyond their years as they bore testimony of Ayati's violation.

Awanessa covered Ayati's body, wiped her face and hands all the time speaking soft, comforting, Cherokee words. But Ayati didn't respond. Awanessa watched her curl up into a ball, her head lodged between her knees. Awanessa decided to just hold and rock her to sleep.

Throughout the night and the next day Ayati sat on the bedroll and stared at the wall. The two women from the previous night came back to offer their help.

Awanessa, feeling helpless, decided to go out for air. She called on Tyanita's uncle whom she had only yesterday located in camp. Tendu was not her favorite person, but he was Tyanita's only relative.

On entering his area of the camp, her stomach turned. He still had his Negro servants to see to his needs. She shook her head, she never understood how some Cherokees could put away the old teachings and own slaves. Much as Tendu had his own plantation and lived like white people, they still forced him out. She shook off her musings and got to the point. "Any word at all of Tyanita?"

He sat back on his cot. "Not a word of my lovely niece," he said. The flesh on his once rotund frame sagged from his jaw line. Even his once ample girth now sloped in the direction of his knees.

"I have searched everywhere, Tendu, and no one knows where she disappeared to."

"Sit down and have some tea my dear? Jonah!" he clapped his hands, summoning his servant.

Awanessa's jaw almost dropped. "You have tea to spare? No, no. I couldn't take it. As a matter of fact, I must return."

"Well, come and see me again my dear; these conditions are most dreadful." He turned a bleary-eyed gaze up to Awanessa.

She left Tendu's camp in a hurry and had to admit the worst had happened. The soldiers must have killed her friend who was like the sister she never had. Tears filmed her eyes for her vivacious friend. Throughout the past miserable hot weeks, she had searched the entire pitiful camp trying to find word of her. No one had seen her run off to the mountains. No one had seen her body. No one knew anything.

"You Squaw."

Awanessa kept walking, her head bent deep in concentration. She pretended she didn't hear or see the uncouth man grinning at her showing his encrusted, brown teeth.

"Squaw, you hear me, gel?"

Awanessa bit her lip and looked at the man in disdain. He took out a filthy rag and wiped the sweat from his mottled red face. He mopped his dirty blond hair and neck.

"You gots lots mo problems ahead a yer, gel." He chewed on his tobacco. "This here whiskey will make you forget it all." He peered at her through close set beady eyes. "Come, just a lil' gold and we be fair and square." He snorted through a bulbous nose, the tip of which he rubbed from side-to-side as if to entice her.

When he realized she wouldn't do business, he craned his neck toward her and aimed a sliver of yellow-brown spit at her feet.

Awanessa side-stepped and quickened her pace. Men of dubious character would way lay her people to spend their last coin on their junk. She doubted whether he had real whiskey in those bottles or some poisonous substance he concocted to annihilate her people. The Council prohibited Cherokees from drinking the poison. She had seen the effects where the liquor addled men's brains.

She walked faster and tried not to look at some of the people caving in to the desire for solace. She hurried inside and found her way to the little area she used to share with Gentle Dove but collided into Rides-With-Wind instead.

He swayed from side to side. She put out her hands to steady him. "Rides-With-Wind," she said, shaking her head in disbelief.

"Oh, isn't it the lovely Awane-sha who prefers a sh-lave over a man of her own kind."

"Stop it at once!" She stomped her foot. "I don't believe you too have succumbed to these vile spirits."

"Wha? Shpirit? His eyes bulged. He looked around him, perplexed, and staggered a step backward.

Awanessa led him back outside for some fresh air and they sat together on a large rock.

"Where," he hiccupped. "Where's your man? Your black man," he added.

"You know as well as I do you ran him off." Awanessa realized he was lucid, even when drunk.

"Nah, he ran off before."

"Well, maybe it's a good thing then. That was a terrible thing you did."

"He's no man. You protected him, but he didn't sh-tay to protect you." Rides-With-Wind took another swill from his jug, swished the whiskey around his mouth and swallowed.

Awanessa looked at him in disgust. She didn't need him to bring up Jeremiah. She felt the keen loss even more and anger he ran off without even saying goodbye. Maybe it was for the best, she sighed. However, she couldn't help the thought everyone she cared about had left her.

"Wa-sh zat sh-mell?" Rides-With-Wind sniffed the air.

"Is it the first time you smell it? What do you expect to smell in this stinking hole we are forced to live in?" She spread her hands wide to encompass the sad conditions of thousands of her people in the inadequate stockades. "You're drunker than I thought." She let out a heavy sigh.

Awanessa looked at the once proud and stalwart young man. His cheeks were sunken, and his shoulders stooped. She felt anger and helplessness when he swilled the flask again and tossed his head back.

"That's not going to help, you know?"

"Nothing can help us." He reclined flat on his back in an awkward position. Within seconds he started a drunken snore, his face within inches from a craggy point in the rock.

A small flock of birds flew in perfect unison, heading south. She envied them and fantasized she was fleeing from these bastards. One look at the hundreds of soldiers guarding them obliterated thoughts of running away.

She decided to leave Rides-With-Wind to sleep off his drunkenness and go back inside. She did not like the way some of the soldiers looked at her.

She had to take precautions to prevent what happened to Ayati and countless other young women in the camp. She felt sad for Ayati as she had only buried little Salali last week. The little boy, Gentle Dove, and many others all left behind in shallow graves along the trail. Awanessa had placed a makeshift marker on her mother's grave, but she knew it would not stand up to brutal weather.

At the beginning of the raid, Ayati's husband had died when he tried to protect his wife and son. And now this. Awanessa sidled past Ayati who remained in the same spot where she had left her earlier.

"Ayati, you must eat something. You'll waste away and be no use to yourself."

Ayati cast a blank gaze around the room, her eyeballs shifted from side to side, not registering Awanessa's presence.

Awanessa offered a piece of raw sap pork she procured for the both of them.

"Here, you must eat so you can live. Remember, you're going on the boat tomorrow. It's a new life for you, Ayati—I'll see you when I get there."

Ayati slapped Awanessa's hand away, turned her head from side to side. Her eyes roamed the camp looking for someone. Turning down the corners of her mouth, she hugged herself and rocked back and forth on her haunches making unintelligible sounds.

Awanessa dragged her tired body over to lie down on the nearby cot. She willed the griping in her stomach to ease. Ayati was better off than she, so was Rides-With-Wind. Both their minds had shut down and said no more. She didn't think hers would ever stop absorbing the suffering.

Weakness overcame her, but just before she drifted off to sleep she saw herself in a strange, exotic place. She was swimming in a clear ocean surrounded by a school of fish in vivid hues. She knew she had glimpsed her afterlife. She'd never make it to Oklahoma.

CHAPTER 7

"Clop, clop, clop," the sounds of weighted feet coming down the stairs penetrated Jeremiah's slumber. He rolled over on his back in alarm and glanced over to see Absalom doing a full stretch on the other bundle of hay. A heavy set black woman, with a white cloth tied in a knot on her forehead stepped in the room. Jeremiah and Absalom waited.

She carried containers of food and the aroma wafted through the room.

"Here's yo food. Yo betta eat plenty." My brother come in at midnight for you. So make sure y'all better not be sleeping."

The men looked at her with questions in their eyes.

"The name is Bertha. Yes, I is free, Lordy be praised." I work for the good Doc Hank and his missus. She raised her eye to the ceiling, and clasped her hands in front, waiting for them to get up.

Jeremiah bounded out of the bed introducing himself after Absalom. Without ceremony, he attacked the food, his first good meal since he left the Cherokee village.

Bertha went on talking, "Massa Hank and Miss Louisa, God bless their souls, they be Quakers and use the cellar as part o' the freedom line.

"But how . . .?" Jeremiah started to ask between mouthfuls of collard greens and fat back. Absalom stayed his hand in the air. "Don't you worry about that, Sonny. This line's been going on fo' you been born."

"That's right and will be going on for a long time too. Ma Timble from the Righteous Plantation send the message. They arrange for y'all to transport to another stop further along. Anytime you feel right safe, you can get off the line."

Absalom wiped the grease running down the corner of his mouth with the back of his hand and said, "At the next stop I is 'bout ready. Get me some work blacksmithing." He ran his tongue over his front teeth and set the plate on the floor.

"You go no further up North?" Bertha asked, looking surprised.

Absalom patted his manumission paper in his chest. "Right here is the ticket to the kingdom." He leaned against the wall with a satisfied look.

You gots free papers? Bertha's eyes rounded like cartweels. She looked over at Jeremiah "You too?"

He patted his waist with his elbow and smiled.

"Lordy be praised. Y'all easy!"

They all looked up when they heard Miss Louisa calling, "Berrrrtha?"

Bertha became a flurry of activity, collecting the dishes in one swoop and hurrying away without another word. She scrambled up the stairs making loud, clomping sounds.

He turned to Absalom still sitting contented in the corner. "How will you know when it's safe to get off the line?"

Absalom shuffled his body on the stool to make himself more comfortable. "I reckon I is far from Massa Robby by now. The next stop will do me fine, Sonny. Just fine."

Jeremiah rested his chin in both palms, his eyes hooded.

"What's going on in that head o' yours, Sonny?"

Jeremiah pursed his lips. "Just want to make it out of these United States—to Canada."

Absalom pulled up from the stool and walked to Jeremiah's pile of hay. He sat next to Jeremiah for a long moment. With a deep sigh, he took the younger man's hand in his own and examined it. "Don't be wanting too much, Sonny. Say thank God you made it this far."

Jeremiah avoided Absalom's gaze and looked over his shoulder.

"Thank God. But can't never rest though until I'm truly free, where no one can force me back."

Absalom worked his lips round and round. "You gonna get yourself kill't. That you will, with them high fallutin ways."

Jeremiah hung his head. "If ever I'm caught, I may as well be dead." He took a deep breath. "Yep, rather be dead. Take my own life, too." He looked off in the distance thinking of a slave he knew from a neighboring plantation who threw himself in the fire after being tortured again and again. All the master said, after the man's death—"a lazy good for nothing, no great loss."

Absalom heaved himself up on the stack of hay shaking his head in defeat. "Brash I tell you—young and brash. No sense God gave you in you head." He flattened his lips in disapproval. After a few moments of silence, he started talking again.

"Listen to a word of advice from your elder. Is better you live out your life—no matter the conditions and plan for a better life in the sweet hereafter."

Jeremiah decided not to comment.

Absalom got comfortable and stretched out his legs placing his hands behind his head.

Jeremiah remained seated at the edge of the makeshift bed, his body hunched over near Absalom's feet.

"So, you think I have no sense because I want to be completely free?"

Absalom looked at him with a baleful stare, "Who run in the middle of the night with no sustenance?"

"Oh no, not that again."

"I is showing you, Sonny, you can't be foolhardy in this here world. No sirree, ain't for the foolhardy. Use your head. Settle down with your trade—"

"And be looking over my shoulder every minute? Bowing and scraping and shuffling my feet for the rest of my life like you plan to do?"

Hurt flared in Absalom's eyes.

"Sorry Abs. Didn't mean that." Jeremiah twisted his neck to stretch out the kinks and rubbed the scar on the back of his neck.

"We's got choices now Sonny. You gots yours. A gots mine. In slavery you ain't got nuthin, not even you own self." Absalom sighed and turned his back to Jeremiah, signaling the end of the conversation.

Jeremiah rose and went over to his own hay stack. He knew they had to get as much sleep as possible for the long night ahead. But he wasn't tired. He felt haunted. He hoped Absalom wasn't peeved with him by his uncalled for comment, but didn't want to disturb him by asking.

He realized he didn't want to lie down and face his thoughts of Nessa. Was she safe? He missed her. Even though annoyed, he had to acknowledge his feelings. This strange part of him he wouldn't dare delve into. He had a feeling he wouldn't like the answers. He believed in 'every man for himself.' He had no room in his life for another human being.

Even with Nessa's face flitting in and out in his mind, he forced his thoughts toward the night ahead. He knew at the next stop he would not get off. With or without Absalom he'd go as far North as he could. He wasn't sure in what direction he headed. But the air of freedom had taken hold and he knew one thing for sure, he must breathe it, at all costs.

* * *

Clad in plaid shirts, brown carpetbag trousers with suspenders, caps, and respectable shoulder bags, Absalom and Jeremiah trudged along the road in their new brogans, trying to look like discreet, free black folks.

If anyone looked too close they would see tension in every line of their faces. They walked with an intense focus, trying to walk straight and not crouch, looking over their shoulder often. They didn't even speak. Absalom, from time-to-time, would shake his shoulders in an effort to loosen up so he would appear natural to anyone who happened by.

They strode along the winding road, the distinct sounds of horses gained on them from behind. The horses slowed to a trot.

"Looky here—never seen these niggers before in these parts"

A second voice chimed in. "No sirree. Boys, I ain't talking to no nigger's back."

Absalom turned to face the men first. Jeremiah saw Absalom's eyes were downcast and his shoulder stooped so he followed suit. He decided to let Absalom get them out of this.

"Sir, ma son here and me jess going to find Parson Deetz down in Rutherland, suh. His horse need some smithy work and ma son is going to make a new baby cradle for the Parson's wife."

"Show them papers, Uncle. You should a had them ready beforehand."

Jeremiah waited for Absalom to hand over his paper and he fished out his, extending it to the other man.

The taller man peered into Jeremiah's face and poked him in the chest. "You, Jeremiah?"

Jeremiah tried to look pious. "Yessuh."

"Y'all come a long way from Athens Georgia." The interrogation continued while the tall man sat straight in the saddle chewing on his toothpick.

"We is free, suh," Jeremiah said, his temper getting the best of him. He stressed the word "suh!" Absalom gave him a quick sharp look.

The interrogator took out the toothpick real slow and placed it in the other corner of his mouth, studying Jeremiah. "Alright, we don't want no trouble. I reckon

we'll stop over at young Pastor Deetz in the by and by."
They handed back the papers. Absalom bowed and
shuffled his feet. Jeremiah bowed too but he couldn't
bring himself to scrape his feet on the ground.

"You gonna get kill't," Absalom mumbled as soon
as the riders rode off. "Mark my words, kill't I say." He
shook his head and sighed. "Wha's gonna become a
you Sonny? You gots to know danger and act longside
it."

Jeremiah knew he was right. He nodded.

"Harumph" was all he got out of Absalom for the
rest of the way.

* * *

The weather turned cool, fall had begun to set in.
The rains last night signaled the end of a long drought.
The heavy rain slowed the men from reaching their
destination, and the ground still looked parched. It would
need more than a shower to quench its thirst, Jeremiah
thought. Despite the incident this morning , his step got
lighter. His spirit soared and he felt bigger than any of
his circumstances—except for one niggling thought, of
Nessa, which he brushed away like a pesky bee.

From the landmarks they had gotten from Bertha's
brother and the other Quakers, Jeremiah knew they
only had about two miles or so left.

"Slow down Sonny, these old bones need a little
rest and a bite to eat." Absalom panted.

Jeremiah wanted to eat up those two miles as fast
as possible, but he pointed to a grassy ridge. "Let's eat
over there".

They found a shady spot with a view of the
surrounding area. Absalom removed his brogans,

turning them upside down to dislodge loose gravel. Jeremiah reached into the knapsack, pulling out some of the cold chicken and passed a big drumstick to Absalom. They ate in companionable silence for a while.

"Freedom's sweet." Absalom said, smacking his lips.

"Not yet." Jeremiah warned. "We have to make it to the next stop."

"I knows it, but it's sweet all the same with my free papers. Don't do nothing to jeopardize it Sonny, nothing!"

Jeremiah sensed another sermon coming. He knew Absalom meant well. So he shook his head in agreement.

They waited for the food to digest. Soon, rumblings like wagon wheels, tons of them, reverberated across the landscape. Jeremiah lay down on his belly and dragged his body closer to the ledge to see what caused the commotion.

Dusk had settled in the valley. A long trail of Indians, most on foot stopped to make camp. The guards sat straight on their horses. Even from a distance, Jeremiah could sense the people's oppression. He noticed their stooped backs and shuffling steps—just like Absalom. His heart broke and shattered in his chest when he thought of Nessa under those conditions.

Absalom snickered beside him. "See what I mean Sonny. You can't fight the white man, yup you bound to lose."

"They didn't even fight them. I was there Absalom; all they wanted was peace and to be left alone." Jeremiah breathed hard, his face mutinous.

"What's got you so riled? Ahhh . . ." a grin of understanding broke out on Absalom's face like a sunflower. "Left your heart with a Cherokee gal huh?" He poked Jeremiah in the side with his elbow.

Jeremiah's eyes fixated on the camp. His heart swelled with compassion at the old and young scurrying about. Babies were strapped to their mother's backs. Babies. His breath stopped for a fraction of a second. Dread doused him like a January downpour.

What if he had planted his seed in her? Even when Massa George made him mate with Hatty Mae and Lola over and over he would never permit himself to spill his seed and beget children to this kind of life. Massa George had concluded his slave must be barren.

His mind reeled.

Absalom held his tongue for as long as he could and blurted, "Sonny, listen to me, don't you go getting no fool notion in you head!"

Jeremiah swallowed hard. "I must try to see her."

"What!" Absalom shot from his seat and sat back down, slow. He rocked back and forth for a minute in silence, his hands around his stomach. He made a keening sound and looked away from Jeremiah. "Now, a knows you done gone coon in the head."

Jeremiah kept his eyes focused on the Indian camp. He spoke in a deliberate tone. "I want to thank you Absalom—for everything. You really are like a father to me—I'll never forget you."

Out of the corner of his eye, he saw Absalom patting the ground behind him for his knife. When he found it, he wrapped it in another piece of cloth and placed it in his knapsack. He eased on his brogans, a size too big, compliments of Doc Hank. Absalom stood, and, one-by-one he flicked the chicken crumbs from his pants with his fingers. He picked up his bag.

A burning started in the back of Jeremiah's eyes. He blinked a few times to get rid of Absalom's blurry image. His throat felt like a stone, lodged at the base and burned. He couldn't speak. Absalom extended his hand. He took it, clasped their fingers, and heaved himself up to face the older man.

Absalom searched his face for a few seconds giving him time to change his mind. He sighed and pulled the younger man into his arms, slapping him on the back a couple of times. Absalom tried to speak, but couldn't. He shuffled away, his back stooped.

"Abs wait—" Jeremiah said on a hesitant note. Absalom paused and half-turned in his tracks.

"I won't get myself kill't." Jeremiah's face broke into a too broad smile. Absalom raised his hands and smiled back with lips downturned at the corners. He kept on walking.

Jeremiah watched Absalom disappear around the bend and wiped the trail of dampness leaking from the corners of his eyes.

They eventually had to part, better sooner than later Jeremiah comforted himself. He squelched the threatening sorrow. He wanted to run after Absalom but he had chosen his path.

The air had turned even cooler. From his vantage point on top of the ridge, Jeremiah studied the camp below him.

From time-to-time he picked up a wispy blade of grass and nibbled. Like a magnet, Jeremiah drew closer to observe the camp. He wondered how he would find Nessa amidst the throng of people. Somehow he knew he could not leave until he found her or at least made a good effort.

He pondered a strategic approach. He decided to search in a systematic manner. He remained on the fringes of the camp and studied the goings and comings. He counted 600 wagons. People were organized in detachments of maybe a thousand, because of the many villages from the North Carolina border and all through Georgia and Tennessee. The Cherokee nation was much bigger than were in this camp. He hoped he could find Nessa in this particular detachment.

The Cherokees had been traveling for a long time before they stopped here in Hiawassee. Old women burdened with large knapsacks on their backs stooped in almost horizontal positions. A few young women, their bellies swollen with babies, carried their belongings on their backs. The caravans housed the sick and very young. Some of them rode horses carrying along pots, pans, and household belongings. But the majority trailed along on foot.

Men brought out dead bodies on a makeshift litter while others, ranging from two to five people dug shallow graves for the bodies alongside the path.

Groups of people left the camp at different times, foraging for food. He knew Nessa, and asked himself "what would she do?" The idea came to him in a flash.

She would search for medicinal herbs to help the sick. She would have to leave camp and go off into the fields, a gamble, but his only hope.

CHAPTER 8

Awanessa awoke to violent trembling. She didn't just have a dream it was a vision, a real experience. She lay quiet, staring off into the crowded room, over sleeping bodies, organizing the shifting landscape of her mind. In one scene of her dream, only half of her people in the camp had made it to this place called Oklahoma. Most had died. Much fighting had broken out between the new arrivals and the existing ones. More white settlers tried to drive them off this new land. Blood. More blood.

The scene shifted to the trail where they walked. Her grandfather blocked the path. She stepped around him, and Etu appeared shooing her back. When she looked behind her on the path, a trail of white flowers sprung up one by one. Gentle Dove waved to her, a serene smile on her face.

Awanessa sat up fast. Too fast. Nausea washed over her. With a sinking heart she wondered what she had caught from all the sick people around. Plus, her family in the vision, wanted her to turn back, to return to their lands in the Smokies. But how and to what? What did her relatives want her to do? Or did they come for her to join them? A confused, disquieting feeling settled over her.

People stirred. An old woman moaned. Another coughed and cleared her throat. A child whimpered, snuggling closer to his mother. Awanessa rose, making herself useful so she wouldn't have too much time to think.

In the last few months, living in these temporary stockades, she realized action was the best treatment for worry. She met Beloved Woman, Quatie Ross, in the makeshift dispensary every day to help out. More often though, they visited and tried to help people wherever they were. Now the weather had changed, the half-naked children suffered most with bad cases of whooping cough.

All throughout the day, she worked alongside Quatie while others helped.

She mentioned her vision to Quatie who replied. "It doesn't bode well." Quatie wore her trademarked hairstyle, parted in the center and pulled sleek behind her ears to show a kind face, but resolute chin. "We just have to keep going; that's all we can do."

"At least your husband put in a word for us to be in charge of our own 'removal,' Awanessa said, all but spitting out the last word.

"Oh, don't say it!" Quatie cut her hand in the air and bent to wrap a little girl in a striped, threadbare blanket. The child whimpered through thin, purplish lips.

Quatie positioned the child on her lap. Her other hand folded a pesto-like mixture into a poultice and wrapped it around the child's neck.

"Where would some of these people be if it weren't for you, out on the boundaries, foraging for wild plants to ease their suffering?"

"A lot of it is dried up from the drought, losing their power. I've searched everywhere in the woods."

Quatie placed the baby down on the makeshift cot. "Oh, do be careful," she murmured, resting her fingers on Awanessa's shoulder.

For some inexplicable reason, Quatie's gentle touch let loose the floodgates. Awanessa sat on a nearby stool, placed her head in her hands and sobbed.

"Come now, tut-tut. We can't have that. You've been so strong."

"I can't go on," Awanessa sobbed. "I can't even find any plants to pick. Everything—" she hiccupped again and again trying to control herself. People milling about cast curious glances in her direction.

Quatie moved her palm in circular motions between Awanessa's shoulder blades.

Ashamed at her outburst, Awanessa stifled her sobs. Finally, lifting a tear-streaked face, she stretched out her arms wide. "Everything . . ." She hiccupped again. "Even the spiderworts you find everywhere are just dried up. Nothing."

Quatie made soothing sounds, continuing to rub Awanessa's back. "Well, let's hope."

"Oh, hope . . ." Awanessa said with a snort. She became a whirlwind of activity, picking up the medicinal concoctions she had strewn about. "Who's going to help us?" She jammed into her bag the empty container of whooping cough syrup she had made. She scrunched the flattened poultice wraps in her hands and shoved bits of discarded stems and barks—from which she couldn't extract an ounce of medicine—no matter how long she boiled them.

Awanessa tossed the bag on the floor and grabbed both of the older woman's hands.

"We both have given away everything we have. Last night when it got too chilly," she continued in a nasal voice, sniffling. "I gave my blanket to a little boy who had a bad case of ague. Winter is setting in. We have no provisions to help our dying people or—" She averted her eyes and sighed with her whole body. "Or even to help ourselves," she ended on a plaintive note.

Quatie gathered the younger woman in her arms. Fortified after venting, Awanessa extricated herself from Quatie's embrace and picked up her bag containing her half-eaten remnants of food and her water flask.

"I'm venturing out into the woods again to see what I can find," Awanessa said, managing a warped smile.

* * *

Awanessa sauntered out of the camp, feeling lighter in spirit. A few guards nodded to her. They knew she tried hard to help her people. Due to persistent petitions by Chief John Ross and other council members to General Scott, the initial widespread brutality had stopped.

The government had gotten what they wanted. Her people were no longer a threat to U.S. expansion. The army didn't see the need to waste manpower guarding disoriented, dispirited and sick people. Only a few soldiers stayed to maintain order.

Sympathy shone from the eyes of a soldier. "No medicine came in today with the supplies?"

"The food and the medicine are never nearly enough, plus . . ." She couldn't resist the jab. "No white man's medicine is as good as ours."

"Well, what about Doc Hank and his nurse that the army brought in?"

"One doctor for how many people? Come on—" She quickened her pace, looking over her shoulder.

"Furthermore, the doc is in the same position— no medicine. He's long gone anyway." She shrugged her shoulders. The soldier said something else but she didn't hear. She knew he meant well, but words were useless when men, women, and children were dying like flies in winter.

Sometimes the soldiers watched her from their posts as she used her right hand to ground plants with her mortar and pestle while stirring the boiling cauldron with her left.

Awanessa passed some of her people searching for food in the nearby woods. Her heart sank in despair. She didn't know how much longer she could make it either.

Already her dress hung loose from her thin frame. Hunger stalked her every day. Last week, black spots appeared in front of her eyes and a dull pain in her lower back slowed her movements. During the course of the week, conditions grew worse. In her weakened condition, she was susceptible to any of the diseases running rampant throughout the camp.

She walked a good distance and found little in the way of herbs to treat the known ailments. The camp stood way off in the distance now but she couldn't return without something to ease the suffering. Excitement coursed through her when she found a few sprigs of comfrey for Onawa and Mai who were breastfeeding and needed to unknot their breasts. It also treated inflammations and gangrene. She had found a double-duty herb.

She meandered here and there, picking up crows foot and dandelion. When she spotted the crawling five fingers, the main cure for ague and whooping cough, she almost whooped in delight. Her excitement waned though as most of it were nothing but dried up twine. She didn't even gather enough to help Taso who now coughed up pure blood.

Tired and dizzy, she staggered past clumps of reddish chokeberry bushes to slump under a majestic, walnut oak tree. The huge canopied branches spread out wide, inviting her to rest; its leaves turned brown, ready to shed. She leaned against the trunk heaving a sigh. Before she closed her eyes, cranes hovered in the sky. She smiled. According to Cherokee lore this was a good omen. Despite her weariness she felt at peace, at one with all of nature and the spirit world.

* * *

She did not know how long she slept. Darkness surrounded her. A sea of white-topped caravans nestled in the night. Good, she could find her way back. But back to what? Feeling unusually warm and comfortable, she stretched, unwilling to leave her cozy enclave. In the next moment her spine stiffened.

She turned on to her other side to face the warmth of a smoldering fire.

"Who—Wha—," she managed to squeak out and froze.

A pair of glittering eyes stared back at her.

A black panther.

Her heart quickened. She didn't have time to run. Her gaze pierced the darkness. When her eyes adjusted to the dark, a man crouched before her.

Jeremiah.

She could only stare, wordless, her heart full of warring emotions. She sat up and leaned against the tree trunk. Despite the warmth, chills rode up and down her arm and she hugged herself.

"Are you cold?" he asked as if he had never left her.

"What are you doing here?"

"Had to find you."

"B-bbut why?"

He rubbed the back of his neck and grimaced before he spoke. "Had to make sure you're alive and . . . well."

"Well, as you can see, I'm fine." She lifted her chin, trying to peer in the dark past him. She still smarted from the way he left her in the village, even though a lifetime ago.

"Not from what I've been witnessing in your camp."

"You've been here all this time, why?" She asked. She felt like she was going around in a circle with him, not getting any answers. "This is as dangerous for you, Jeremiah, as it is for me. It's best we go."

"Yuh. Let's go."

She rose unsteady. His big arms snaked around her waist.

"Come with me," he murmured nudging her hair with his nose.

She looked at him, feeling her eyes widening. "What do you mean come with you? You have no place to go—do you?"

He smiled again, this time without showing any teeth. "Don't worry so."

Tears filmed her eyes. "You're being hunted and I'm being chased from my home. Be sensible."

He pointed to the camp. "Look Nessa, is that sensible? What you going back to?"

She hung her head and bit her lip, remembering their lovemaking when he first shortened her name. "I must go." She walked away from him without looking at his face. She felt alone and cold without his arm around her waist. His question, "what are you going back to" echoed through her mind.

A few yards away, black spots danced in front of her eyes again. In one split-second she had a deep knowing. Every step she made toward the camp moved her one step closer to the grave. She would die in this no-man's land and not set foot out West.

She cast a stricken look over her shoulder in time to see a shadowy figure flying in the air toward Jeremiah. A scream gurgled in her throat and died as the man wrestled Jeremiah to the ground. Jeremiah soon recovered from the surprise attack and they traded equal blows.

"Why don't you stay away," said a muffled voice.

She gasped. "Rides-With-Wind." He didn't even cast her a glance.

"Stop it this instant!" She yelled, stomping her foot and feeling helpless. They paid her no mind but rolled on the ground.

Warning shots from a rifle shattered the night air. Awanessa involuntarily covered her mouth to stifle the scream. The men stilled. Rushing feet trampled through the chokeberry bushes.

Jeremiah reared in the air like the bullet had gotten him in his chest. Rides-With-Wind struggled to his feet shouting. "No! Stay here Awanessa!" He picked up a rock to let sail at Jeremiah's head. Jeremiah grabbed it and slammed Rides-With-Wind over the head. Rides-With-Wind crumpled to the ground.

In two strides he reached Nessa's side, grabbing her arm. "Come," he said, his voice urgent.

"Stop—, Right there!" The voices sounded closer.

"Soldiers," Nessa whispered, her voice cracking.

"Come," Jeremiah said, his voice urgent as he pulled on her arm.

Her heart beat at triple speed. Without a second thought she placed her hand in Jeremiah's and they ran.

He all but carried her as they fled. She leaned into him, grateful for his strength, feeling safe and protected even though she knew it was superficial. She glanced over her shoulder to see if anyone followed; only the caravans stood like sepulchers in the dark.

She murmured a quick prayer for Rides-With-Wind, hoping he survived the blow. The soldiers probably stopped to see to Rides-With-Wind, preventing them from pursuing her and Jeremiah.

If the soldiers had any intentions of giving chase, Jeremiah soon lost them. Throughout the night Jeremiah kept up a steady pace, still half carrying her. They stopped twice to rest and he tipped her chin up to slake her thirst.

On the second stop her stomach rumbled, so he gave her a chicken drumstick. She looked at it in amazement as if it had materialized out of thin air. She noticed a bulging knapsack tied to his back. She hoped he filled it with food to last for a while. She took a couple of bites and hadn't tasted anything so good in months. A piece of flatbread would be perfect.

As if her thoughts manifested her wishes, Jeremiah proffered a broken chunk of bread. Not quite the flatbread, but it was wonderful sustenance. They sat in companionable silence, each wrapped up in their own thoughts, not daring to speak and alert any would-be patrollers.

After they ate, Jeremiah gestured they had to go. Not of a mind for conversation, Nessa understood the need for silence between them. Jeremiah pushed on. The moon came out in full force, illuminating their path. In her befuddled mind, she wondered at how purposeful his strides were as if he had a home to go to. Or, even that he knew where to go.

For once, she surrendered the reins to someone else. Without any effort at all, she flowed with the rhythms of his hips—two harmonious beings in the solitary night.

Far off an owl hooted, lending eeriness to the night. The staccato sounds of crickets pierced the air causing her body to twitch in fear. Jeremiah pressed her closer to him, leaned into her and whispered, "We're getting closer."

She wondered closer to where.

Nessa ran her tongue over dry lips. Jeremiah always addressed her by the shortened name. Awanessa belonged to her old life. She realized she had spent all of her time taking care of everyone else, but did not take care of herself. She needed water and didn't want to deplete their supply. The pain in her lower back intensified and a wave of dizziness swept over her. Her knees buckled.

In the distance, the sound of bloodhounds rented the stillness. In one fell swoop, Jeremiah picked her up like a corn cob doll and flung her over his shoulder. He pressed a reassuring hand in the middle of her aching back and burst into a sprint.

CHAPTER 9

A cloak of darkness enveloped Nessa. She floated in a cocoon. Fragments of elusive skeins entwined her lashes. She fluttered her eyelids, forcing them to open wide, but she couldn't. She wanted to reach up and peel away the cobwebs, but not even her fingers moved.

Images of the man she killed floated in front of her, his face accusing, forefinger pointing at her. A cry bubbled in her throat. She wondered why Jeremiah didn't help her. Maybe she had dreamt she saw him. Maybe she had died at the camp. Maybe.

A weakness seeped down her arms and legs, and she sank back, deep into the welcoming, engulfing darkness.

Nessa drifted in and out of consciousness. Often, she felt hands administering to her body lifting her and forcing liquid in her mouth. The disoriented feeling passed. She didn't open her eyes right away but tried to re-orient herself.

She knew she had left the camp to gather herbs but did not meet with much success. She met Jeremiah. Her chest swelled with the thought. Then she left with him and he picked her up when they heard bloodhounds. Jeremiah started to run, dodging branches and trees.

A long time after the sound of barking dogs diminished, he kept on running. His heart pounded next to hers. Somehow its steady beat gave her comfort. Despite his exertions, he remained calm, his grasp on her body never loosened. She couldn't remember anything else.

Still befuddled, she rose from the cushy bed of leaves to rest on her elbows. They were in a smoky, enclosed space. A smell of cooked game hung in the air. Water trickled nearby. A quick glance took in the abandoned lean-to, covered with vines and shrubs.

"Welcome back."

Nessa's heart lurched at the gentle voice. She swiveled around and Jeremiah sat cross-legged directly behind her.

"How long have I been like this?"

"A few days."

Her eyes flew to his in alarm. "What happened? I laid here for days?"

He touched her forehead and cheek for any fever.

"Not quite a week. Carried you when it was safe to travel. You had me right scared, you know?"

"I'm so sorry." She bit her cracked lips. He brought a cool cloth to her lips and offered her water.

"Don't be sorry. God knows you'd be dead if I'd left you in that mess." He slowly covered the water canteen and sat back against the cabin's wall. "If it weren't for Providence."

"I must have been such a burden . . ."

"Hush now. Was I a burden to you when you saved my hide?"

"No, but this is different—." She stopped. The memory of her losses washed over her. "I had so much then," she whispered in a strained voice. Clearing her throat, she spoke stronger, "now you have to save yourself; you shouldn't have to worry about me too."

He leaned forward and brushed her forehead with his lips. "Now we have each other. If it's enough for you, it's enough for me."

She felt warm all over and light-headed. He eased her back on her pallet of leaves.

"You must rest. You need to recover before we make another move."

"Just stay here and talk to me a little."

"Hardly going anywhere," he said with a chuckle.

She smiled too. "Can anyone hear us talk, you think?"

"Nah, no one can hear us from outside or see us. And we still get good light in here."

"But where are we J?"

He smiled at the shortening of his name. "We're headed south."

Her eyes dilated in alarm. "South? No, no-no-no, you can't head deeper south. That is too dangerous for you." She furrowed her brows. "How do you know where you are anyway?"

"Followed the North Star. When I left your village I stumbled on a man who became my friend. His name's Absalom." Jeremiah's eyes tinged with regret. "We traveled together for a while following the North Star."

"But, if you followed the North Star how come we're heading south then?"

He grinned, "Tha's right."

She rolled her eyes and sighed.

His grin became broader. "Just went the opposite direction of the North Star."

"Don't tease!" On a sudden inspiration, she said, "do you know my people recognize seven different directions —north, south, east, west, up, down and center?" When Jeremiah gave her a puzzled look she continued blithely: "North means trouble or defeat and South means happiness —so we're going in the right direction."

Jeremiah chuckled. "That's mighty convenient. Your Great Spirit's with us then." He stretched his long legs in front. After a few seconds he said, "Reckon we're now in South Georgia near Florida."

She turned startled eyes on him. "You must have wings!"

He chuckled. "Sometimes I think so. I'll outrun bloodhounds, trackers, even the entire United States Army."

"You've done this before, haven't you? I saw the old welts on your back."

His eyes dropped. He shook his head. "Still outran them. A so-called friend betrayed me."

"Oh?"

"Against my better judgment, I waited for this friend by the Savannah River. He showed up with Massa George, those same slave catchers, and some more riff-raff with dogs and all."

Nessa felt like retching. She placed her fingers over her mouth, "Oh my God. I don't want to hear anymore."

"Realized afterwards Ole Massa George believed I had the good life working as an artisan and not out in the hot sun picking cotton."

"It would seem so."

He laughed without humor. "Massa George got a way of draining a man's lifeblood." He pursed his lips. "You know what burned me up the most, Nessa?

"What?"

"When he would harass me to death about finishing a chifforobe or table—so he could collect the money."

She waited; she knew when he worked his lower lip he had more to tell.

He looked down the length of his nose at her. "It's a simple thing really . . . compared to all the cruelty and everything else. He—he just couldn't wait to sign HIS name on all the fine furniture I created. HIS!"

She searched his eyes and found pride running deep to his core. She wondered what kind of man stood before her, whose spirit could not be broken no matter what they did to his body. He had no fear and was so different from some of the other slaves who were resigned to their fate. Etu used to tell her their passivity was a ruse. It was to lull their owners into thinking they were obedient and couldn't think for themselves. And when the opportunity to escape came, some would seize it, displaying the most cunning in their quest for freedom.

"You're talking too much you know." He studied her face for signs of fatigue.

She chuckled, "I'm just listening."

"Something to eat?" he asked.

Maybe her light-headedness was from hunger. She looked around, a now alert, curious expression on her face. "What do we have?"

"A rabbit." It was staked on a stick over a smoldering fire in the other corner of the cabin. He moved to poke it with his knife.

Her stomach growled. He handed her a morsel on a big green leaf. She bit into the succulent meat and he added more to her leaf She ate until her stomach started to roil. "I don't want to eat too much too soon."

"Good thinking—you don't want to be throwing it all up."

She sat back contented and watched him put some of the uneaten rabbit back on the makeshift hearth.

"Where did you come from J?"

He looked at her in surprise. "Where did that spring from?"

"Well, I know you came directly from Athens, Georgia and before that from Augusta. But were you transported from Africa or were you born here?"

"Here. But my father and mother were Coromantine people on the West Coast of Africa, they told me."

Nessa not wanting to interrupt kept silent.

"My father drove the carriage for Massa George's family. He was well-schooled, son of a chieftain. Had his own religion too."

"From a chief's son to a slave?" She murmured. "So J, you're the grandson of a chief!"

He chuckled. "Tell that to Massa George. Much good it does in these parts. You know what?" His eyes became animated. "My father, he led a mutiny on the ship that brought him here. They threw half of the sailors overboard." His eyes sparkled in the telling.

"Then what happened?" she leaned forward in rapt attention.

"If it weren't for a Dutch ship pulling up alongside and taking over, things would have been different."

"So I guess they slapped him back in irons, huh?"

"Yes. My father was a warrior too. When he came here he never gave up his old ways. He tried to escape many times."

"He would leave you and your mother?"

"It was the only way. We knew he'd come back and buy us." He shrugged. "It was just the only way." He stared off into the dark depths of the room. "Bloodhounds circled him and mauled him to death." His voice sounded distant, sad.

"Oh." She slapped her hand over her mouth. "I bet you're like your father."

"Yes."

"And what of your mother?"

He refocused on Nessa. "Well, she worked in the big house. She wasn't easy either," he said on a smothered chuckle. "Every week she'd steal a book or newspaper. We had quite a hidden stash. I even taught her to read."

"So how did you learn?"

J's face softened. "Through Devlin, Massa George's son. We were tight growing up."

"But wasn't it illegal?—I mean for slaves to read?"

"Sure was. Devlin was a good sort though. A living devil his father would call him. He never changed either. He'd sneak all kinds of books and some poetry books to me too."

He laughed out loud at the memories."When he heard I sprung from the Coromantine people, he brought me this book of poems. It's so precious; I know it by heart."

"Tell me; tell me what does it say?" She said inching closer.

He raised himself up in one graceful motion to his feet. He faced her. With a pokered face, dramatic arm flourishes and pregnant pauses he recited:

"Yet, if thine own, thy children's life, be dear,
Buy not a Cormantee, though healthy, young,
of breed too generous for the servile field:
They, born to freedom in their native land,
Choose death before dishonorable bonds;
Or, fired with vengeance, at the midnight hour
Sudden they seize thine unsuspecting watch,
And thine own poniard bury in thy breast."

Jeremiah clutched his chest and staggered back, making a final downward swoop with his right arm. He collapsed to the ground, joining Awanessa in muffled laughter.

"That's just like my father," he said trying to be sober. "Sounded just like him."

"And you too," she whispered. He reached over and clasped her fingers. They held each other's hands while wrapped up in their own thoughts.

"What happens now? Where do we go from here?"

His face turned serious and he clasped both hands in front of his face. "Can only try my best to keep us out of harm's way."

"You never answered me though; why aren't we going north?"

"My father, once when he ran away, became friends with this Indian chief, or I think he is a chief."

"So?" Nessa knitted her brow, "A Cherokee?"

"No, a Seminole chief named Osceola. They became friends. Remember, my father went about all over with the carriage. Anyways, this Osceola and his band waited for him on the other side of the river but the patrollers got my father. He never made it. He didn't die right away either. For a week my mother nursed him . . . But—." He shook his head to clear the memory flooding his mind. After a few seconds he continued. "But before he died, he told me how to get to the Seminole village."

"So, that's where we're trying to get to then?"

He nodded. "You need your full strength though."

"Wait. One more question. Originally you were headed north ... before I found you."

He shrugged. "At that time I wanted to find my own way. But with you here, south is the best course to get help from Osceola."

She had more questions but decided not to burden him. Even without knowing what the future will bring, she knew they were going to face it together.

She stretched and yawned. "I feel so much better."

He smiled when her stomach growled in contradiction.

She looked at the half-eaten rabbit smoldering on the makeshift spit. "You didn't go out and hunt did you? What would you hunt it with anyway?"

"I told you, I can outrun anything ... even a rabbit."

She stifled a giggle behind her fingers, picturing this huge man running after a tiny rabbit. "Serious though, if anyone had come by, you could have been killed."

He got up and fixed her something to eat, muttering to himself, "Gonna get kill't, gonna get kill't," he mimicked Absalom. Her brows knit in confusion. "Been hearing that a lot lately," he explained.

"But you could have!" she emphasized. "Anyone could have come along and spotted you."

"Do you think we've come this far to get caught?" He shoved an ember into the fire hard. "I'd die first."

Little by little the mood changed to somber. The weight of their situation sank in. Jeremiah stoked the dying fire.

"What are you thinking?" She asked.

He left her to lie down on the other side of the fire. "Thinking we need to stay here another full day then head out tomorrow night."

She stretched out on the leaves, yearning to reach out to him but something in the rigid set of his back gave her pause. She shivered, whether from the chill or the lurking thought in the back of her mind: What untold dangers waited for them on their journey south tomorrow?

* * *

Nessa felt much stronger the next day, almost back to her old self. They ventured outside, one looking out for the other, while they foraged for food to build up their supplies for the journey. They found corn, apples, berries, and a possum or two to roast. She was thankful the little stream behind the lean-to ran crystal clear. They filled every container they had.

Once back inside the hut, Jeremiah stared in puzzlement at the brilliant red flower Nessa had picked. "What are you going to do with that?"

"Oh that's *Scarlett Bee Balm*. After I boil it and drink it for tea—I'll be good as new."

He tried to suppress the amused smile tugging at the corners of his mouth. His eyes crinkled in merriment and he folded his arms on his chest. "Begging your pardon, Lady Awanessa, what'll you do for a teapot ma'am?"

She gave a curtsy and almost cooed. "Oh Lord Jeremiah, I'm always disposed to have my necessities at hand sir." With a flourish she plucked a tin can she had in her satchel—now empty of herbs. She tossed her head back at an angle, giving him an arched look, and sauntered to the stream, eliciting strangled laughter from Jeremiah.

She stifled threatening giggles, rinsing and filling the can with clean water.

Soon after she made tea, Nessa sat down, giving him an expectant look. "Shall I pour milord?"

"No milady, can't have you burning those tender fingers." Jeremiah used some of the leaves from their beds to hold the tin can and remove it from the flame. He let it cool awhile then offered it to her.

She sipped the tea and closed her eyes as the warmth seeped through her body. Jeremiah turned from her and proceeded to roast all the corns on the coals. He handed her a perfect roasted cob.

"I've never eaten corn this way. But it's good. We make hominy out of it back home," she said brushing the stray grains from her lap then looked away, her eyes growing misty. Jeremiah touched her arm and shook his head.

She sniffed. "No use, right?"

In a quick stride he folded her into his arms. He'd wanted to do this for so long. He held her tight. He finally raised her chin and started to rain kisses all over her forehead, eyelids, cheeks, and lips. She felt so right in his arms. As soon as their lips met, molten fire shot through her body and she pulled his head down. She was flying, her senses abuzz like bees searching, searching deep for the sweet nectar embedded in her flowering plants.

Before she had her fill of the ambrosiac nectar, she heard a loud, "Pop, Pop," like rifle shots behind them. They froze. Their eyes flew open in horror and they sprang apart. Jeremiah pushed Nessa behind him in one swift motion.

Nessa clutched his back while her eyes scanned for the intruder. Jeremiah did the same until she realized his shoulders were shaking with uncontrollable laughter. He couldn't speak; he just pointed.

Nessa stepped from behind him. The remaining cobs of corn leaped up in the air with sparks shooting off as they became over-popped. Her face crumpled with hysterical laughter. She held her belly and sank to her leafy bed.

"Popped off by a corn," he said, trying to restrain his chuckles.

Nessa used her skirt hem to dab the corners of her eyes while her laughter subsided. "A deadly weapon; I wouldn't want to get close to another one for sure."

Jeremiah removed the blackened specimens and popped one kernel in his mouth. "A little crispy, but still good." He grinned and dusted off the ash.

"How can we be having fun when we're in so much danger?" she whispered, suddenly sober.

She watched his face grow grim. He continued to toss the kernels in his mouth, one at a time, staring at the fire. He rose and strode to the unhinged front door.

He returned and began to pace. "We have about seven, maybe eight hours before we leave. Now we've eaten, we'd better get as much rest as possible," he said.

"Why don't we leave as soon as it gets dark—that way we'll have even more time?"

"Nessa dear," he sucked in one of his cheeks hiding the tiny smile on his lips. "You don't know much about what goes on outside of your village. Do you?"

"Yes, I do! We had a very good relationship with white people. I even had a friend Clarissa; I'd attend community dances with her family. They were really nice." Her eyes flashed, and she looked him dead in the eyes. "So don't tell me I don't know what's going on outside my 'little world.'"

"Tut-tut, temper, temper darling," he chided, wagging his forefinger.

She lowered her eyes, disarmed.

In a more serious tone, he continued. "Patrollers usually scout the outside of towns and borders from dusk until around midnight and all during daytime. So I'm reckoning that's when we should light out—at midnight."

"Oh," she mustered in a small voice. He walked back to the fire. In a methodical manner he packed their foodstuffs and scarce belongings. He obliterated any other signs of their presence with his foot.

* * *

Jeremiah wanted to lie down and snuggle next to her. Just hold her. He banished those dangerous thoughts. He felt ashamed—after all she had gone through. She had lost the baby during her week-long sickness. He didn't think she knew she was expecting. He wasn't going to tell her and cause her more worry. He had to be careful from now on. Jeremiah nestled his chin on his palms and considered the dangers inside and outside the cave.

He watched her while she slept. The weak fire sparked a deep, rich chestnut brown glow through Nessa's hair. He could get a similar glow by rubbing and layering linseed oil into those exotic woods Massa

George brought down from the Territory. Jeremiah could never resist stroking a table, especially when buffed to a most brilliant sheen. Her hair held the same attraction. He bit his lip and looked away from her.

When it came to Nessa, his traitorous body belied everything in his brain. How can he stop from getting close to her when his whole body and mind yearned to hold her all through the night? He decided he'd find a safe place to leave her where she'd be happy. He had his free papers; he'd try to get work on a schooner bound for Boston.

Yes, he decided he'd leave her with the Seminoles.

He felt quite pleased with himself for having a plan until another thought struck him. His heart dropped in his belly.

When they reached the Seminole camp, would Osceola even remember Jeremiah's father and welcome the son?

"DRAPETOMANIA, OR THE DISEASE
CAUSING NEGROES TO RUNAWAY
It is unknown to our medical authorities, although
its diagnostic symptom, the absconding from service,
is well known to our planters and overseers ... "
- "Diseases and Peculiarities of the Negro Race,"
Dr. Cartwright (in DeBow's Review, 1838)

CHAPTER 9

Even though it was good travelling with Absalom, it was even better with Nessa. All through the night she made a most pleasant companion. By example, she taught him how to walk the surefooted Indian way using all his senses, avoiding men or wild beats. They travelled hand-in-hand, along the light of the moon. Jeremiah felt as if they were making good progress, their next challenge to find a place to hide before daybreak.

Without warning, Nessa's hand wrenched from his grasp.

Jeremiah!" Nessa shrieked his name, pain lacing her voice, eyes wide with terror.

She sank to the dew-covered grass. Jack rabbits darted in fright at her scream, fleeing into the maze of shrubs and trees.

Breath left his body for a split second. His eyes widened in horror. Jeremiah dropped to his knees in the grass beside her.

A snare clamped her left ankle tight.

Silent tears flowed down her cheeks, her face contorted in pain. He tried to pry open the snare with his bare hands. With every tug and pull, the snare clamped tighter. His heart sank heavy in his chest. Brute strength could not pry it open. If he continued, the snare would hold her ankle until all her flesh disappeared. The snare would hold to the bone. He knew from experience only a key would open it. And he knew who had the key.

Under a blanket of faint stars, and a pale sliver of moon, he pulled her close, hugged her and put her head in his lap.

"Save yourself. Go on without me," she said on a sobbing breath.

"Never," he whispered. He looked at her foot twisted at an odd angle, already growing welts. He could have battered the trap until it opened. She'd lose her leg in the process and possibly bleed to death. He'd seen it happen over and over. He couldn't bear it. Trackers set traps all the time for runaways and critters. "We'll face it together," he said on a half sob.

She began a steady cry, fading to whimpers as she slept. He held her through the wee hours. Now and then his huge body racked with dry sobs. Keen disappointment melded to his bones; bile rose up in the back of his throat. His vision blurred with images of whippings, torture, back-breaking work, and even death.

No help for it, he'll fight till death. He had nothing else to live for. But for the first time in his life he felt fear for another human being. He would use the one trump card he had left, his free pass.

Even though he knew, and the slave catchers knew, no sane free black man would be roaming these parts at night. And how to explain Nessa. His head throbbed.

He tucked her tight braid under the collar of her dress. He leaned against the slender trunk of a nearby chokecherry tree, closed his eyes and waited. He dozed on and off, dreaming of free falling from a cliff when voices and yapping sounds seeped into his consciousness.

"Looky here boys, looky here!"

Jeremiah cracked one sleepy eye to see the cause of this ruckus—enough to wake snakes. Menacing dogs surrounded him, pawing the ground, their eagerness held in check by a bunch of plug-ugly-looking men.

Jeremiah bolted upright and shook Nessa's shoulder. Her eyes opened, filling with awareness. He raised her to a sitting position, to their impending doom. He held her hand and she clasped his in a clammy grip.

It may be the last time they would touch each other. The thought robbed him of breath for a second. It wasn't about what happened to him so much. No, he could not protect her—as a man.

Rage boiled in his chest, his nostrils flared and his chest heaved. How would Absalom get out of this mess? Abs would bow his head, stay humble and not make any funny moves. He glanced at her ankle, now swelling. Yes, he'd do the same; he cannot do anything to cause her undue harm. The dogs in their excitement scampered around while the four slave catchers clapped their hands and slapped each other on the back.

"My word, not one, but two turtle doves caught in our trap." The leader said, with a toothy grin.

"A strapping buck and a juicy squaw!" said his crony with the gourd for a nose.

They circled like buzzards.

"This is the big time Sarge," said the one with a giant cowlick shooting from the top of his head. He hunched, rubbing his hands together as if cold.

"I is a free man. Ah have mah papers, suh!" Jeremiah said in a voice just enough to be heard by the nearest man. He hung his head, defeated, but not before he saw Nessa bite her lip and glance away. Shame scorched his face and he drew a steadying breath. So much for Abs' way of handling the matter. He'd bide his time.

"You heard that gentlemen? This here boy says he's got something to show us" Sarge said in mock surprise, slapping his leg and stalking Jeremiah. "Something mighty official too," he continued, while the others guffawed.

One of the men waddled over to Nessa. He hoisted his trouser waist over his pot belly to show several keys in a bunch, along with a dangling knife. He stooped to insert a long, rusty key into the snare. He jiggled it back and forth. After a click, he extracted Nessa's foot.

"Careful now—no damage. She can fetch a good price," said Sarge, the obvious leader.

"Sarge yer gonna look at his papers?" Cowlicks asked, glancing at Jeremiah out of the corner of his eye.

"Sure, let's examine his papers like the proper gentlemen we are," Sarge said, his pock marked cheeks had deep grooves like sweat could gather and settle there for a while.

The rest of the men burst out laughing. "We's proper gentlemen," they nodded one after the other.

Jeremiah handed them the paper, his heart thudding erratic.

"Ha! George Sylvester Browne, indeed!" Sarge said.

The others laughed until they held their sides. "George Sylvester Browne never freed no slaves in his lifetime. This is sweet!" said gourd nose.

"He'll pay some pretty shiners for this one." The pot-bellied one all but wheezed when he said it, his pink cherub face aglow with greed.

Nessa was free.

Jeremiah moved fast. He clobbered Cowlicks over the head, stunning him. He wrestled with Potbelly for the knife while the other man jumped him from behind. He elbowed the man who fell to the ground. But before he could turn to get Sarge, the unmistakable sound of a revolver clicked at Nessa's ear. Jeremiah's arms stopped in mid-air, like a statue. His shoulders slumped and he gave up his hands, like an offering.

Nessa's hands covered her mouth to choke back sobs.

"Get me the handcuffs from my bag," Sarge said in a stern voice. "You bunch of hens, it takes a man to do a man's job." Cowlicks fetched the handcuffs and clamped them on Jeremiah's wrists while another shackled the defeated man's ankles.

"You getting the squaw ready to go?" Sarge asked Potbelly, whose eyes looked decidedly crossed from the blow Jeremiah gave him.

"Aw Sarge can't we have a wee bit of fun with her first?" The others turned to Sarge, ready to pounce on Nessa if he gave the word.

"Y'all fooled around enough with this property. I want this Romeo and Juliet clean, you hear? No bruises, not even a scratch." Sarge walked back to his horse with resolute strides. "I want every penny of this reward—twill be much more than selling them in the deep South."

One of the men smirked when Sarge turned his back. "Ole Sarge can't git it up himself, that's why he don't want nobody else to have her."

"Old geezer's pecker stuck at half past six," another said with a chortling sound.

The others stifled their disgruntled comments when Sarge sauntered back. Jeremiah watched Sarge roll out an advertisement from the bulging pile in his pocket. Jeremiah closed his eyes. Sarge read:

"$2000 Reward for Dangerous Runaway Male, 6ft 3, Medium brown complexioned, named Jeremiah Browne. Black, shiny eyes, high cheekbones, no facial scars."

A low whistle went through the group while shooting Jeremiah, "wish we could kill you glances."

Sarge continued. "The squaw ain't worth more than $250, but we'll sell them together to the good Mr. Browne for a package of $2,500."

"A package deal," one said.

"One he can't refuse," The whoops echoed in Jeremiah's ear. They hoisted him behind Nessa into the back of a wagon, pushing him face down in the cart, a boot planted in the middle of his back. The cart rumbled away. He felt a need to retch. He had failed her. He turned his face from Nessa sitting next to Sarge, not wanting her to see his utter despair.

* * *

Bright streaks of orange slashed across the azure sky and the sun set low over the horizon. The slave catchers completed their business with Massa George.

Jeremiah watched Nessa, hands unbounded, limp with an uneven gait toward the main plantation house with one of the house slaves. A profound sense of loss weighed him down.

Massa George paced in front of him, his hands locked behind his back waiting to pounce. His celestial blue eyes, looking out from a handsome face, belied his intent. His blond sideburns, sprinkled with grey, moved in and out when he clenched and unclenched his jaw.

"You'll rue the day you crossed me boy!" Massa George's angular face turned mottled red. "After I break your leg you'll never run again. But first your hot-headedness is gonna be broken boy."

He peered into Jeremiah's face; his eyes turned an even paler shade of blue. "You hear me?" He reached up and grabbed Jeremiah by the collar and slapped his cheek twice.

Jeremiah gathered his saliva to spit in Massa George's face. But the spittle drooped down his collar instead. Massa George fired several slaps across Jeremiah's face in rapid succession. Jeremiah's head snapped sideways at the force of the last one. He felt the sting, but knew those were only mosquito bites compared to what's ahead.

"Noah," Massa George called to the overseer standing nearby. "Take away this pile of refuse and you know what to do."

"Want me to wait till morning sir? He'll set a fine example to all the other wretches harboring any such grand ideas."

"Good, good, but for tonight shackle him to the wall in the mess room and sprawl him like a spider. After he's lashed, we'll do the cathaul." Massa George strode away.

Jeremiah's skin crawled. He had witnessed the cathaul, one of the most dehumanizing tortures inflicted on slaves. He pictured them tying him down flat upon the ground with stakes and cords. They would borrow the huge, fierce tom-cat from the Killerman plantation and haul the cat backwards along his bare back. He could almost feel the animal's claws digging deep grooves in his back. He flinched at the dousing of salted water he'd get after the cathauling. He had to find a way to get out of here. But what of Nessa? He massaged his temples to relieve the throbbing.

"Noah, get Caesar and Hercules to guard him all night. No food!" With those directives, Massa George stalked toward the house. Halfway he turned and said in a deliberate tone. "Gather everyone first thing in the morning. That will show them what happens when they interfere with what's mine." He strode with quick determined strides toward the house.

* * *

Harmony Plantation's main house looked much grander than the other plantation houses Nessa had seen in North Carolina or Georgia. She limped past the imposing white columned porch, following Mirtilla to an out building. All the time she kept looking back to see where they were taking Jeremiah.

The two women entered a wide room with a great stone fireplace in the center where dozens of pots hung from a contraption. Mirtilla duck-walked around her domain, barking orders to two scullery maids whose elbows were buried in sudsy water.

She cuffed two little boys on their heads, "Don't I tell you no marble playing in here?" The boys scurried out. With one hand resting on her ample hip she gestured with the other. She laid out the rules of the house and general duties she expected Nessa to perform.

Mirtilla re-wrapped her head with a red and white checkered cloth and tied it with a knot in front as she talked. She pointed to where Nessa would sleep nearby. Nessa guessed she must be about middle age. Mirtilla's unlined skin gave off a luminous sheen but her popping eyes had a deep knowing.

"Lordy, that Jeremiah. He gots no call to be running like that. He sharp as tack but don't have sense that boy!" Mirtilla handed Nessa a broom and looked her up and down. "Heh, heh, Miss Lucretia not going to like you one bit. Especially now Mr. Devlin come back home to visit."

The name "Devlin" rang a bell in Nessa's memory of the agent in her village who bothered Tyanita. "Who is he?" she asked.

"That's Massa George and Miss Lucretia's only son. As she says all the time 'Dev is heir to all this.' She punctuated the statement with a wave of her arm. "A disappointment he be too.'"

"How so?"

Mirtilla grinned. "He be just a real devil, that's what he be. Always into one scrape or the other."

Nessa didn't need to encourage her.

"Master Devlin always chasing the women. Well, the women likes him too. A fine figure he be. No ma'am, can't blame them." She winked at Nessa. "Jeremiah was his body servant when they were young. Real tight they be. Then Massa George made him whip Jeremiah for nothing."

"Why?"

"Good Lord chile, just to show who's master and who's slave and they mustn't cross the line or forget.

That's what." She looked at Nessa as if she couldn't believe she didn't know the answer and had to ask. "The old Massa couldn't do nothing with young Devlin though. After that? He get even wilder. Then, Massa George force him in the army to make him straighten up and fly right. That's what."

Not interested in hearing about Devlin's exploits or his relationship with Massa George, Nessa chewed her bottom lip thinking about Jeremiah.

"What's going to happen to Jeremiah now Mirtilla?"

A distressed look flashed across her face. Her eyes popped a notch. "Only the Good Lord knows, chile," she whispered. "All I know is he won't be too long for this world after they be done with him." She directed a furtive glance at the door. "They going crucify him tomorrow! That's what."

She became brisk in her movements and business-like as if she regretted her talkativeness.

"You can't be working looking like that." She fished out of a cupboard a pile of clothing—an ugly brown, homespun dress. Heavy brogans clattered on the wooden floor at her feet.

When Nessa put on the dress, it hung from her shoulders like a crocus bag without sufficient yams to fill it out. She sniffed the dress. It reeked of cured fish. Pulling the ugly brogans on her feet, she winced in pain. The brogans hugged her tortured ankle but she realized her ankle now had some support.

"You ready chile?"

Nessa nodded, "Yes ma'am."

Mirtilla looked pleased with the deference Nessa gave her. "Come, we have work to do—just watch the other servants—the way they do things." She wiped her hands in her apron, swaying from side-to-side out of the kitchen.

Nessa followed her to the dining room where the dinner table needed clearing. Her jaw dropped in surprise. In less than a second, her gaze flicked over the black and white toile with scenes of plantation life papering the high walls. Golden fabric shirred across the high ceiling in soft pleats. An elaborate chandelier, with twenty white candles and tear-dropped crystal nuggets hung from the center. On the oval dining table, two gleaming silver candelabras anchored the white damask tablecloth at both ends. At the centerpiece, a low arrangement of white magnolias gave off a fragrant scent. She had never seen such splendor.

Two servants scraped the leftovers from the table into a container. Miss Lucretia stood in a corner, watching them. Mirtilla beckoned Nessa to help with removing the tablecloth.

Miss Lucretia moved over to the sideboard and poured coffee over the leftover scraps of food. A woman of medium height, she had bright sharp eyes, darting back and forth, taking in what everyone did all at once.

The sideboard had gleaming silver platters with a few oysters, rice, and string beans leftover from dinner. A portion of roast beef still floated in gravy. Nessa's stomach growled in anticipation. She took the folded table cloth into the kitchen along with some dishes, wincing in pain as she walked.

The other two servant girls looked at her with curious eyes, not certain of her position in the kitchen. She gave them a wobbly smile. But they turned back to their work. In a few minutes, Mirtilla returned with three more servants in tow carrying scraped dishes and platters. Her stomach growled again.

Nessa couldn't believe her eyes. The leftovers weren't given to the servants. "No dear, Miss Lucretia she count everything," Mirtilla told her.

Awanessa sat down and tried to eat the unpalatable fare of crackling bread, sappy collards and hog maws Mirtilla had prepared for the slaves earlier.

While she ate she looked out the window. About five or six small black children pushed and shoved each other vying for the cornmeal in the trough.

Her eyes roamed the surroundings, noting the huge carpentry shed where dozens of young men hauled in slabs of wood. The shed blocked her view of the cotton fields in the distance. To the left, neat rows of slave cabins looked forlorn in the shadowed evening. Further off, she saw the dilapidated barn where they held Jeremiah.

She wished she could talk to Devlin to find out if he's one and the same. Maybe he'd know the whereabouts of Tyanita. Maybe he could help Jeremiah.

As if she had conjured him, Devlin strode down a path. His hands buried deep in his side pockets, his lips pursed as if whistling a jaunty tune. Her heart quickened but steadied when she thought maybe his father had sent him to her village to inquire about Jeremiah. She preferred to believe Devlin would help, especially after she remembered Mirtilla's words. She focused on him helping her. A plan started to take shape in her mind.

She turned to the two women with urgency in her voice. "Where can I go to the privy?" They looked at her and twittered. One removed a sudsy finger to point down a path adjacent to the slave quarters. Nessa crouched, clutched her belly and asked where she could find herbs to help her ailment. They pointed in the same direction.

Nessa dragged one foot behind her out of the kitchen. Loud giggles followed. She decided to remain crouching. She grimaced, making a few audible groans in case anyone wondered.

People milled about and glanced at her but no one bothered her as it was obvious what she was about. She made her way down the path and, to her delight, found a field of bushes and herbs perfect for her plan. She snapped enough for her purpose and wandered about on the pretext of gathering more. She watched the house to make sure no one was paying attention.

A horse's whinny caused her to turn around. Devlin directed three little boys to stack bags of produce in a cart. He stayed his hand for her to stop. She crouched down amidst the bushes, her heart doing double-time to her breathing. Soon he had the cart piled with sacks and the horse tethered to a tree.

Devlin shooed the boys away. He looked left and right and strode towards her. His blue eyes bore into hers. He dragged her by a braid, pushed her and pulled her back a couple of times, all the time speaking in a low, rapid tone.

He did something strange but she didn't complain. He used his knife to slice off her long, silky braid up to her ears. He turned around and held it up like a trophy to the somber-faced onlookers.

"She doesn't need this anymore on Harmony—we can't have her tempting all the men." He threw the braid in the air. It undulated like a snake and landed in the bushes. Four little slave girls and boys, clad in sack cloth down to their knees, scrambled to find it.

Devlin pulled Nessa forward and thrust a cold metal between her breasts. She clutched her chest, really needing to go to the privy now. She ran with a lumbering gait toward the lean-to, amidst a burst of laughter from the onlookers.

Darkness sneaked over the plantation and the path back to the kitchen merged into the night. A warm amber glow illuminated the many windows of the big house. Nessa saw Miss Lucretia's and Massa George's head bobbing by the window in the parlor. Nessa ducked in fright. All they had to do was spot her lurking outside and she would be chitterlings for the slaves' dinner tomorrow.

She remained still in her hiding place. In single file, slaves passed down another path to their cabins. They had just come in from the fields. Stony-faced, they walked with their feet shuffling across the ground. No whistling. No singing. No talking. When the last one passed by, she minced her steps back to the kitchen.

The kitchen bustled with activity. One girl stirred a pot of beans while the other dried a pile of dishes. Mirtilla peered over her mending in the lamplight. Socks and undergarments piled up to a mound at her feet. She squinted at Nessa through bleary eyes.

"Where you been?"

"I went to gather some herbs, ma'am."

"Herbs? Who's got the bellyaches?"

"It's to make tea for my ankle, ma'am. She stretched out her leg to show Mirtilla who looked at it and grunted.

"You watch, after I drink this, my ankle will be good as new by tomorrow and I can help you better."

Mirtilla grunted again. She turned her attention to the scullery maids. "Gals go on out and feed your pickaninnys now; this one here will take over." Mirtilla shooed them out with a pushing motion of her hands. She turned to Nessa. "Even if you have to hop on one leg, you need to keep stirring that there grub until it's done then take it down to the barn."

Nessa couldn't believe her luck.

Mirtilla continued. "Massa George want me to feed the guards so they can guard your fool man all night."

"Yes ma'am."

Mirtilla sat hunched over her mending again, rocking back and forth, humming the refrain of an elusive hymn.

It was pitch black when Nessa found her way to the barn. She leaned to one side from carrying the heavy food pail.

"Ooh wee, a nice little squaw from the big house to keep us warm the whole night through."

A voice shouted from inside. "Did she bring vittles?" The guard rubbed his hands together and salivated. From the gleam in his eyes, Nessa was sure he wasn't salivating for food. "Let's make a deal, squaw: Spend the night." He smacked his lips. "Then you'll know fer sure the brute in there is alright."

Alright? Alright until tomorrow, then what? Nessa thought watching him, her expression wary.

The guard advanced, his hand scratching his crotch. She dropped the pail of food on the path; one of the cornbread rolled out. She lifted her skirt and ran as fast as she could, the men's' laughter echoing down the path behind her.

Even though she didn't see any signs of Jeremiah, she knew for sure they held him in the barn—alive.

They wouldn't guard a dead man. She breathed a sigh of relief.

It had to happen tonight.

* * *

Nessa counted Mirtilla's snores and the low whistles to gauge the depth of her sleep. She took her knapsack, stuffing it with cornbread and whatever else she could find. She inched her back against the crude stone wall in the dark toward the door. She didn't lurk in the center of the room because she knew there would be obstacles in her way.

Mirtilla made two loud snorts and Nessa jumped. Mirtilla let out a long deflated whistle and the steady snores resumed.

Nessa now knew if she could make it to the door and unlatch it before the snorts came again she would be home free.

The snorts came at the more vulnerable moments. Mirtilla's eyes would pop open with each snort or she'd jerk and wake up for a brief moment.

Nessa stepped out on the stoop. The cool night air fanned her cheek. She looked right and left, crouched low, and scampered toward Jeremiah's prison, despite the nagging pain in her ankle. She pushed the door in, giving a silent prayer of thanks when it opened with only a tiny squeak.

Peering in, she noted a dim lantern in the corner. She gave a cursory glance at the two guards slumped in the corner. The sleeping draught worked. She had crushed the leaves so fine and dispensed it throughout the meal she delivered to the men earlier. Even if they woke up they would be too weak. They wouldn't even have the energy to move or call out. Her eyes soon adjusted to the lighting. She scanned the room and her eyes opened in horror.

Jeremiah was a spider; legs spread-eagled and manacled facing the wall.

She assessed the situation and wasted no time. She whispered his name but he only grunted. She poked in her bosom and found the key Devlin had dropped there earlier. She released the shackles from his legs first so he could land on his feet. With his feet dangling, she grabbed a stool and climbed up the length of his body to get to his arms. Without losing a precious moment, she freed both his arms.

Disoriented, he slurred her name in shock.

Nessa wasted no time. She took his arm and led him outside toward the horse and cart Devlin had tethered nearby. Her ankle had begun to feel better immediately after drinking the tea. The swelling had subsided, but not enough to bear his bulky weight. She struggled with him to the cart and hoisted him in.

She took command of the reins in haste, steering away from Harmony. Jeremiah's dazed expression quickly faded. He checked the position of the North Star and gestured to Nessa he'd take over now. Nessa gasped at his busted lips and the cuts running diagonally from his temple to his chin.

In the cool morning air, Jeremiah's nose and forehead beaded with sweat. "Must go before bullhorn sounds."

She caught his low mumble and agreed. She knew from her overnight visits to Cecelia's plantation, or even on visits to Tendu's plantation, when the bullhorn sounded at 4:00 a.m., the slaves had to rise. She had looked out of her window and seen them scurrying about, feeding their families. Soon after, they marched off to the cotton fields where they'd work from sun-up to sun-down.

Within moments they headed in the direction of the Georgia-Florida border. All this time not a word passed between them.

Nessa got busy in the back of the wagon. Amidst bags of grain she found food, water, and clothing for both her and Jeremiah. Now she understood why Devlin had cut off her hair. He had left boy's clothing and a cap to disguise her. She changed out of her dress. Somehow, she knew she wouldn't see her Cherokee garb again. She rolled it up in a tight ball, donned her cap and jumped in the seat next to Jeremiah.

"Howdy partner!" She plopped herself on the buckboard seat beside him, her legs spread wide apart.

Jeremiah took his gaze off the road, his eyes registering shock. The laughter died in his throat to a chortle. "Nessa, how …the heck did you…manage this?"

Nessa explained everything leading up to their escape while she dribbled cool water then some healing salve over his cuts and bruises . She showed him the two passes allowing them to deliver grains. It stated they would return to Harmony by 9:00 p.m. the following day.

Jeremiah shook his head. "That Devlin is something fierce."

"Oh my God, he cares for you so much! And guess what?" She grabbed his arm in excitement." He has Tyanita in Florida. She's safe! He's going back to St. Augustine. He says we're to make our way there Jeremiah."

"Let's lay low with Osceola's people first. We can't wear out the horses too much. It's much closer to stop with them, and we can decide what we'll do."

"That makes sense."

"If we could just make it to the river—hope when they start looking for us, they'll be heading north. No slave runs south, you know?" He chuckled and glanced at her garb. "What's your name, boy?"

"Ned, sir," Nessa deepened her voice.

"You'll do," he said and suppressed a smile she knew was painful for him.

Nessa looked ahead, sideways and several times over her shoulder. In the wee hours of the night everything looked ominous—even the deep, purple-streaked sky. The horse whinnied and she flinched in her seat. Thick underbrush loomed on both sides of the road. Leafy branches stretched out from the dark trees like giant arms waiting to pounce on them as they passed.

The long hoot of an owl followed them down the road. Awanessa sneaked a look at Jeremiah, suspecting he too felt eerie. He quickened their pace, his face somber. They rode for miles in silence. She had never seen such a creepy place. Her heart dropped when she caught sight of the inhospitable-looking swamp.

"The villages of the Indians have all been destroyed... the swamps and hammocks have been everywhere penetrated, and the whole country traversed from the Georgia line to the Southern extremity of Florida; and the small bands who remain dispersed over that extensive region, have nothing of value left but their rifles."
- General Thomas Jesup, U.S. Army (1838)

CHAPTER 10

Okefenokee Swamps, Border of Georgia and Florida

"Are we lost?" Awanessa's voice tremored. Without answering, Jeremiah parted the sinewy grass embedded in the marshy ground. It sprouted as far as the eyes could see over the flat landscape. "We're where we supposed to be." He knew he didn't sound convincing. He didn't want to admit he was indeed lost.

No sign of life, but two cranes shifted from one foot to the other. Something long and dark, like a log, glided in the water of the nearby creek—in their direction.

"Come," he said, scrambling over to a tiny bluff. The ground was solid even though sandy. Nessa brushed away the moss dangling from the tree while

Jeremiah tethered the horse and cart, all the while casting surreptitious glances around him.

He looked for a path to take them deeper into Seminole territory. He gave a start when lily pads brushed by his ankle. A big red-bellied turtle stuck out its head. A smile tugged the corner of Jeremiah's lips when he heard Nessa's stomach growl. They wouldn't be short of food, he thought. They would set up camp and wait.

A day later, a Seminole scout found Jeremiah and Nessa by the Okefenokee Swamp. He led them to the tribe's settlement across the Georgia line into Florida. Jeremiah found out the Seminole Leader, Osceola, had been captured by the Army and died in prison earlier in the year. But, the tribe's fierce spirit lived on with or without their indomitable leader. The people received them warmly and rejoiced for the grain.

* * *

Even though they'd been with the Seminoles only a week, they felt comfortable. In amazement, Jeremiah scrutinized the makeup of the tribe. Black Indians moved easily amongst the Seminoles, like one. Whoever heard of black Indians? He learned this was the result of interbreeding between runaway blacks and the Seminole Indians who offered a safe haven. The settlement in no way had the amenities of the Cherokees.

One day, several Seminole men approached Jeremiah and Nessa bearing logs. "Come, we build chickee," one of the men said. They all grinned, nodding their turbaned heads.

Nessa looked at Jeremiah in disbelief. "I can't believe we're going to have our own house."

"No, no, we won't be here long enough to have a house," Jeremiah protested.

"Doesn't matter—easy to put up, easy to take down—that's why we use them," the Seminole man said, walking toward the spot for the chickee. Several women dragged palm fronds to use for a roof. The men dug a hole for each of the four posts to hold the dwelling in place.

For the next few hours, Jeremiah, Nessa, and their new-found friends worked side-by-side.

A few days later, Jeremiah slumped down on the damp grass next to her—a little distance from their chickee. Like the other chickees, it had no sides, as was the Seminole custom, it kept away the elements. "These people are so warm and friendly. No one's ever been so good to me. Not used to this at all." He glanced at Nessa. "They sure don't look like the Indians I'm used to."

"I was thinking the same thing." She rolled over in the damp grass lying on her side, facing him. "My people adopted the white man's ways so much—trying to fit in." Her face turned pensive.

Jeremiah sank into a contemplative mood too. He sat up, hugging his knees, peering at her over one knee. "We been here dilly dallying for a while now. We need to keep moving."

Nessa shot to a sitting position. "Why?" Her pensive mood turning agitated. "At least there's safety in numbers and the people here are so welcoming."

"They can't keep running deeper and deeper into the swamp," he said, looking around him, lowering his voice. "No future here for us. Eventually the soldiers will remove them—all of them and send them out West."

"No they won't!" She jumped to her feet looking down at him, hands on her hips. "Did you hear Wild Cat and the others at Council yesterday? They'll fight to death!"

He sighed. "Fight, fight for what?" He stood, brushing the clinging blades of grass from his trousers.

She scrunched her eyebrows together. "So what do you want to do just give up and run? Her upper lip curled in a sneer. "Run, like we've been doing. For what?"

His cheeks burned like when Massa George slapped his face. He tried to be reasonable. "Doesn't make any sense Nessa. We just can't win, can't you see that?"

She rounded on him. "What are you, liver bellied? I'd think you'd want to seek vengeance for all they did to you." She stalked away, her feet making plopping sounds on the sodden ground. An egret peered at them, but flapped its wings and flew off when Jeremiah rushed after Nessa.

With quick strides he caught up with her and turned her shoulders around to face him, his face grim. "You think your people should have stayed on their homeland and fight. Don't you?"

She nodded, her eyes bleak and distant.

"Well, I tell you what would happen. You and your people would all be dead." He shook her shoulders again. "Do you hear me? Dead!" He pulled her resistant body closer. "If we stay here we'll be hunted. Think they're joking when they say all the Indians gotta move from the Southeast and me and my kind kept in chains?" He took a deep breath, looking up into the sky as if for inspiration. "That's not living Nessa."

"Well, I'd rather stand with these Seminoles and fight." She swatted a pesky mosquito on her arm. "I'd rather be dead. Do you hear me? Dead! Rather than give up everything I am. You have no honor!" She turned and spat on the ground. "Coward!"

His eyes glittered with rage. "You call me a coward? You who want nothing more in life than to live in this," he threw his hands out wide . . . "this swamp?"

"Yes, this swamp! It's better than being caught in a snare, running in the middle of the night scared of your own shadow, beaten almost to death." She paused in her tirade, her chest heaving. "It's better than being hung or marched to death on foot to parts unknown. She paused for her words to make an impact on him. His face stayed implacable so she flung the words at him, "you are so ungrateful."

He leaned into her, their noses barely touching. "Yes, I want more. I want what is due me as a man." The murky water oozed up around his brogans in a puddle. "You—should have been a man. You shouldn't have changed into a dress, the boy's clothing you wore here suit you well."

Her nostrils flared. She jabbed him in the chest with her forefinger. "And you, should be a woman!" she said, giving him a level stare. Her eyes reminded him of hardened honey, crystallizing in a jar. She stepped back, lifted the hem of her Seminole dress and flounced off toward their chickee.

Mist settled over the area like a damp sheet. Jeremiah stood stunned by the heated argument between them. Mosquitoes so loud brushed by his ears, he thought they were bees.

He looked around at the unfamiliar surroundings with its wild grass sprouting from puddles of murky water. A snake as big as his forearm slithered away in the mist. He shuddered. He didn't like this place one bit. He felt a deep stirring inside of him to move on. Nessa could remain with the Seminoles or take her chance with him. Just the thought of not being with her or not seeing her again made a chilly path through his veins. But he would give her the choice.

Jeremiah approached the chickee he shared with her. They had no privacy. Nessa complained often about the lack of walls so he couldn't understand her desire to remain.

He admired Wild Cat and all the Seminole Braves but he knew deep in his gut, fighting made matters even worse. He resented her accusations. Couldn't she realize he wanted to live as a free man—in peace, or die trying? He was no different from the Seminoles in spirit he concluded. He only wanted to find a place where he wouldn't be hunted and always watching his back.

A fresh surge of anger stirred inside him. He turned and walked away from their chickee. He decided they both needed time away from each other to cool off. He wandered through the marshy village. Women in their own chickees prepared for bed. Others sat talking in small groups.

"Come over here Jeremiah," one man shouted, beckoning with one arm. They sat around a dwindling fire and shifted their bodies to make room for him. They were all in their mid-twenties—around Jeremiah's own age. They told him their plans.

"We have to leave now," another said. "In a day or two we'll be there."

"Hope they're not bringing any children," the oldest of the bunch muttered. They stomped out the fire.

Jeremiah wanted no part of their escapade. He didn't come this far to get himself caught again or worse, get killed. But, he didn't know the way to St. Augustine and this trip would help him make it there safely with Nessa. If she wanted to go with him. His heart rolled over in his chest. He brushed away the doubts.

He decided to leave with them now and not go to Nessa in her present mood. Maybe she would reverse her unfair thoughts after he returned to camp.

The five braves and Jeremiah commandeered their horses and left the camp. For about a day and a half Jeremiah kept pace, only stopping to break camp the next night. They didn't talk much so he mentally noted the route. His neck chafed with the air getting warmer the further south they rode.

On a hissing breath the leader signaled they stop. A big white plantation house loomed out of the shadows. The men tethered their horses and Jeremiah followed them closer. Jeremiah's heart palpitated, but stilled with the thought he was here to do good. He tried to remember what Absalom said. "One man's poison was another man's stew?" He shook his head, the point eluding him. He realized he used Abs in his thoughts, like a guiding angel, when the moment called for caution.

A low sing-song whistle erupted from one of the braves. It sounded like any other wild bird's call. He repeated the sound in measured intervals but not like the randomness of the birds.

Out of the backdrop of bird calls and the darkest night, five, massive, black silhouettes emerged from the swamp's underbrush like one form. They waded toward them, mist swirling all around. Jeremiah recalled the lochness monster in a swamp he read about in a poem. The silhouettes separated, and he saw they were men just like him. The whiteness of their eyes held no fear but a feverish brightness. The Seminoles led them to the tethered horses and gave them each a weapon. They traveled all night and throughout the day to return to the Seminole village.

* * *

Nessa's anger had dissolved into shame in the wee hours of the morning. She wondered if Jeremiah had left her. She deserved to be left, she thought in self-pity. She wondered where he slept. She needed to see him and apologize for her rash words. She wanted to do something special to atone for her tongue, unhinged by anxiety.

After she washed in the stream, she ate some sofkee which tasted much like hominy. One of the friendlier women, Hakiseah offered to take her to the sewing chickee. In the hut, women gathered and chatted while they sewed clothing for their families. She watched them for a few minutes. The amount of beads they wore around their necks amazed Nessa.

She felt better. She would fashion a long shirt for Jeremiah.

"You need lots of calico for him," Hakiseah said. "His shoulders big."

"But won't it be too hot though?"

"Long shirt, hot? No." Hakiseah said. "Protect from mosquito bites and ticks and from traveling in the woods—you know thorny underbrush."

"Oh that's so good." Exactly what he needs for our long journey ahead, she thought. If he returned for her. All day Nessa worked with the women only stopping to eat. She had chosen a black long shirt the Seminoles wore. All the better to hide while they traveled. But where was Jeremiah?

Nessa learned a handful of braves had taken Jeremiah with them to 'rescue' several runaways. Hakiseah said they increased the Seminole 'army' that way—to fight their common enemy. She prayed in silence for his safe return. Guilt, like a pestle pounding corn, almost overwhelmed her. His decision to go was due to her vapid tongue. What if he got killed or hurt? She closed her eyes tight to block out the thoughts.

The sun sank in the sky bathing the village in coppery hues. Nessa decided she'd prepare dinner for him and leave it on the smoldering fire. Hakiseah helped her to fix boiled swamped cabbage and Indian bread.

"Are your people ever going to move out West?" Nessa asked curious despite herself. She cut out the heart of the cabbage palm and stripped off the outer tough fronds to reach the actual white heart.

"Oh, so many already left—even some relations. Many settlements torched by army. We forced to move further and further into swamp."

"So why are you staying then?"

Hakiseah chuckled without mirth. "For same reason why you here. This all we have. This our land." She threw up her hands to encompass the flat landscape.

Nessa thought the Cherokees did more uprooting. After all they had established real houses, schools, and even a newspaper but she remained silent.

Hakiseah changed the subject. "Best if you cut into small strips." She pointed to the fronds. "Then most tender," The two women cooked the fronds slowly in a little water until soft.

Nessa brought out the flat bread and heard a big commotion outside. "What's going on?"

Hakiseah sighed. "John Horse is back." When she saw the puzzled expression on Nessa's face, she explained. "He sold out. He one of our best leaders after Osceola died. Went over to white man's side and persuade people to go west. So he's back. Try and round rest of us up. He won't get Chief Wild Cat to agree." She said proudly.

"But why would he sell out and assist the army after he fiercely resisted removal for so long?"

Hakiseah shrugged. "I guess because most other bands like Alachuas, King Philip, Holatoochee and all his chief friends surrendered. As far as me and the rest concerned he not Seminole anymore." She continued to stir the fronds in the pot, the smell permeating the air.

John Horse rode into camp in full regalia. Two long feathered plumes sprouted from his bright colored turban. He was about the size and height of Jeremiah but not as handsome. His skin wasn't copper-toned but jet black. He was fine though, Nessa thought admiring his long shirt studded at the lapels with silver clips. A wide sash, gathered at the waist supported a handsome dirk. Even his leggings were decorated with colorful fancy ribbons. Many of the Seminoles followed him to hear what he had to say.

"Shouldn't we go too?" Nessa asked her friend.

"If you want to, but is no interest to me."

"Mama, mama," Hakiseah's little toddler Nensu ran to her, his eyes wide open in fear, pointing to the thicket.

"It's only a little itsy bitsy frog my dear." The little boy jumped up in her lap with his thumb in his mouth. "Want story." He pulled his finger out making a popping sound.

Hakiseah smiled at her son. "How about little green frog?" Nensu jumped up and down in her lap, "little gween fwog, little gween fog." He settled back in her arms, and started to suck his thumb again.

Nessa overheard some men, when they passed by, saying John Horse asked them to leave the territory and give in to the white man's demands. Nessa felt fear for these people and realized Jeremiah was right. Removal to the West was inevitable.

She listened closer and most of the people shouted back at John Horse. They were only going to move further inland. How much further? Nessa wondered. Soon, there won't be any place to go but the sea. She had to admire them for their fortitude. When she couldn't hear anymore, she listened to Hakiseah's story.

"The little green frog was sitting on the edge of the water lilies sleeping away. A big ole' rabbit came hopping along, came upon the frog and said, "Hi there! Why are you sleeping?"

"It's too pretty a day to sleep. Wake up! Wake up!" chimed in Nensu.

Hakiseah continued, *"I don't have to do anything,"* *said the irritated little frog. But that pretty ol' pesky rabbit kept on until the little frog got really mad and told him, "I'll fix you up." So little frog started singing his funny little song or noise he makes to call the rain. Within a few minutes, the black cloud came and the wind started blowing. Then the rains came and soaked the ole' rabbit so much he got cold and ran home. Whenever you hear the frogs singing away today, better be near shelter, because they are warning you that rain is coming soon.*

"The rain is coming soon. That why?" Nensu asked.

"Yes, that's why."

"Oh," he yawned and his eyes drooped. Soon he was fast asleep in Hakiseah's lap.

Nessa chuckled. "Did you make up that story?"

"I tell it to him every night." The two women laughed. The light glinted off Hakiseah's glass bead necklace, blinking red with varying shades of blue.

Even though Nessa spent an enjoyable day with Hakiseah and enjoyed little Nensu, she decided to retire. She would wait for Jeremiah in their chickee. Hopefully he'd return.

* * *

Scouts informed Jeremiah and his band of what transpired during John Horse's visit. The men stormed off to convene with the other Seminoles in the camp.

Jeremiah was glad to be back and anxious to see Nessa. Now more than ever he was ready to leave. But first he stopped at the stream and washed himself. He entered the chickee careful not to make any sound. She slept on the pallet, her back away from him. He removed his brogans and lowered his still damp body behind her. She pretended to be asleep, but he knew different. She breathed shallow and irregular.

He ran his calloused hands up and down the length of her bare arm.

"Nessa." He waited for her response. "Um… would like to leave here . . . tomorrow." When she didn't respond, he continued, "Don't know what's out there or what will happen. But you have the choice—." He swallowed and closed his eyes, "come with me or stay here." He stilled his caressing motions and suspended his fingers over her flesh—just grazing the fine hair on her upper arm. He waited for long minutes.

"I'm sorry," she said.

His breath caught and his heart dovetailed to his toes. She wasn't coming. He withdrew his hand, balling it into a fist by his side. Deflated.

"I'm so sorry J about the argument. I – I've thought about it." She said, making little sniffles. He laid next to her quiet. "About what you said, you're right," she continued.

"About you staying here?" He faked nonchalance in his voice.

"No, you goose!" she turned to face him and poked him in the side. "We need to go. We need to make a way that's right—for us." Her voice sounded tremulous, "or I guess we'll just die trying."

"You know I can't offer you anything sure," he breathed the words. He loved her so. But he couldn't offer her even love right now. He belonged to Massa George and he wasn't free to love. He wondered when did this love malady strike him. He had avoided it all his wretched life. It only brought shattering loss and overwhelming despair. He vowed he must find a way so he and Nessa can live in peace or he'll have to make a way.

She gazed up at him, her eyes swimming with unshed tears. "I'll go to the end of the earth with you J – if I can."

He inhaled deep, his chest rising in exultation. His eyes misted. He tried to speak but his throat constricted.

He could only manage to swallow. Overcome with emotion, he buried his face in the groove of her neck and clutched her tight.

They laid there in the quiet night, their chests pressing close, feeling the synchronized rhythms of their hearts. "Do you still think me a man?" She whispered in an impish voice. Her hands enfolded and caressed his broad back.

"No!" he uttered in a low growl, "God No!" he repeated in a stripped, ragged voice. His lips traveled up to her face and hovered over her mouth. "I'm sorry for that jibe."

As their lips met and fused, she chuckled deep in the back of her throat. Their renewed trust inflamed and ignited the passion smoldering between them. They didn't care whether anyone saw them, lost in their own misty world.

Jeremiah laid back sated—all was well. They would worry about tomorrow when it came. In the meantime a plan began to hatch in his mind.

CHAPTER 11

St. Augustine, Florida

On their way to St. Augustine, Jeremiah and Nessa lost track of the days. Even though Jeremiah heard of Florida being always warm, a winter's chill still hovered in the air.

After they arrived, Jeremiah used the coins Devlin had slipped them to secure a room in an old two-story building. Jeremiah soon found work repairing furniture he thought was inferior quality. Sometimes he even worked as a caulker on the St. Augustine docks, a trade he learned in Augusta, Georgia, before his former master sold him off up river to Massa George.

Nessa stayed in the rented room while he worked. Jeremiah didn't want her to seek employment. The government could pick her up and transport her out west. He had forged another manumission paper and kept it on him at all times. However, he was wary of slave catchers so he didn't speak much to anyone.

He knew Nessa missed the camaraderie of the Seminoles. To an extent he did too. It was a community in which he felt truly accepted and free. It felt good. They'd been here many weeks now and they had talked about earning passage for Canada or Massachusetts. He wasn't keen on Massachusetts because he could still be shipped back to the Deep South by an unscrupulous catcher.

Mingling with the free blacks in St. Augustine, Jeremiah had easy access to news. He often looked for discarded newspapers—even if they were a few weeks old. In those papers, they learned the Cherokees' plight. Nessa found out her good friend Quatie—the wife of Chief John Ross had died. Thousands more had died enroute and they still didn't get to Oklahoma yet, traveling through a long and bitter winter. Nessa gave a silent prayer. She knew she would have died like Quatie. She felt relief she wasn't in the swamps either with the Seminoles.

One evening Jeremiah brought home to their little room two different newspapers. One for colored people and *The Florida Herald* for everybody else. After they ate dinner they spread them out on the floor and devoured the contents.

"Ness, did you see this?"

"What?" she scuttled closer to him.

His face brimmed with excitement. Up North, they're getting a ship and sending free colored people to a place called Liberia."

"Forcing them?"

"No, no—if they want to go"

"Hmm, that doesn't sound like the government—must be some trick." She turned back to the paper and kept on reading.

He jabbed his finger at the article. "Just look, Ness, let me read this to you."

As she listened, the dawning light of hope entered and left her eyes.

"What?" He searched her eyes wanting to clear the resistance he saw there. He smiled. "You don't think we can go together, right?"

She nodded.

"Trust me. We will so." He pictured the plain gold band he kept making payments on in the tiny shop by the waterfront. He had been trying for weeks to find Devlin. If anyone could get them on a boat it would be his pal.

She took up the paper and read the article for herself. "This Liberia sounds…"

"Free!" he blurted out the word with such exuberance they gurgled with laughter.

She continued to read. "But it's in Africa," she said, her voice rising to a wail. "Where there's nothing but jungle, lions and tigers and . . . and. . . savages . . . oops!" She put her hand over her mouth.

"Oops is right," he said, looking at her disgruntled. "Not sure where in Africa this Liberia is but they brought my parents from Africa. And they were the best and kindest people."

She squirmed and didn't look at him. "You're right. This is the savage land." Her eyes clouded in remembrance and she closed them tight to shut out the images.

"Nessa, there's good and evil in this world. But right now, in this time of our lives evil is winning out." He wondered how many Devlins, Mr. Hank and the abolitionists up North, how many were there? Not enough!

"Another thing, you can't believe everything you hear or read. Who do you think wrote the books?" He warmed to his subject. "They only stating their opinions. I know you heard some Spaniard discovered America, right?"

She nodded.

"Well, how long your people and all the other Indians been here?"

She nodded again in agreement, stunned by his knowledge.

"Shucks, they twist anything to make themselves look good. When I worked in the furniture shop I overheard some boys bragging how the Army whupped the Seminoles. You saw for yourself, they didn't whip nothing. Most of the time the Army got whupped then went back and sing a different tune." He took a deep breath. "I tell you Nessa, living in a jungle, surrounded by lions, tigers and any other wild animal seem like heaven."

"As long as I'm with you." She wet her fingertip and turned the paper.

He caught her gaze and winked at her. His heart overflowed with love for this woman. He returned to reading his paper. A comfortable silence enveloped the tiny room only disturbed by the turning pages. He gathered more information for his plan.

* * *

One week later, Jeremiah rushed through the front door. "We have to get out of this place Nessa."

"What happened?"

"Do you know?" He swiveled on his heels to face her. "New law in this city says every free black must have a guardian, a white guardian. Have to carry around a paper saying "I, Mr. Sonafabitch, consent to be the guardian of Jeremiah Browne—a free black."

She covered her mouth so she wouldn't gape at him.

"Plus, I have to always carry my free paper. You know what will happen if I don't?"

Nessa's eyes bulged, her heart leaped with fear.

He sat down heavy on the dining chair. "Could be sold back into slavery!"

A pounding started in Nessa's temple. Is there any end to this? "But, but, St. Augustine is a territory, it's not even a state."

"Might as well be," he said, sounding disgruntled.

"What do we do now? Can you forge one of those guardianship papers like you did the free paper?"

He laughed without humor. "Much good is that going to do. It has to be filed down at City Hall."

"Oh no! Well, what about the man you work for. Would he do it?" She grasped at straws now.

"My last resort. I've been trying to find Devlin for weeks now."

Mulling over this new development, they lapsed into silence.

Jeremiah started to massage the back of his neck. Nessa became even more alarmed, seeing Jeremiah's extreme state of agitation.

"Sit down here with me." He took her palm and studied it, his brows furrowed. "Been working on a plan, a crazy, hair-brained plan, but my only reservation is you. Don't want to put you in any untold danger you know?" His worried gaze drifted over her face.

She clasped both of his hands in hers. "There is no danger that is worse than being here—just sitting here like stool pigeons. We must take action."

He covered her hands with his big meaty one. "Got to thinking. After I close up Mr. Libbert's shop in the evening, I could go down to the port and see if they need a hand loading the indigo and provisions on to the schooners."

"Yes?"

"Got to thinking too—I could find out which ones setting to go up North."

"And?"

"Get on the ship to Liberia from there but first I have to find us a way to get out of here."

Her face broke into a wide grin. "You mean like stowaways?"

His face looked sheepish, but he nodded.

"That's brilliant!" Her face became animated. "I still have the boy's clothing. I just need a bigger hat and we'll just have to cut my hair shorter."

He looked at her hair curling onto her neck in spiky wisps. "If you cut any more—you'll be bald. But I don't care." He jumped from his chair, grabbed her in his arms and made a jig around the round.

She started to sing, making up words in time to their dance. "We'll be stowaways, stow-awaaay. . ."

"No," he stilled their pace when a tune from a chain gang passing by Harmony Plantation seeped from his memory. He rocked her from side to side while the words of an old spiritual bubbled in his mind. He replaced the original words "Steal-away" with "stow-away" and crooned:

Some glad morning when this life is o'er, I'll stow-away;
To a home on God's celestial shore, I'll stowaway.
I'll stowaway, Oh Glory
I'll stowaway; –in the morning
If I die, Hallelujah, [you're at my side,]

I'll stowaway (I'll stowaway).

If the shadows of this life have gone, I'll stowaway; Like a bird from prison bars has flown, I'll stowaway (I'll stowaway).

Just a few more weary days and then, we'll stowaway; to a land where joy shall never end, we'll stowaway home (we'll stowaway home).

Nessa didn't know the words but she caught on to join him in the chorus, whispering the refrain like a solemn chant. When the song ended they continued to hold each other and rocked.

They remained in each other's arms, wrapped in contemplation. Shards of light marking the day's end descended from the tiny window, projecting ghost-like shadows on the wall behind them.

* * *

Jeremiah felt lucky to secure work at the port loading supplies on to schooners. Soon he had his vessel marked. He worked extremely hard and showed up every day. He wanted them to trust him. They did and paid him well. Soon after, he made a deal to receive payment in food instead. The purser looked surprised but glad to oblige.

Jeremiah made sure the food he packed would not spoil easily. When the night watchman walked in the other direction Jeremiah would sneak off to his hideaway, carved out behind the huge bags of grain, at the front of the ship. Getting Nessa on board would pose a challenge.

One night he had it figured out and told Nessa to meet him at the docks.

At the appointed hour, Nessa crouched amongst the bags and scooped out half its contents. She crept into the bag, wrapping herself in a blanket she had brought to smooth out any odd angles. The ship's horn let out a mighty blare. Jeremiah picked up the bag and heaved it over his shoulders; his back bent low with the increased weight.

"Mighty heavy bag you got there," one free black sailor said to him.

"Yeah," Jeremiah panted. "Glad it's the last one. Well nigh beat though." Jeremiah quickened his pace. This was no time to be engaging in small talk. "Hope you have good weather when you sail."

"See you around," the sailor went about his business.

Jeremiah walked on deck, his head down carrying his bag while everyone scurried around making preparations to sail. No one paid him any attention, so accustomed to seeing him coming and going. Plus they took it for granted he was free.

Jeremiah got to the hold and dropped to his knees. He looked around careful not to attract attention. He loosened the bag. Nessa stuck out one foot and wiggled her bottom out. Jeremiah dragged the rest of the bag into their hideaway thinking it would make a good pillow for them.

With the bags piled high like little hills, Jeremiah directed Nessa and they disappeared into the darkness. Later, they felt the ship's movement as it started to glide out into the ocean, away from land.

Jeremiah had packed enough food and water to last them for a whole month if they were careful. He wasn't taking any chances. He even secured a spot to do their necessaries. He believed they could live with anything as long as they were on to a better place. They had enough room to walk around and they could even look through a porthole.

Nessa whispered in his ear "J, I can't believe we're doing this, we're on our way!" Her voice sounded hoarse with suppressed excitement, fear and anxiety.

He patted her cheek and expelled a long sigh of exultation. He knew the hard part of getting off the ship was coming up. But, he'd cross that bridge when he got there.

He leaned back against Nessa's bag of grain and took her with him. They lay in each other's arms, lulled by the swaying vessel until they were fast asleep from sheer exhaustion.

Nights followed unbroken days. Jeremiah and Nessa didn't mind. They talked about everything. No one ever came into the hold so they weren't worried about detection. But they were still careful to speak in low tones.

"How much longer do you think?" Nessa asked.

Jeremiah's brow furrowed. "We should be there pretty soon."

"Are you sure it's going to Massachusetts, though?"

"Actually Nessa, we should be there already. Have no idea what's going on."

Her eyes widened.

"Sailors told me it sailed to Massachusetts—that's the route. Didn't want to ask too many questions so they become suspicious, you know?"

"It's better than being on land. At least we're getting somewhere." She tried to joke, but her apprehension grew on par with his. She chafed to get a whiff of fresh air. It was difficult looking out the porthole and returning to the quarters that were so spacious earlier but now cramped.

Day and night, torrential rains formed a thick glacier over the porthole masking their view of the outside world.

They talked way into the night about how they'd get off the ship and where they would land. Nessa spoke about her childhood and how she missed Gentle Dove and wondered what her people's life will be like in their new land. After a while they slept.

During the night she shook Jeremiah awake to tell him she dreamed her people were all starving and drunk. All the other tribes who were already in Oklahoma were killing each other. Jeremiah half-listened, all the time thinking something was wrong. The ship rocked and creaked more than usual.

Sometime during the night or before dawn, Jeremiah couldn't guess, he grew dizzy from the incessant rocking. The ship made a long creaking sound, groaned and screeched to a halt.

The ship pitched him to a nearby wall, his head connected with a resounding thud. His entire world looked black. He shook his head to gather his senses and slithered on his belly whispering "Ness, Ness, where are you?"

Frantic footsteps rushed back and forth above board. Screams rented the air, giving way to muffled directives. The ship was not level. It tilted at an odd angle. Nessa careened down the slope and grabbed on to him muttering in an urgent voice, "Jeremiah, the ship, oh my God, the ship is sinking."

CHAPTER 12

They held on to each other, steadying themselves, while the ship dipped and floundered. Water gushed in.

"Hold my hand; we must make it above board." Jeremiah crawled out of their space and dragged Nessa along, wading through rushing waters to the stairs. He hoisted himself up, and helped Nessa. They rushed headlong into the melee.

No one noticed them, they crept silent, like shadows in the dense fog.

Jeremiah stopped short and Nessa careened into him—just in time to hear him gasp.

Fire spread fast throughout the ship, breaking off sections and casting parts into the water.

The few remaining crew members piled in the lifeboat like a haphazard stack of wooden logs. They rowed from the disaster.

Jeremiah could see a dim, disembodied light off in the distance. He wondered if it was a lighthouse, he'd heard of them. He scoured around looking for more lifeboats.

None.

Nessa skidded across the deck. Strong gales whipped his body and he ran toward the stern. The ship in its death throes gave off its last warning knell.

"Hold on. Hold on!" Jeremiah shouted through the pelting rain. Nessa slipped. His arm reached out and snaked her waist, twining tight. The stern broke away, pitching them into the riotous sea. Nessa landed a few yards away out of his grasp, away from the stern, her head disappearing beneath a wave.

Jeremiah clung to the stern with all his might but it kept capsizing. He fought to stay on but a forceful wave crashed into him, throwing him far from the stern.

Instinctively, he threw his arms up in the air and gulped, filling his lungs with air. The sea claimed him. His feet flailed wild, aimless. Sinking. A thousand bells went off in his ears. He would die with bells ringing. At least he would join Nessa into this watery grave.

A sea creature, a shark, or something else pushed Jeremiah's body, shooting him upward, cutting clean through the water. The moment his head broke the surface he sputtered and gasped for air. His mind registered the small, firm hands and knew. It was Nessa.

Hacking and retching, he managed to grasp the broken off stern Nessa found. "Hold on, keep your head up," she screamed.

He pulled himself up to lie face down. Water spewed through his mouth, deep from his gut. After a while, miraculously the sea calmed, he could feel it. Small fists pounded his back.

Again, she saved him.

The makeshift raft was just big enough to carry them both. They laid exhausted until the night sky shifted to stacked rows of pink and blue. The ship had broken apart and disappeared without a trace, as if nothing out of the ordinary had occurred.

They slept and woke to the raft's gentle rocking motion. Soothing waves lapped at his ear. He tightened his grip. "Ness," he whispered. "I don't see any land."

Nessa's red-rimmed eyes were huge orbs in her face.

She scanned the horizon in all directions before settling back on his anxious face. "We're still alive and we're together."

"Thanks to you ... again." He felt for her hand and held it tight. He silently pledged if they came out of this alive, he'd do everything in his power to be a real man for her. He'd protect and cherish her, so help him God.

"I sure hope there are no sharks around here—or else we'll be their breakfast," Nessa said in a disquieting tone.

"Hush!" He said, flinching when a wave washed over his legs. He breathed in the salty air and thanked God the air was relatively warm or they wouldn't have lasted this long.

She snuggled under his armpit and they drifted along in dejected silence, losing sense of time and their location.

They woke and slept. Only when their throats were parched and lips stiff from lack of moisture did they resort to sipping from the precious flask of fresh water Nessa always kept tightly around her waist.

Jeremiah scanned the horizon while Nessa dozed again. When his gaze discerned a black dot, way off in the distance, he blinked several times to clear his eyes. He opened them and the dot grew bigger.

It was a ship.

He could even make out the mast. His heart thumped in his chest and he felt his skin flush with heat. "Ness, wake up, Ness a ship."

Nessa opened unfocused eyes and closed them again. When his excitement finally washed over her, she scanned the horizon. She bolted to a sitting position, all vestiges of lethargy gone.

A ship was indeed coming in their direction.

"We must get their attention," she whispered on a trembling breath.

Jeremy tore off his once-white shirt and waved it into the air.

"Wait J; wait until they've gotten closer and able to see us."

"Shucks, and take the chance they miss us?" He waved again.

An hour or so later the ship got a little closer, heading in their direction.

"What if it runs over us?" Nessa said, fear choking her voice.

"They have to see us." Jeremiah said clinging to hope.

They took turns waving Jeremiah's shirt.

* * *

Jeremiah felt insignificant when he put his head back and looked up the sides of their big rescue ship, *The Serpentine.*

A group of curious onlookers peered over at them while the sailors threw them a lifeline. Nessa grabbed the rope, and they hoisted her up, her body swinging back and forth in the wide expanse to the ship. He watched in trepidation.

"I love you," he whispered. It was the first time he said it and he knew she didn't hear.

When his turn came, anxiety made him sweat. He did not know what was ahead of him on *The Serpentine*. But he knew for sure he didn't want to be left to potential sharks.

As Jeremiah's feet touched the deck someone shoved him forward by the neck. "Just stay right here boy, until the Cap'n comes."

He could feel the air around him becoming thick and oppressive. Jeremiah hung his head knowing what to expect. Pointy-heeled shoes peeking from beneath ruffled hems swirled away. A silver tipped cane tapped by without a break in rhythm. Men in black Hessian boots, with unhurried strides, didn't pause their conversations. Water oozed through Jeremiah's saturated brogans and puddled on the wooden deck. He glanced from the corner of his eyes down at the mysterious blue depths of the sea. He almost chuckled to himself when he realized he was caught between the proverbial devil and the deep blue sea.

"Don't you be having any funny notions boy; you're worth more alive than dead."

Jeremiah looked up and wished he hadn't. The silver gray eyes staring down at him reminded him of the mean Siamese cat which nearly tore him apart when he went near her kittens. Young Devlin had held his side with laughter after Jeremiah flew off the balcony to escape her wrath.

"Am a free man. A left *The Hermina* when it sank." Jeremiah muttered, sullen.

"On *The Hermina* were you? We'll see about that." He rubbed his chin while the other arm folded across his chest.

"Yes, suh!"

"Well, all the crew made it safe and accounted for at Cape Hatteras including one free black sailor." Jeremiah's heart sank. "Wonder why you two were left?"

"We were below deck, suh."

"Hmm. Hmm. Tell you what, after a short stop we're headed back to Wilmington, North Carolina. Then you can state your case to the authorities. It's my moral duty."

Jeremiah's heart rolled over twice and took a dive to flounder in his soggy shoes. "Where is my partner?"

The man chuckled but his eyes still looked like impenetrable iron. "Don't worry, you'll join her soon."

"Cap'n" what do you want me to do with him?" a burly sailor with weeks of new beard asked.

"It's too inconvenient to tie them up but secure him and the squaw together in the lazarette below deck."

The burly sailor turned a questioning gaze at his captain.

"Oh they can start making plenty babies for their new Massa, compliments of *The Serpentine*." The Cap'n said, shoving his hands in his pockets and chuckling to himself. "Don't forget to give them their daily grub," he said, walking away.

The sailor turned to Jeremiah and grinned, showing broken teeth like stumps of seaweed. "Come on boy." He grabbed Jeremiah by the arm.

Jeremiah followed him anxious to see Nessa. He memorized every turn, scanning the area for exits and entrances.

In one shove, Jeremiah found himself in the room with Nessa.

"Oh God, thank God!" she blurted out. She hugged him tight and wept.

Holding her, Jeremiah felt a gentle uncurling of his insides. The turning and click of the lock resounded through the empty room.

They slid down to the floor still holding on to each other. Light streaked through the porthole, and Jeremiah felt grateful. Now at least they'll know the difference between night and day. He grazed his face along her warm dewy cheek, thankful she had come to no harm.

After a while, footsteps shuffled up to the door and the lock turned. "Here's your vittles." A tray skidded into the room, most of the drink spilling on the ground. Before they could take note of who brought the food, the door slammed and the key rattled in the lock from the outside.

Two bowls of lumpy oatmeal, two slices of stiff bread and a cup of water. It was a feast.

When they had eaten and not a crumb left, Nessa knitted her brow at the thoughts racing through her mind. "What now J? We almost made it." She bit her lip to fight back the tears.

He spread his hands out and rubbed them together. "I don't know Ness."

"I almost wish we had stayed on the raft you know? Our future would have been unknown. Now we know for sure what we're heading for. And it's not good."

Jeremiah sat in silence; he pulled her head down to rest in his lap, stroking her cheek. "Yes, our imaginary sharks are looking better by the minute."

She giggled, a little hysterical.

"Let's not talk about this or even think about it right now, Ness. Just know we'll find a way when it's time. Let's be quiet for a while knowing we're safe and together."

She sighed in his arms. He cradled her head, inhaled deep, put his head back and listened to the air coming in and going out of his body. No thoughts of their predicament entered his mind. He closed his eyes and breathed with the rhythm of the undulating waves. He had to wait for the right opportunity to make his move.

* * *

Jeremiah did not know how long they sailed, maybe a week or so. He kept a constant vigil by the porthole. One day he looked out as usual, expecting the same. His body recoiled, his gaze filled with alarm.

"What do you see, J?"

"The sea, it's not right."

"What do you mean 'it's not right?'"

"We seem to be in strange waters. The color is . . ."

She jumped to his side nudging him to the side with her hip. "Aqua?" she said, peering out in disbelief.

"Exactly. Look Nessa you can even see the fish! Oh, don't like the looks of this." He said, drawing on a ragged breath. "Plus, we should be feeling chilled by now from the Northern drafts that I hear about but instead we're feeling uncommonly hot."

He shoved his hands in his pockets to control his agitation. He fingered the gold ring he had tied to a string in the bottom of one of his pockets. It still was not the right time. He slipped it on and up to the knuckle of his third finger, but it couldn't pass, so he slipped it off again.

"So you don't have any idea then?" She asked.

"No, apart from the states belonging to the North and the ones belonging to the South, I don't know much more about the United States. Do you?"

"I know there are islands, a lot of them called Indies.

"Islands? Reckoned we were going to Massachusetts."

"Maybe we are but not directly, if you know what I mean." She bit into a piece of hard tack.

She inched away, giving him room to join her again at the porthole, their faces squishing together. "My grandfather told me that on an island belonging to France, the slaves killed off all their masters and governed the island by themselves." She thought for a moment. "That be Haiti. Yes, I'm sure that's what he said."

Jeremiah felt his body tremble with pleasure. He thought over the possibilities then decided to forget about the future for now. After a while, he felt a finger poke in his side.

He eased his body down to the floor and pulled her down beside him.

"How come you know all about old time things and places and Europe but don't know anything about where you live?" She asked.

"When I steal books from Massa George's library or when I deliver furniture to other plantations, I grab the first book I see. Didn't have time to read titles, you know?"

"Did you have many books?"

He chuckled. "Stole so many, one at a time though, had to dig a big hole in the dirt floor of the cabin, under the bed, so I could hide them."

"So you have the Bible?"

"Yes, my mother stole it from Miss Lucretia's mother for me. She said it would comfort me. But it didn't really. Often wondered what kind of God he must be, probably Massa George's personal God that says: 'Servants obey in all things your masters.'"

She cleared her throat. "Well, First Corinthians also said:

Art thou called being a servant? Care not for it: but if thou mayest be made free, use it rather. For he that is called in the Lord, being a servant, is the Lord's freeman: likewise also he that is called, being free, is Christ's servant.

Shock registered in Jeremiah's eyes. His face broke out into an incredulous smile. He put his head back and laughed. "Thought you and your people believed in the Great Spirit?" His shoulders shook from laughing.

She gave him a level stare. "Blasphemy won't get us anywhere." She turned and leaned her back against his chest and stretched out her legs. "You don't want any bad luck to come upon us now do you?"

"No." He whispered, his laughter subsiding.

"So let's not talk things we don't know anything about. All I know is we need to have something or somebody watching over us. So, I'm not laughing about the white man's god, the Indian's god or anybody else's god."

He smoothed the nape of her short spiky hair. "Right now we need all of them."

He changed the subject. "Shucks, wouldn't it be grand though if this ship went to Haiti?"

"Jeremiah, we don't even speak French. Stop being fanciful and worry about how we're getting off this ship without being clamped in chains." She went back to the porthole.

He followed and rested his chin on the top of her head. The reminder sobered him.

* * *

The next day, sunshine streamed through the little porthole like molten gold making teasing dances over Jeremiah's prostrate body. Nessa's mind flooded with the danger and their hopeless situation. They had been sailing for days, but now the ship had stopped.

As if sensing a change in the air, Jeremiah bolted upright to a sitting position, looking disoriented for a second. Finally awareness dawned over him. As if in one accord they rose to look out the porthole, their faces colliding. Nessa realized at once they had docked during the night.

Outside, seagulls swooped down and up while seaweed floated on the white crested surf. Off in the distance steep mountains rose resplendent in the sun. Above board the ship, brisk footsteps created staccato sounds amidst the splatter of running feet.

One particular set of footsteps became louder as it approached their room. Jeremiah sidled up against the wall to the doorway. Her heart flip flopped to her belly.

The footsteps slowed. The lock turned and when the door cracked open to shove the tray inside, Jeremiah sprang like a panther. Tray, plates and food flew everywhere. The startled man opened his mouth to yell but Jeremiah clobbered him hard. The man's eyes rolled back and he sank to the floor. Jeremiah ripped off the man's shirt, tore off the sleeve and gagged him. He also bound his mouth, wrist and feet.

Meanwhile Nessa searched the man's pants pockets. She found a purse with a few gold coins tied to his underpants and a pocket watch with a broken minute hand. She secured the treasures to her person, doffing the man's cap. Jeremiah led her out, locking the door and depositing the key in his pocket.

No one heard the commotion. She felt a gentle tug on her hand. "If anyone happens by, just look busy."

She nodded, her mouth felt dry.

They walked like normal but hid in darkened corners. Nessa waited and watched for Jeremiah's cue. She wondered how he knew the path leading to the outside.

"Hey you!" a voice interrupted the silence.

Nessa skulked and receded into the shadows.

Jeremiah acted as if he didn't hear. He started to pick up a bucket lying around.

The sailor came into plain view, "Hey you, I never see you before on this–"

Nessa clobbered him from behind with a plank of wood.

Jeremiah grunted with appreciation and hauled the sailor into the shadows giving him the same treatment as the other guard. This time, Jeremiah removed the sailor's cap and forced it on his own head. Nessa secured two more gold coins and followed Jeremiah's lead.

They climbed the stairs the sailor had come down. Their heads bent and their caps pulled down. People were leaving the ship in rowboats. Two cabin boys poured water over the decks while others scrubbed.

No one paid Nessa or Jeremiah any attention. Jeremiah walked out in the open while Nessa stayed behind. He beckoned and she walked in a nonchalant manner toward him. They walked down the plank and

Jeremiah stopped. His eyes looked wild. She held his hand and they eased into the warm soothing water.

She sneaked a glance at Jeremiah. His face showed sheer panic. His hands flailed the air. Her blood ran cold.

"Just hold my hand—don't let go," she said in a loud whisper.

"I can't . . ." He turned stricken eyes toward her. His Adam's apple bobbed. "I–I can't swim!"

"Shut up, I know." She swam with him like one of the fish beneath her. She grabbed him by the waist and pulled him closer to the base of the ship.

They were secluded from anyone's view. "Move your feet back and forth like this."

He did it. Her hand continued to buoy him from his middle. "Now watch me how I move my arms. Any trouble just hold on to me alright?" She kicked off toward land. Jeremiah dog paddled with awkward and over powerful foot motions.

"Relax and be natural," she whispered back to him, hearing the loud splashes he made.

She glanced behind again and he was holding his face clear out of the water, his chin pointed to the sky and his nostril pumping in and out. If their situation wasn't so dangerous she would laugh out loud.

She slowed her pace. "You'll go faster if you relax your neck and not fight so hard."

When he sputtered and gasped she decided to take matters into her own hands. She buoyed him whenever he started to sink but his weight was too much. She couldn't continue much longer.

". . . Oh, Englishman! thou ne'er can'st know
The injured bondman's bitter woe,
When round his heart, like scorpions, cling
Black thoughts that madden while they sting!"
- Thomas Pringle

CHAPTER 13

Nessa guessed Jeremiah sensed the exact moment when the water turned shallow because he just stood up. The waves lapped seductively under his nose. His head looked like a blob, bobbing on the water's surface.

She swam ahead and waited for him to catch up; she luxuriated in the sun-kissed crystal waters. Shoals of fish dodged her every movement. She noticed how the rippling waves caressed the white sandy beach. She drank in the sight of this strange beautiful land. Lush green mountains framed the background. Palm-like trees, almost like she saw in St. Augustine, dotted the beach in abundance.

Off to the right, black fishermen rowed past in dug-out Indian canoes not even sparing her a glance. Ahead, native lads tied up their boats.

Nessa could not put a finger on it but the air felt different here and it wasn't only the landscape. The ship must have stopped off in Haiti, she thought. She waited for Jeremiah, her chest heaving with excitement.

Jeremiah emerged on the beach breathing hard. He grabbed her arm, propelling her forward across the beach. Between breaths he announced he wanted to go as far from the ship as possible.

Soon they left the beach area, not exactly on the road, but keeping it in sight.

"Shouldn't we make sure the ship has left?" Nessa asked.

"And then they start to look for us?"

"But J we don't–"

His face tightened with tension. "Nessa we don't have time to weigh the ups and downs now. Let's keep moving."

"We might just run in to the ship's crew. Jeremiah we don't know where we're going. She ran along beside him trying to keep up with his swift strides. "Let's take stock of what to do first."

"They'll run into us if we sit around here taking stock." He grabbed her arm, moving even faster.

"Shouldn't we at least ask——"

"Don't trust anyone."

She sighed and stumbled to match his pace. His face looked like an immovable rock.

"We can't let anyone see which direction we're taking." He turned to her. "We're not getting back on that ship." His eyes glittered in the bright sunlight.

They kept close to the dirt road and walked for hours without meeting anyone. Jeremiah's stomach rumbled and hers rumbled in echo.

* * *

Jeremiah glanced down at Nessa, her feet begun to drag. They came upon a shallow brook, with clear water, the rocks smooth and white creating little waterfalls.

"You're beat aren't you?"

"Yes, I need to rest a while." Her face looked taut.

They found shade under a huge tree, bearing long brown pods. He stopped and bent to scoop water with his hands and drank. She did the same. Afterwards she used her wet hands to wipe the sweat from her face and moisten her neck.

He watched her wet the hem of her skirt and used it to pat her neck and between her breasts. He licked his chapped lips and decided he had to find something for them to eat.

Jeremiah jumped in the air and grasped a handful of long brown pods from the tree. He showed them to Nessa. She ran her fingers over the smooth brown shell and when she found the indentations at the side she twisted. The shell cracked to reveal a moist meaty inside.

"I hope it's not poisonous," she said giving the pods a wary look.

"Hell, we'll die from poison fruit or starvation. So I'll take my chances with this." He bit off a portion and the sourness curled his tongue; but it was not unpleasant. The more he ate, the more his mouth filled with saliva. He spit out the smooth shiny seeds embedded in the fleshy portions.

Nessa still stared at him.

"Watching to see if I'm going to keel over first?" He asked.

She chuckled, cracked a shell and took a bite. Jeremiah laughed when her eyes popped from the sour taste. But she continued to crack the shells with her teeth, ate the fleshy fruit and spit out the seeds. It took the edge off their hunger.

They kept moving, not yet daring to walk on the road. Lush vegetation obscured the ocean. They trudged on, avoiding the dense mangrove thicket with their gnarled roots knotted and embedded deep in brackish swamp water. A rank smell emanated from the slimy pools. They tried to stay on dry land. Nessa scratched at the mosquito bites on her arms and forehead.

At last, Jeremiah thought, it may be safe to get on to the dirt road. No one had passed by for miles except swarms of little red and black speckled crabs darting across their path on tiny pointy legs. This would send Nessa screeching and clinging to his arm. He laughed and held her close until the visitors passed.

The sun beat down on their heads relentless. A summer's heat in Georgia never burned like this, he thought. They were both drenched with sweat. The top of his head felt like the scalp was peeling away inch-by-inch and would soon melt his brain if he didn't do something.

Jeremiah toyed with the idea of picking one of those big leafy plants just to cover their heads. He changed his mind though when a rustling in the underbrush conjured crocodiles in his mind. The thought made his steps quicken, despite his weariness.

Later, the sun descended in the sky and the relentless heat had softened somewhat. Birds in every hue flew about, feeding their young and lending a rich cacophony of sound. Away from the swampy area, the air smelled better. Now and then a welcoming, light breeze would waft by. All of a sudden, just like the Serpentine had loomed out of the vast sea, a crude hut appeared in the distance.

Jeremiah scanned the area. He spotted a vegetable garden at the front of the house with neatly arranged produce. He recognized corn growing on the left side of the house but not much else of the other viney plants.

Two barefooted slave girls, about seven or eight years old, frolicked by an almost dry creek. They wore tent-like dresses, made from thin cotton fabric, barely grazing their ankles. When they saw Jeremiah and Nessa they stopped. They stared, their white eyes sharply contrasted with their dark complexion. Nessa moved toward them but they ran away.

"Mama, Mama, smaddy a come, smaddy a come," the little girls shouted in unison, running inside the house. In the ensuing silence, a three-legged mutt barked at them. It made two steps forward and retreated in twice as many steps. The mutt tried to circle them, yapping at their heels, but an invisible rope pulled him back. Finally he skidded and sat back on his haunches turning rheumy eyes expectantly toward the house.

A tall, straight-backed Negro woman without breasts, waist or hips came from the corner of the house. She stopped, folded her arms across her chest and stood like an unmovable pole waiting for them to get closer.

Jeremiah gave a slight bow. "Ma'am we're coming from afar and wondered if you could spare a bite to eat."

Only her eyeballs moved, sizing them up. Her gaze flashed across to Nessa and examined her with equal interest. Finally, the pole bent and whispered instructions into the older girl's ear who took off in the direction of the dense woods behind the hut.

"Yes, yes, come in, de name is Miss Ilda." She wiped her hands on her smock dress. "Me just finish boiling some porridge."

Jeremiah put his arm around Nessa's shoulder and introduced them and followed Miss Ilda inside the hut.

"Me just send for Marse Clifton, me husband." She pointed to a few stools in a corner. "Make yourself comfortable while me share out de porridge." She ducked through the doorway and disappeared to an outside kitchen.

Jeremiah had no idea what porridge tasted like but his stomach rumbled with anticipation.

"I wonder where we are," whispered Nessa.

"Let's not give away too much information until we know what's going on," he said in a low cautious voice.

Jeremiah looked around him with interest. The hut had two rooms. A neat bed stood in one corner. A crude table stood covered with a tablecloth and four stools in the center. He didn't see a hearth. He wondered how they managed in the winter. Two low benches were at catty corners on the opposite side. Funny pages torn from the newspaper covered the entire back wall.

"Ness, he whispered "why do you think they cover the wall with newspaper?"

"Probably to keep out the chill in winter." She shrugged. "Or maybe it's for decoration."

He rose and examined the newspaper-lined wall. He read out loud, *The Daily Gleaner, Kingston, Jamaica, December 18, 1838.*

Nessa slapped her hands to her mouth, her eyes wide. "We're not in Haiti then!"

Jeremiah sat back down on the bench. His chin propped up with his fist. He studied the well-swept dirt floor and a movement captured his attention behind the curtain at the window.

He'd never seen a slave hut with curtains before, even if only patched sheets. A head bobbed from behind the curtain. The other little girl appeared. Her hair parted and braided in sections, peeked from behind the curtain.

"You pretty." She said with awe in her voice to Nessa.

"Thank you. What's your name?"

"Me name," She stretched out the words in a sing-song voice ending on a high note. She started again, never giving a direct look. "Me name . . . hem . . . Hannette!" she blurted out in a triumphant tone.

"Ha-nette, what a beautiful name." Nessa slowed her words to match the little girl's speech rhythm.

"And me sister." Hanette dug her big toe into the ground, making little circles. She looked up, from the corner of her eye. "Name is. . . hem . . . Hangela!" She grinned showing tiny teeth with about four missing in the front.

A loud clatter resounded against the side of the house. Hanette's neck snapped to the window. "Me father come!" she announced to no one in particular. "Him carry back a heap of wood." She dashed off through the back door to investigate.

Soon after, Miss Ilda and her husband entered the room. Jeremiah noted he and Marse Clifton were about the same size and age. The resemblance with the high cheekbones and the same build startled him.

"Howdy mon," he said, going straight to Jeremiah, his hand outstretched. He turned and shook Nessa's hand.

"Marse Jeremiah and Miss Nessa, me and me wife pleased to make your acquaintances. We don't have much you know but whatever we have we willing to share with strangers." His tone sounded friendly.

Miss Ilda waited while the little girls spread the tablecloth and aligned the edges over the table. They stepped back and their mother nodded in approval.

"Where is the plantation around here Marse Clifton?" Jeremiah asked.

"Call me Cliff mon. Up de road—you never pass it?"

"We came from the opposite direction." Nessa piped in.

"Didn't meet anyone on the way." Jeremiah added.

Clifton and Miss Ilda looked at each other. The little girls twittered behind their fingers.

Miss Ilda laid out bowls of steaming porridge in front of them. The top had swirls of brown in the middle and a sprinkling of some kind of copper dust.

Jeremiah's mouth watered. He took up a spoon and inhaled the aromatic contents in the bowl.

Nessa skimmed the contents with her spoon. She sniffed, wondering how it tasted.

Miss Ilda face pokered. "Don't smell me food! Is nothing in de porridge but a lump of sugar-head with a sprinkle of cinnamon and little nutmeg."

Jeremiah had no idea what she meant but he started to shovel spoons of it in his mouth. It was the most delicious food he had ever eaten in his entire life.

"Ooh delicious," Nessa swallowed a spoonful of the porridge. "We didn't mean to upset you Miss Ilda. It's just that I've never eaten this before or tasted anything so good."

Miss Ilda's expression softened.

Jeremiah nodded and grunted in agreement. The little girls twittered again and Hanette dropped her spoon splattering porridge over the clean tablecloth.

"What do I tell you about misbehaving at the table. You want me to get the guava switch?" Miss Ilda said, directing a dagger stare toward her children who sat up straighter.

"Easy Miss Ilda, easy." Clifton patted the back of her hand. "Them's just little pickneys."

Jeremiah's head snapped up from his food. He wondered why Clifton would call his own child the derogatory "pickanninny."

Miss Ilda unwrapped the other plate and distributed two cakes each. "You don't know what this is either?" she looked at Jeremiah and Nessa out of the corner of her eye as if testing them.

"You mix any beberidge?" Clifton piped in.

"Hangela go get de big jug of beberidge." Miss Ilda continued. "Me couldn't find any sibble orange to squeeze in there so is so-so sugar and water."

Jeremiah bit into the salty flat cake. Midway he stopped, his face frozen in pain. He rose from the table and walked to the backdoor, shoving his fingers in his mouth to remove particles of bone lodged in his gum.

When he returned to the table, the mangy dog ran limping before him and nestled at Hanette's feet. Miss Ilda and Clifton stared at Jeremiah hard. Jeremiah gave them a sheepish smile. Nessa fixed her eyes on the fish cake, looking for hidden bones. The girls took big bites but he noticed they chewed slowly. Ever so often they removed a bone.

Clifton cleared his throat and Miss Ilda sat up straight, becoming the pole again.

"Alright, me see and hear enough." Clifton folded his arms across his chest. He darted a curious glance at Jeremiah and Nessa. "Every man, woman and pickney—even de backra in Jamaica know not to nyam fritters without searching for bone. And everybody in this world know cornmeal porridge. Oonu talk very strange, now where you come from?"

They all leaned closer to hear. Miss Ilda chased the children. "Go on outside and sweep up the yard and stop listening to big people argument."

The girls scooted from the table calling to their dog. "Come Delicate, come outside." They ran through the back door with Delicate hopping at their heels.

By the time Jeremiah and Nessa recounted their stories, the beberidge in the jug disappeared. Leftover particles of porridge formed crusts around the sides of the bowls.

Jeremiah did not know what these people would do with the information but they looked like good people. Clifton looked dazed. Miss Ilda blinked several times, refocusing to the confines of her little hut.

"So oonu don't even know say we free." Clifton mused aloud.

"Your owner freed all of you at once?" Jeremiah said in disbelief.

"Hemancipation," Miss Ilda muttered.

When Clifton saw the blank look on their faces he explained. "From the first of August this year . . ." He paused for effect. "No more slavery!"

Jeremiah squinted at him not knowing whether he jested.

"You hear me mon? Every black man, woman and pickney free!" Clifton said, ramming his fist on the table.

Jeremiah hung his head—he felt like the blood had stopped circulating through his veins and receding like a big ocean wave. He lifted his head and looked at Miss Ilda, "Say it again if it's true."

"Yes, de Queen of Hengland make us free."

Nessa's hand slipped into his and she leaned in to him. All of a sudden, a powerful new surge of blood coursed up his neck, down his arm, his legs and tingled through every toe. His insides felt like the blood couldn't find places to go so it just crisscrossed in his veins. He couldn't speak for a minute.

He heard Nessa ask, "Who's working the plantations then?"

Both Miss Ilda and Clifton threw their heads back and laughed. "Dat is one piece of joke—you hear me?"

Nessa looked puzzled.

Miss Ilda rocked back on her stool. "Ole Buckra no like it when the slaves get free. No like it all. Dem want to pay us pittance to work. Everybody walk off and left them. Now dem have nobody to work."

"So you mean all the negroes can now live anywhere they want?"

"Yes, mon, even though de missionary dem want us to stay in de free villages near all de old plantations."

"Why?"

Clifton shrugged. "I guess dem think dat they can see us and watch us. But dat's not the way we see it. Every man want to strike out for himself."

Miss Ilda peered through the back door to check on the girls. She walked back to the table and started to stack the dishes. "Everybody now just scatter. Some gone way up into the mountain dem to farm and build dem own house."

"Can I help you Miss Ilda?"

"No dear, you sit right there."

So who's doing all the cotton picking now? Jeremiah asked.

"Cotton?" Miss Ilda looked at him puzzled.

"No mon, we plant cane—sugar cane." When Jeremiah didn't reply he continued. "De cane make sugar and rum."

Jeremiah's eyes widened with understanding.

"See Miss Ilda have four fingers? De machine dat make sugar chop off her finger. We was so glad when dat old Lord Barclay hightailed it back to England after we free."

"He just up and left?" Jeremiah couldn't believe it. "Just like that?"

"Yes mon, I tell you. He give everything to his mulatto son, now the overseer."

"So, wouldn't it be easier to work for him?" Nessa asked.

Clifton and Miss Ilda dissolved into chuckles. "Him just as bad." Miss Ilda volunteered. "Him think him white, so him lording it over everybody. Want to work us like we was still slaves."

Clifton interjected. "And for pittance too!"

"Everybody want to know what it feel like to be truly free so we don't want to go back there—even if we have to starve."

"But me hear dat him put him mother and his sister Portia out of de big house because they shame him. They look too black." Clifton said on a chuckle.

Miss Ilda removed the table cloth revealing a thick sawbuck table with x-shaped trestle legs. The surface had deep grooves down the middle and burnt marks at the end.

"Nobody want to go back on Barclay Downs Estate anyway—not even to work for pay." Clifton said pulling his shirt from his pants. He casually raised his shirt to expose his back. "This is what dat ole Lord Barclay's overseer left me with."

Nessa gasped and visibly flinched at the sight of Clifton's back. Jeremiah's throat constricted. For a split second his mind flashed to the numerous beatings he'd received and witnessed in his lifetime. This was the result. The healed welts formed massive ropes intertwined like dozens of serpents, interlocking and choking each other. If he was not mistaken, he could even make out a serpent's head with its tongue darting all the way to Clifton's right shoulder blade. No words were said, none needed to be said. Clifton pulled down his shirt and tucked the ends in his pants.

The warm breeze constantly wafting through the hut had stopped and the air became heavy. Clifton inadvertently left a section of his shirt untucked. Miss Ilda came up behind him and forced the shirt tail down in his pants. She smoothed out the creases all around his waist and stepped back to view if everything was in place. She turned and walked to the back door calling out to her children. Jeremiah felt suffocated. He wondered what was in store for he and Nessa in this place.

CHAPTER 14

January sailed in balmy with not even the slightest bit of chill in the air. Nessa stood on the verandah looking toward the mountains. She wondered what lay beyond this settlement by the coast. Even though they had left Montego Bay where the ship arrived, this town of Falmouth bustled with commerce and activity.

Lady Barclay dozed in her rocking chair with gnarled fingers clasped in front of her chest. Nessa reached over to adjust the mosquito netting around Lady Barclay's slender frame and the lady groaned and stirred. Nessa felt sympathy for her when the woman called out. "Wallis, Wallis?" Her eyes stayed unfocused until it settled on Nessa. It was a never ending refrain since she had gotten this job to be Lady Barclay's companion and nurse.

"His ship didn't come in yet ma'am. It takes a long time for a ship to cross the water from England."

"Of course I know that, Wallis would not abandon me in this God-forsaken place with all these free savages running around," she said to convince herself.

She sat up, her back straight and her eyes lucid. She groaned from the arthritis in her joints. "Thank God for you Nessa because I couldn't abide any of those women tending me."

Six months had passed without any sign from Lord Wallis Barclay. Lady Barclay had moved into this white clapboard house in town with a wrap-around verandah. She left the estate in charge to a mulatto, former slave, rumored to be Wallis Barclay's own son. He had the child with a former slave woman.

"Would you like some of my special tea, ma'am?"

Lady Barclay's eyes crinkled into fine lines at the corners. "You mean some of your Indian medicine?" Her lips stretched over a good set of long teeth and she laughed out loud. She pasted behind her ears, strands of strawberry blonde hair threatening to form ringlets on her sweat-tinged cheekbones. "Your remedies are really helping me you know."

Nessa smiled and patted the back of Lady Barclay's hand before she rose to make tea. Little did Lady Barclay know she got all her "Indian medicine" from Miss Ilda down by the Martha Brae River. Nessa did not recognize any of the plants grown on the island. But Ilda taught her to find cirhossee leaves for belly aches, peppermint leaves, bizzy and some she didn't remember the names but recognized by the shapes of their leaves.

She stooped to place the pot of water on the hearth. A dangling pot crashed to the floor, accidentally overturning a stool. Instinctively, her hand moved to protect her thickening stomach. She righted the stool and sat, waiting for the water to boil.

Her heart ached for Jeremiah. She missed him. He is living his own life now – an independent one. The weekends were worse—after they had lunch on Fridays, he made no attempt to see her again until Monday. And she always had to go to him. He convinced her to take this job with Lady Barclay, under the pretext she would be safer than living atop the furniture shop where he worked. But she knew better he wanted total freedom.

She decided she wouldn't pressure him and if she told him about the baby he may feel forced to marry her. She needed to know he wanted her for herself, not because of circumstances. Nevertheless, away from everything familiar, she felt alone and adrift without him.

She returned to the verandah with the tea tray laden with sconces. Nessa poured a cup for Lady Barclay and some soothing peppermint in a flowered china cup for herself. They sat back to watch the sunset.

After a few minutes the rumble of a carriage coming up the winding path broke the companionable silence.

Lady Barclay leaned forward, eager to catch a glimpse of the visitor. But she sat back with a faint sigh when she realized it wasn't her husband. Her face set, she cut hard into the sconce with her knife and slathered imported, lemon butter with jerky motions.

Despite Nessa's problems, she enjoyed working for Lady Barclay. In the mornings she taught reading, writing and simple arithmetic to the former slave children at the Moravian Church. She'd have lunch with Jeremiah upstairs in the room he shared with another worker or under the banyan tree at the town square. In the afternoons, she'd stay with Lady Barclay and sleep in the next room.

Nessa ate two of the sconces, laden with coconut and currants, cook had made this morning. She brushed the crumbs from her mouth while the handsome mulatto strode up the steps, his back straight.

Lady Barclay took little sips of tea. Her index finger pointed up in the air with each sip.

"Good evening mum," he removed his hat and bowed to Lady Barclay. He nodded to acknowledge Nessa.

"What is wrong now Kendrick?"

"Am here to talk to you 'bout the conditions at Barclay Downs mum. It's time to cut the cane and I can't find anyone to do it."

Lady Barclay's lips compressed into a thin line.

"If we don't cut the cane by next week . . ." he examined his hands . . . "there won't be any money to run the estate and distillery. Plus—"

Lady Barclay cut him off by chopping the air in front of her chest. "You mean to tell me that all these lazy wretches won't work for wages? They're used to working for free then is that it?" She didn't wait for him to answer but continued, "Then don't pay them!"

Kendrick stood, his hat in his hand. "Lady Barclay, the people don't want to work unless they are paid decent wages mum."

She darted from her chair, her arthritic condition forgotten. She paced around him like a little sparrow protecting its turf. "Decent wages," she said with a smirk. "Who determines that?" She wagged a bony finger. "You give them an inch and they want a whole mile. Ungrateful wretches!"

"Yes mum."

Kendrick, not wanting to turn his back to her kept turning on his heel. Nessa had to stifle her mirth. She bit into her sconce and hoped she wouldn't choke.

Lady Barclay finally stopped pacing and leaned over the banister. She turned to him. "What about all the other estates in the parish, Wilberforce, Atherton, Vale Royal, Montpelier and all the rest?"

"It's the same thing all over mum."

She threw her hands in the air, "So what's going to happen to decent people on this island?" She said, turning aghast eyes to Nessa.

Nessa looked down at her saucer and took another bite of the delicious sconce. She washed it down with the dregs of the now tepid tea, smacking her lips with an exaggerated show of relish.

She looked up to see Kendrick watching her with a twinkle in his golden gaze.

Nessa stood, her ankles peeking out beneath one of the many too short dresses Lady Barclay had given her. She gathered the tea tray, Lady Barclay's empty cup and marched off to the out kitchen. Kendrick's gaze followed her through the double French doors, a wistful expression on his face.

* * *

On a Wednesday, more than any other day, Falmouth bustled with activity. Nessa sauntered down Cornwall Street, made a swift right onto Duke Street, which opened right onto the south side of Water Square. The square had a giant reservoir in the middle. Former slaves peddled their vegetables and produce right along with the other merchants.

The town boasted department stores, craftsmen such as gunsmiths, goldsmiths, tinsmiths, carriage-makers, and hotels, taverns and brothels. Nessa looked around wide-eyed, not even Athens, Georgia or St. Augustine looked as developed.

She shopped for lunch to take to Jeremiah where he worked. She bought a loaf of round bread at the bakers. She still had trouble with the currency of pounds, shillings and pence. She also bought two pieces of cured red herrings, a jug of beberidge and for dessert, two coconut drops from the old woman wearing a red bandana.

Nessa pulled the straw hat down on her head, trying to ward off the relentless mid-day sun. With basket in tow, she made her way to the cone-shaped building called *The Foundry*. Inside, several men bustled at their tasks. An attractive tall, black woman sporting a wide-brimmed hat strolled amongst the men, both hands on her hips. She circled Jeremiah who still focused on his work, an amused look on his face.

"Portia, a man can't concentrate on his work when you swinging them hips you know?" One worker yelled out.

She threw back her head and laughed, a wild throaty laugh.

Alarm ran down Nessa's spine but she squelched it. She strode over to Jeremiah's side. He acknowledged her with a big smile but he continued to polish the mahogany foot rail to a rich sheen. He stepped back to admire it while he wiped his hands on the nearby brown-streaked cloth.

"It's beautiful, J," Nessa said, her eyes gleamed in appreciation. She tried not to look at Portia who was busy examining her from head to toe.

"Tried to make it the same deep, rich color like your eyes," Jeremiah said, backing away and turning in time to see her hang her head.

She gave him a coy look. "You weren't even thinking about me, much less my eyes."

He reached for her free hand. What do you have in that basket?" He sniffed. "Smells so good. And you look so good."

She batted his hand and laughed. "You're just flattering me for food Jeremiah Browne!"

"Mr. Kingsley, I'm going for a bite to eat with the missus." Jeremiah yelled across the room. The wiry man glanced up from his pile of papers for less than a second, but he grunted in acknowledgement.

"What a lucky man—fancy a pretty package like that bring us lunch eh boys?" One of the other workers said.

"Y'all just jealous." Jeremiah shot back in a good-natured tone. "C'mon Nessa, let's walk down Victoria Street. We can eat under the banyan tree."

They walked out hand-in-hand and she felt Portia's eyes throwing daggers at her back. Nessa felt uneasy. She wondered if this woman occupied Jeremiah on the weekends.

Jeremiah took the basket and they walked in step. Nessa dismissed her feelings and chatted about her new activity, teaching former slave children how to read.

"Some are very bright and eager to learn, but some? Good Lord Jeremiah I can't even get a peep out of them; they just stare."

"Because they've never seen anyone so beautiful that's why."

"Oh stop! What's gotten into you all of a sudden? She chided him but felt pleased with his flattery. They arrived at their spot under the banyan tree. Nessa spread one of Lady Barclay's tablecloths on the grass.

As she laid out the food, Jeremiah tucked her hair behind her ear and kissed her on the lips. She swatted him for the second time. "Jeremiah Browne stop, let's eat!" she reprimanded.

"Been wanting to do that since yesterday." He said, grinning at her.

He took one of the cured red herrings and twisted off the head. Roasted to a crisp perfection it crackled when he bit into it.

"Watch for the bones," she warned him.

"Darn nuisance that's what it is, but so good."

She chuckled, remembering the time he almost choked at Miss Ilda's and Clifton's house. It seemed so long ago. It amazed her how easily they settled into their new life.

After they had eaten their fill, Jeremiah leaned against the tree patting his belly in satisfaction. "Have to head back soon Ness. This was so delicious." He looked at her his eyes filled with warmth.

She started to gather up the remnants of their picnic. "Remember I told you I'm going to Milk River Bath with Lady Barclay in a few days?"

"Isn't she on vacation all the time. What is she going there for?" His expression turned sulky.

"Silly," she punched him in the side. "Lady Barclay has an arthritic condition—she swears every time she goes to Bath she feels better for months afterwards."

"Didn't that Bible thing you rub on her do any good?"

She giggled. "It's called *Sinkle-Bible* , silly."

"That's a foolish name for a rub I've ever heard— no wonder it's not working." He pursed his lips and looked her full in the eyes. "So what am I supposed to do while you're gone?"

She cast him a sidelong gaze. "Portia will be more than willing to take my place."

"Portia . . . why do you bring up that brazen woman?"

"Just saw the way she was circling you and making eyes at you that's all."

He sucked air through his teeth in irritation much like all the people on the island do. "So, when will you be back?"

"I think Lady Barclay said a week or so."

Jeremiah groaned.

She scrunched her teeth in the sugared coconut drops. "Is that a groan for the food you'll miss or is it for missing me?"

"Won't even answer that." He stared at the coconut drops in his hand as if counting each piece of diced coconut.

"Ness, I'm wanting to get my own land and put down some roots."

Nessa became quiet and waited.

He didn't look at her. After a prolonged silence she stood up and placed everything in the basket. "Yes, that's a good thing," she said with forced brightness, not wanting him to see the film of tears gathering in her eyes.

They walked back and he talked about all his plans and his dreams. Not once did he ever mention "we."

At the entrance to *The Foundry*, he dipped his head and kissed her soundly. "Can't wait for you to get back," he said touching her cheek with the back of his hand.

She picked up the basket and crossed the street while he went inside. Her heart sat like lead in her chest. A vague feeling of dissatisfaction settled over her but she couldn't give in to her thoughts now. She was running behind her usual schedule, so she pondered the quickest route to Lady Barclay's house. Just then, a familiar looking carriage pulled up alongside her. "Good afternoon Miss Nessa."

"Oh, good afternoon Mister Kendrick."

"May I offer you a lift back to the lodging? I'm heading right there, mon," he said extending his hand. She dimpled and climbed in beside him.

"Thank you so much. It's awfully hot out here today."

"Is hot everyday, mon." He looked at her with appreciation. At the moment the carriage disappeared, she glanced back to *The Foundry* and saw six policemen disappear inside.

CHAPTER 15

"Wait!" She clutched Kendrick's arm in rising alarm. "Why are so many policemen entering *The Foundry?*"

He chuckled. "It's probably old Benjie. He work there, you know. The mon drinks pure rum for his lunch. At least twice per week the police have to cart him away when he get too rowdy or if he pass out."

She leaned back in her seat and dismissed her fears. Jeremiah had mentioned such an incident last week. He also mentioned Benjie was the only true friend he had where he worked. She turned to Kendrick. "So how come they haven't fired him then?"

"Mon, the old coot is the only one skilled for making parts for the ship—so they need him bad."

The carriage turned down George Street then King Street. "Oh I've never been down these streets," she said, marveling at the architecture. They passed two and three-storied townhouses built in the Georgian style. With stone on the lower floors and wood upstairs, some even had wrought iron balconies. No doubt, a passerby on the street could hear conversations taking place on the wrap-around verandahs. She decided she didn't like these houses as they rested on tall wooden columns extending almost to the sidewalk. No privacy.

Further on, Kendrick pointed out the police station, Town Hall, and various places of interest. "Thank you for this sightseeing trip. And I get back to Lady Barclay in a much shorter time than if I had walked."

He tipped his hat. "My pleasure. Mon, the sun is too hot to walk."

"I had no idea this place had so many different streets. I only walk down the main street."

"Yes mon, and they always building new buildings."

After a moment's silence, he glanced at her through the corner of his eye. "Remember I'm taking you and Lady Barclay to Milk River?"

"Oh great! but, who'll look after Barclay Downs when you're gone?" She asked.

"Not much to look after to tell you the truth."

"Did you get the cane reaped though?"

"Yes, half of it. Lady Barclay doesn't know I had to pay more. She going to be in one pile of ants nest when she finds out." He said chuckling to himself.

She listened to the cadence in his voice. She loved the way the natives used their voices almost like a musical instrument.

Kendrick cleared his throat. "Ahm, Miss Nessa are you involved with anyone?" His voice sounded cautious.

"Involved? Why . . . yes."

He glanced down at her third finger and smiled in relief when he didn't see a ring. "I hope not too involved that I couldn't invite you to a function on Saturday night, eh?"

"A function?"

"Yes mon. At the Town Hall. Sometimes they have dances and balls, and they having one Saturday night right before we leave on Sunday."

She looked at him in surprise and he continued. "Sometimes even traveling dramatic troupes pass through from time to time."

Nessa couldn't believe how civilized this place was. She would love to go to a dance but with Jeremiah. The carriage pulled up in front of Lady Barclay's lodge. Kendrick stopped the carriage and waited for her answer.

"Sounds exciting, Kendrick, but I have a lot to do with Lady Barclay before the trip."

His face fell but he jumped from the carriage and helped her down.

"Nessa is that you?" Lady Barclay asked, rushing through the front door, hair parted in the middle and slicked down across her forehead. "You're late this afternoon."

"I'm sorry Lady Barclay I got delayed."

"By whom? Hope it's not that ne'er do well by *The Foundry*." She flounced out on the verandah. "You can do better than him my dear. 'Esther . . .'" she called out,

The cook came rushing out. "Yes, mum?"

"If you've finished with dinner you can go—just leave it in the warmer." She turned to Nessa. "Plus, I don't want him hanging around here."

Nessa swallowed. Anger pulsed at her neck, especially when she saw the smug expression on Kendrick's face.

"Kendrick, any word?" Lady Barclay said, startling him. He looked a bit dazed before he refocused and handed her a stack of letters he had brought from the Downs. She flipped through them, her eyes scanning the return address for a familiar handwriting. She passed them all to Nessa and addressed Kendrick again. "I need you to drive me and Nessa to the ball at the Town Hall on Saturday." Kendrick's head bobbed as if his neck was on a loose coil. A streak of gold shot through his amber eyes and his face radiated pure pleasure.

Nessa pursed her lips. "I have nothing to wear to a ball, Lady Barclay."

"Oh tut." Lady Barclay said, waving her hand. She turned to Kendrick. "That's it for now, you'll pick us up at 8 o'clock on Saturday night."

Kendrick's face burst into a wide grin, which he halted when Lady Barclay said, "Wait . . . You can wear one of Wallis' black tail suits. He has so many he won't miss it."

"Thank you mum," he said, bobbing his head and fingering his cap.

"Shoo now," she said, waving her hand, already regretting her benevolence.

Kendrick backed away as if he'd just finished addressing Queen Victoria herself, not wanting to turn his back on her. Finally, he went down the steps, slapping his cap in his left hand and hopping into the carriage. Nessa didn't believe his smile could get any wider; the entire bottom row of his teeth showed.

"Doesn't he have a lady friend he might want to go with?" Nessa asked Lady Barclay.

"You're both in my employ and I expect you to do as I request." Lady Barclay said, with a regal flounce of her head. She relaxed and flashed Nessa a smile, her eyes more animated than Nessa had ever seen. She walked to the side of the verandah peering around the side of the house, clapping her hands. "Clothilde, Matty!" When she didn't see anyone she mumbled under her breath. "Where are those confounded women when I need them."

Clothilde appeared like an apparition. Her smooth, ebony skin shone with a film of perspiration. A small pointy head sat disproportionate on an elongated neck and wide sloping shoulders. Nessa had never seen her smile. The only sign of life on her face were dark eyes absorbing her surroundings.

Soon after, Matty rushed to the verandah lifting the front of her skirts so she wouldn't trip. Everything about Matty was rotund, even her cheeks. Her lack of height didn't help. Nessa could see she was older than Clothilde though. In contrast, Matty chatted like a magpie.

"Larks mum, me hear you call and me was clear in the back rinsing out the clothes and by—"

"Ok Matty," Lady Barclay stilled her with a hand. "Listen, I want you and Clo to go in my wardrobe and take down my apricot ball gown."

"Hapricot? Oh you mean the peach one with the plenty ribbon round the waist, that you—."

"Yes," Lady Barclay cut in. "That's the one! Iron out the ribbons and lay it over the chifforobe to air out then the blue one with the empire waistline."

"You mean the sky blue one with the cord under the breast mum that you wear last year to the christening over at Vale Royal and you say you don't want to wear it again because—."

"Yes, yes, press that one too for Miss Nessa. And Clo, I want you to take several empty jam jars with the lids from my cupboard. And at eve tide, I want you to catch as many peenie wallies as you can and place them in the jars."

"We going make peenie frock, Clo!" Matty explained to the taller woman who only nodded.

Nessa looked puzzled but Lady Barclay patted her hand and said, "You've never seen such a splendid sight my dear. You'll witness it for yourself when the peenies start to glow all over the gowns. It's dazzling in the ballroom."

Nessa recoiled in horror. "You mean those glowing insects that look like fireflies? We're going to sew them into our gowns. Don't they crawl and bite?"

Matty threw back her head and laughed. Lady Barclay chuckled and Clo's lips twitched. Matty clutched her heaving breasts. "And Miss Nessa when the peenies shine you only hear them go click! And if all of them go click at the same time you don't need no music to dance with." Matty glided across the verandah in a mock waltz.

"Alright now go back and finish rinsing the clothes. Make sure you put two bars of blue in the final rinse, especially on the white clothes." Lady Barclay said, trying hard to keep her face straight.

"Yes mum." Clo made her way to the back of the house.

After exerting herself with the waltz, Matty used her apron to dab beads of sweat from her forehead. "Me will have everything ready for you, mum."

After Mattie left, Nessa sat with Lady Barclay on the verandah for a long time. Lady Barclay told her about the upcoming ball and who would attend. She also named all the women whose husbands were abroad.

From time to time, Nessa massaged the *Sinkle-Bible* rub on Lady Barclay's shoulders and joints.

Lady Barclay stretched out on the divan with her arm draped across the back. A medicinal smell lingered in the air. Nessa massaged more of the slimy potion. She kneaded and rubbed until Lady Barclay's head lolled to the side.

The sun descended in the sky, a glorious orange orb. Nessa fixed Lady Barclay's special tea and joined her with shortbread biscuits.

"Get out the Jane Eyre book. I'm impatient to hear what happened to Jane," Lady Barclay said with a half yawn, covering her mouth with four fingers. Nessa opened the drawer underneath the divan where Lady Barclay stored her fashion magazines. "You know Wallis told me Indians were savages, can you believe that? I don't know which ones he saw."

Nessa's heart sank. Not her wild Indian stories again, please. She made no comment but flipped through the book to find where she left off.

Lady Barclay prattled on. "I wish my eyesight was better for reading. Every word looks backwards and jumbled on the page. This reminds me, I need you to pen some letters for me."

"Are you ready ma'am?"

"Certainly," Lady Barclay said. She reclined on the divan with her hands crossed on her chest. Her eyes took on a dreamy look. Nessa picked up where she left off yesterday. The main characters, Jane and Mr. Rochester were separated because of Mr. Rochester's deception and Jane headed off alone. Nessa read for a while until Lady Barclay started a light snore. She continued to sit in silence, looking off into the distance. Her mind flashed back to the policemen entering Jeremiah's workplace. She wondered, who were they looking for?

CHAPTER 16

"Mighty fine specimen old chap, mighty fine." Mr. Kingsley let out an appreciative whistle. "Don't be getting into any trouble you hear? I'd sure hate to lose a fine craftsman like you." He walked to the foot rail where the squat bookkeeper was attaching the gold plate: "Kingsley 1839" on the underside of the bedstead Jeremiah completed.

"A work of art," the little man beamed. Jeremiah wasn't sure if he marveled at his own neat script or the beauty of the furniture.

The bookkeeper and Mr. Kingsley continued to talk between themselves as if Jeremiah wasn't there. "This will fetch a few pounds in London—"

"But Mr. Kingsley," the bookkeeper interrupted. "Lady Marston commissioned one last month, remember?"

"No, not this one. See the workmanship?" He skimmed his fingers along the side. "London will pay royally for this. And it's mahogany too?" The bookkeeper nodded. "Send her the one that Lenny built. She won't know the difference between mahogany and pine."

"Lenny!" Mr. Kingsley shouted across the warehouse. "You finished with the bedstead you're working on?

"Yes sah. Me polish it with the walnut stain."

"Good, good, when it's dry I want you to add the darkest stain you can find—when it's almost black call me."

"Yes sah." Lenny, a big strapping man with a bullish neck, cast a malevolent glare at Jeremiah.

Mr. Kingsley turned to Jeremiah. "Let it air a few more days, then package it with the matching chifforobe."

Jeremiah nodded in agreement.

Mr. Kingsley rubbed his chin. "Come back into my office with me."

In his office, Mr. Kingsley counted out several shillings and a guinea. Jeremiah's pulse raced with anticipation. Mr. Kingsley patted him on the shoulder. "I'm pleased with your mighty fine work," he said.

Jeremiah accepted the extra money with appreciation. This had become a ritual each week with his boss. When he left Mr. Kingsley's office, he returned to put away his carving tools, rags and stains.

As he completed cleaning up and got ready to leave, several of his co-workers blocked his path. Lenny rounded on him. "You think you a big shot. You think you can just come here from God knows where and take away other people jobs?"

"You have a job don't you?" Jeremiah asked in an irritated voice.

"You hear him? A talk like say him a Queen Victoria's husband. Same thing with his Coolie gal."

Lennie rejoined. The other men guffawed. "You think me didn't hear? You a get more money than everybody else—like say we a quashie." Jeremiah started to collect his tools. The other men avoided his gaze.

"Don't know where him come from with his high fallutin talk either," one man grumbled. "Come here on ship from foreign, because you can't tell me say is Jamaican talk that." Lenny agreed and continued on his original track. "Everything him do, the old fart in his office heap on the praise like is only him one can work."

A huge young man who liked to flex his muscles, more when Portia came around, joined the group. "Kingsley and dwarfie, they act like man and woman."

"Batty man them," Lenny said. The room exploded in laughter.

Jeremiah had no idea what they laughed at. He still didn't quite grasp all of the island lingo. But his blood chilled at their conversation.

He had always kept to himself because he didn't want anyone questioning him about his whereabouts. When their laughter subsided, another of the men chimed in.

"You wait, the police after him too—you didn't hear them yesterday? Them ask him a whole heap of questions."

"Hm," Lenny grunted. "Story soon come to bump. T'will all come out in the wash—you wait."

Jeremiah completed his tasks and stalked out of the shop. He did not want any trouble. He felt uneasy and unsettled.

He yearned to see Nessa before she left for Milk River Bath. He missed her closeness—even though of late she had put emotional distance between them. He remembered Portia laughing in his face yesterday telling him, her mulatto brother Kendrick was whisking Nessa away in his carriage—right under Jeremiah's nose. His insides churned.

He soon dismissed the discontented men inside *The Foundry* from his mind. He ambled down the cobblestone streets, stopping at the butcher. He selected a hefty chunk of 'round' beef for Miss Ilda. From the sidewalk vendor, he chose pink-on-top coconut bars for the little girls. In the pub, he secured a flask of rum to share with Clifton. He visited them every Saturday. Miss Ilda would cook a big pot of tripe soup while he talked with Clifton and worked on carving a special chifforobe for Nessa. Today he'd have time to put two coats of varnish on before he tried to see Nessa later in the evening.

He didn't get to see Nessa as often as he'd like because he was on a mission. He wanted to offer her something besides a ring. A real solid life. It probably wouldn't matter to her but it did to him. This was what being a man was all about.

It wouldn't be long before he could put his plan in action. His chest heaved with pride. Clifton had taken him to see the middle-aged Moravian minister about a parcel of land last weekend.

Reverend Kersey had counted the money one-by-one. He spread a drawing on the table. "See here?" he pointed. "We are here." His fingers traveled up a long way in the hills. "This place is Clarksonville—Mr. Clark's son owns that huge tract of land. Making an entire village I hear."

"One man?" Jeremiah queried.

"Yes, and right down here is where I'm sending you to a place called "Try-See.""

"Try see?"

The reverend turned pink with suppressed laughter. "Yes, try and see what you can make of the place." Jeremiah laughed too.

Reverend Kersey offered him some lemonade. "And if it doesn't suit maybe you can try something else. But there's plenty available up in those hills, the Dry Harbor Mountains."

After more discussions, Jeremiah left with directions to meet Clifton who accompanied him driving his wagon. But when they got to Try-See, both men didn't like the lay of the land. They found one nearby which suited even better. "This is it!" Jeremiah stood on the hill overlooking the valley and felt at one with this land.

"Yes," Clifton agreed. "This is good land. Try and See . . ." they exploded in laughter at the unintended pun. "Try and see if the reverend will swap." Clifton continued. They slapped each other on the back. Jeremiah walked off away from Clifton with visions forming in his mind. He swallowed in exhilaration.

The next day he had gone straight to the reverend and made the swap and got a bigger parcel than Trysee. He had already named his new land Brownsville.

He couldn't wait to tell Nessa. The thought of her brought him back to the present. Earlier she had displayed no interest when he mentioned getting land. What if she was interested in the mulatto? His heart beat wild in his chest and he felt unsure. He would not rest easy until he saw her tonight.

Later in the evening, Jeremiah walked back to town. Dusk had arrived, the air balmy. With a spring in his step he sauntered down the streets. He buried his hands deep in his pocket, fingering Nessa's ring and whistling a jaunty tune.

Jeremiah approached Lady Barclay's house on the edge of town. It had much more privacy than these other houses with their verandahs sitting in the street. He turned off onto the tree-lined path leading to the house. He knew he had to go to the back entrance. This place was liberated but not so liberated. He knocked on the back door, two or three times, but no answer. The sound of carriage wheels rumbled up the path. Jeremiah inched his body sideways against the house, hiding behind the bramble bush.

His eyes popped when the mulatto, Portia's brother, opened the carriage door dressed up in a suit like a white man. Nessa descended the stairs with Lady Barclay.

Nessa looked magnificent in a fancy, pale-blue dress with what looked like dazzling diamonds twinkling all around her wide skirt. Her hair, parted and smoothed in front, piled to the back of her head and secured with a pale blue ribbon. Her hair cascaded down her back. She looked as regal as a queen.

His mouth went dry when Kendrick turned and helped Nessa into the carriage, after her mistress. Lady Barclay, wrapped in an apricot ensemble, looked like an overly sweet bonbon Devlin used to save for him. Nessa smiled up in the man's face and looked so happy. Kendrick's brownish curly hair, amber eyes and copper skin complemented Nessa's looks. Jeremiah admitted, with some reluctance, they looked good together. A perfect match.

Kendrick's hand lingered on her, suspending over her even after he seated her in the carriage. He looked besotted. The little woman, probably the maid, ran around like a little hamster. She clapped her hands and chatted to no one in particular. Soon the carriage rumbled away.

So that's the way it is, Jeremiah thought. A slow burn in his chest settled into a festering wound. He sat on the ground and placed his head between his knees. What a fool he had been. He could not offer her the kind of life she was living. It would even be unfair to propose to her. She might just accept out of loyalty because of what they'd been through together. After a time she would be miserable with him thinking of the life she gave up, going around with people who treated her like an equal.

It was a gone conclusion. Portia had said Kendrick's father was leaving him with property and a rum distillery as his legacy. The father had even had him schooled for a while by a tutor. How could he match anything like that? He would be doing Nessa a disservice by forcing her hand, he reasoned. Now he finally knew why she was so cool toward him.

Thoughts of the mulatto turned to rage. If the man came within a hair's breadth he could scalp him and hang his head on a totem pole high up on the hill in Brownsville. See how he would look without all those big brown curls.

Jeremiah spat on the ground. He couldn't even swallow with the mulatto in his mind. The thought of Brownsville felt like the dregs from Miss Ilda's beberidge drink.

The loud chirping crickets inspired him to raise his head. A couple of them chased each other. The bigger one caught the other and hopped on its back. Another loud chirping filled the air; the other cricket raced from the left to the victim's rescue. The aggressive one dethroned the other and they all raced off into the bushes.

He did not know how long he stayed at the base of the bramble bush. He was stretched out, so he must have fallen asleep. However, sleep didn't ease the way he felt. His chest squeezed in and out from the sides like an accordion player the black-haired man played down at the docks. He could almost hear the man crooning in a foreign tongue, *Ave Maria*. The man always had a look of longing on his face.

Jeremiah waited in empty silence. A pair of fireflies, peenie wallies, swooped in flight traversing the night. They danced and cavorted, the apparent male emitted a bright orange flash every few seconds as if he guided the female through the dark. It's the flight of the fireflies, he mused wondering what chased them. After a while, no answering yellow-green flash from the female, she had disappeared. The light from the lone firefly dimmed. Jeremiah felt great empathy and oneness for the lone male firefly. The night stretched on—taut like a drawn bow.

CHAPTER 17

In the melee of attendees at the ball, Nessa had to admit she was having a good time. Never had she seen such fancy people in one place or such a variety of people either. At times she couldn't tell the whites from the coloreds. Nessa looked around but could not find any darker-skinned people, only the servants. How she would love to dance with her Jeremiah but she knew they'd cut him dead.

Lady Barclay pointed across the hall with her chin. "That one with her blonde tresses is a mestee."

"Mestee?" Nessa whispered back. "But she's white."

Lady Barclay chuckled behind her fan. "That's a mixture of quadroon and white." She laughed again. "I guess you want to know who is a quadroon. That's a mixture of mulatto and white."

Nessa furrowed her brow. Ninety-five percent of the occupants in the room had black blood. So, if this were a sample of the people on the island, mulattoes and their offshoots far outnumbered the whites.

A well-dressed mulatto in cutaway tailcoat approached Nessa and Lady Barclay. He looked over Nessa with interest.

"May I present my companion, Miss Awanessa."

"Delighted." He bowed over Nessa's outstretched hand.

Nessa curtsied and smiled.

"Delighted to see you Mr. Jordon." Lady Barclay said shaking his hand and smiling. "I heard you had a big pimento crop this year."

Nessa didn't wait for his reply. She excused herself to refill her glass with more warm punch. She crossed the room, taking the opportunity to absorb the ballroom's splendor with its walls lined with gold brocade paper. Two huge, brass-ringed chandeliers hung from the ceiling, like hundreds of candles, suffusing the room with soft light. On the walls several candelabras glowed throughout the large rectangular room.

Nessa sipped her punch and admired a slender woman wearing a satin, emerald dress with puffy short sleeves. The neckline, cut straight across the collarbone, anchored silky, burgundy ribbons on both shoulders. Her male companion wrapped his arm around her fitted waist, which flared off into a full layered skirt. The couple danced the quadrille with others, Nessa watched every movement so she could pattern their steps.

Music flowed throughout the night, except for a brief intermission. The orchestra mainly played music for the quadrille dance. At one point they played the waltz, the new dance craze, but the older couples didn't know how to dance it so they resumed playing the quadrille. She spotted Kendrick making a beeline for her so she decided, on the spur of the moment, to try the dance. Giving her empty glass to a passing servant, she stepped in place to join the ladies on the floor. The women offered their right hands to each other as they passed and their left hands to the opposite gentlemen.

Kendrick's eyes bore into her. He hurried through his steps to get to her. She bit back a smile when all the ladies had to turn and face the opposite couples, leaving him with another partner. This went on for a while with more complicated sets. Nessa sighed with relief when the dance ended. Not that she didn't enjoy the dance but Kendrick's obsession rankled her nerves. The men bowed and the women curtsied. Soon Kendrick appeared at her side offering his arm. She steered him in Lady Barclay's direction.

"Mon, you've been sticking close to Lady Barclay. Are you avoiding me?"

Nessa fanned her face and neck with a pleated fan. "No. I'm not, but I'm Lady Barclay's companion, remember?" She smiled up at him with false sweetness.

He made a tsk, tsk sound through his teeth and changed tactics. "You look quite bonnie tonight," he said looking deep into her eyes.

She gestured across the room. "Everyone looks so splendid don't they?"

"Would you like more punch?" He asked.

"Yes, please." She was relieved he would be gone for a while. Her eyes searched the room for Lady Barclay and saw she was laughing with two older women. She didn't need her.

The night progressed and the dapper looking men looked wilted in their cutaway tailcoats. How smothered they must feel in their snowy cravats tied high up on their necks. As if to punctuate her thoughts, they flashed white, embroidered handkerchiefs to dab at their damp foreheads. Kendrick returned with the punch and it made her stomach even queasier. A teeny bit flattered at first by Kendrick's attention, it relieved some of her pique toward Jeremiah. Now he was too much.

Feeling stifled by the sultry heat she turned to Kendrick. "I need to get a breath of fresh air." Her heart sank when he followed close at her heels.

On the verandah, she stepped out in the moonlight and gulped in the cool sea breeze. It revived her. They spent a few quiet minutes exchanging pleasantries but the conversation turned.

"Lord Barclay will soon come back to the island you know?"

"I hope so," Nessa replied. "Lady Barclay is dying for him to return."

"Then what will you do?" he asked, giving her a sidelong glance.

"I'll probably get another position," she said, plastering him with a smile she didn't quite feel. She didn't like the way the conversation turned.

"You know I'm his son." He said in a hushed tone.

"It would seem so."

"He promised me Barclay Downs when he goes back to England for good."

Nessa was glad for him. "That's just wonderful Kendrick."

"Mon, we could share it together," he said in a hopeful tone.

Her face grew pensive. He reached for her shoulders and turned her into him. Before she could see his intent, his mouth swooped down to her lips and planted a sloppy kiss. His tongue darted in and out like the big green lizard outside her bedroom window. She stepped back and pushed him away, wiping her mouth with the back of her hand.

"I'm sorry Miss Nessa. Just got carried away."

He looked so contrite, she nodded. She gathered her skirts and started for the ballroom. She glanced back over her shoulder at his silhouette in the shadows. "I think Lady Barclay's looking for me." She disappeared inside to stay by Lady Barclay's side for the rest of the night.

Soon after, the party waned and Lady Barclay made her farewells. Nessa's feet dragged to the carriage. The fresh air fanned her face as the carriage rumbled down Duke Street. Exhaustion closed in on her, her eyelids drooped.

Too soon, the carriage rumbled up the path toward the house. She wondered how she'd keep Kendrick at arm's length on the trip to Milk River. Lady Barclay noticed his attraction and encouraged it, so she wouldn't be getting help from that quarter. She wondered if Lady Barclay knew Kendrick was her husband's son. It's possible, but she'd probably ignore it, not wanting to make waves with her husband.

Kendrick helped Lady Barclay down and she strode up the stairs ahead of them. "See you at noon, Kendrick," she called over her shoulder and went inside.

Nessa was fast on Lady Barclay's heels, but he grabbed her arm and pulled her to him. "I have to get Lady Barclay ready for bed," she said in protest. But he held her tight. She decided to give him a quick peck on the cheek to get rid of him. He had other plans and embraced her. He did the lizard again. She endured it for a few moments only to pacify him. She managed to break free and ran inside.

By the time she removed the pins from Lady Barclay's hair and helped her to bed the woman was asleep. Nessa blew out the light.

Inside her own room, she untied the sash at her waist to remove the peenie gown. It was weird, insects blinking their yellow-green and orange lights. She stuffed it into the bottom drawer and put on her night rail. Her stomach fluttered, she patted her small rounded stomach. It was the first movement from her baby. She paused to see if it would happen again.

A steady rapping at the window over her bed distracted her. Her eyes darted to the window in alarm. The fluttering intensified not only in her belly but all over her body. She knew it was not the baby this time. It was alarm spreading through her. Jeremiah stood outside her window. Her heart pounded. What if he saw everything?

She felt as if she was going to be sick, her eyes flew to the chamber pot in the corner. As soon as it came, the sick feeling passed. He wouldn't understand. She pulled on an old pelisse over her night rail, shoved her feet in a pair of slippers and squeaked the back door open. He stood there silhouetted in the moonlight with his arms folded across his chest. His face looked sculpted and implacable.

She pushed by him and they walked in silence. At the opposite side of the house she stopped. "How long have you been here?"

"Long enough to know exactly where I stand."

She reached out to touch him, he backed away a step.

"J no darling, it's not what you're thinking."

"Don't have to think, Awanessa, seeing is believing."

"Please . . ." she implored. "There's nothing between me and Kendrick. I didn't even want to go to the ball, but Lady—"

"Oh shut up. And you're going away with him tomorrow for a week? Spare me please!"

"J, that's not fair, he's just driving us!"

He waved his hand dismissing her. "Look, I waited because I wanted to let you know . . ." He glanced up at the moon and refocused on her face. "You don't have to feel guilt or loyalty towards me." His face turned cruel. "After all I never promised you anything now, did I?"

"No you didn't, but—"

"So now we're both free." He squared his jaw and started to stride away.

The baby kicked and she rounded on him. "You can't be free of me . . . ever!" she said on a wail, following him around the side of the house.

"I can't? Watch me!" He increased his stride.

She caught up with him and clutched his arm. "You can't leave me . . . us like this Jeremiah."

He looked back at her as if she had grown two heads.

"Listen to me J . . . I'm . . . I'm having your baby." He stood stock still. "I didn't want to break it to you like this," she said in a tremulous tone. "Our baby J…"

He rounded on her with a low bitter laugh. "If it's mine. How do you know I'm the father?"

Her face registered horror at his words, "If it's yours?" she shrieked at him, her eyes glazed with shock. She rocked back on her heels and slammed her fist into his jaw.

His head snapped to the side. He almost reeled from the force of her punch.

"If it's yours? . . . If—it's—yours?" She repeated the words in near hysterics, not caring if she woke the dead. She sprang on him like a feral cat. Rage contorted her face. She raised her hands again, clawing his face all the way down to his throat, making little mewing sounds from the back of her throat.

He stood immobile and didn't try to ward off her attack. Her energy spent, she battered small fists on his chest while dissolving into a mixture of weeping and hiccups. He reached for her.

"Go to hell!" She hissed, springing back in a crouch as if she had two hind legs. Her chest heaved. With her back still arched, she turned and ran inside the house, one hand protecting her stomach.

* * *

After a disturbed sleep, Nessa woke to unusual noise and bustle in the house. She could hear Matty nattering away and Lady Barclay's high pitched voice, which became even higher when she was excited about something. Heavy footsteps walked the wood floor and a deep man's voice boomed through the house.

A team of horses trampled through her head. Nessa groaned and crawled out of bed. She pushed back scenes of the night before from her mind and got dressed.

She had to face a new life without Jeremiah but first she had to meet the new day. She splashed cold water from the wash basin on her face, rinsed her mouth and went out into the living room.

Lady Barclay beamed up into the face of an aristocratic looking man with lacquered, silver hair. He tapped his pipe on the sideboard while she talked.

The lines of the man's face resembled Kendrick's except for his sharper, longer nose.

The man fumbled in his breast pocket and took out an ornate, quizzing glass. He held it up to one eye and peered at Nessa, his eyeball enlarged. "And who might this be my dear?" Nessa felt like one of those peenie wallie bugs, warranting close inspection.

Lady Barclay spun around, her eyes and smile bright. Nessa had never seen her so alive and animated. "Oh Nessa did we wake you up?" She turned back to her husband, "Milord, this is my companion from the Colonies I told you about."

He nodded to Nessa and dropped the quizzing glass in his breast pocket, the handle protruded.

She addressed Nessa. "Our trip to Milk River Bath is canceled. Lord Wallis returned just in time, didn't you Milord?"

"I'm only here for two weeks. After that we pack up and go home."

"I know you said it before, but are you really serious this time?" Lady Barclay clasped her hands together in a prayer.

"Of course I'm serious. Do you think I'm going to stay on this God forsaken island with savages let loose?"

"Oh Milord, I'm so glad you gave me permission to move into town." She grimaced, "I shudder at what would happen to me out there on the Downs."

"Mark my words." He tapped his pipe on the sideboard. It will soon be anarchy on this island. You give them an inch and they want a whole mile. After the mile they want more. Where does that leave decent folks?"

Lady Barclay nodded in commiseration.

He warmed to his subject. "The gentry back in England are all pleased as peacocks with their self-righteousness that they've abolished slavery. I tell you Florence, it's a feeding frenzy back home. The once revered plantocracy who turned these islands into the sparkling jewels of England's crown are now reviled."

"You mean we shall not have a place in society when we return?" Lady Barclay's face clouded.

"We shall retire to the country my dear—in Bedfordshire. I've secured a respectable manor with a bevy of servants and a prim rose garden."

Her face brightened. "How about neighbors?"

He chuckled, "Yes you'll be able to attend your balls. Lots of neighbors around . . . and yes, they are titled."

She clapped her hands in delight and turned to Nessa who looked for a break to escape. "Nessa how would you like to live in England?"

Without waiting for Nessa's response, Mr. Barclay chuckled and addressed his wife. "Oh you'll be the talk of the town, alright. An Injun for a companion. Lady Abbot would swoon. Not to mention the gents holding on tight to their wigs."

Lady Barclay laughed out loud with him and Nessa slipped away into the kitchen. What a relief to get away from those two. Nessa's stomach rumbled, anticipating food. She prepared a breakfast tray for herself and then Matty trapped her.

"Miss Nessa, what do you know? Last night me dream of this fish, just swishing his tail back and forth in the water. And you know what they say when you dream of fish?"

"No," Nessa spooned ackee on her plate and added two johnny cakes.

"Somebody breeding." She whispered in an ominous tone.

"Breeding?" Nessa tried to follow her train of thought.

"Yes, mum, breed, in de family way, soon have baby."

"Oh," Nessa said, her voice rising to a slight squeak.

"A hope is not me daughter for as God loveth, I'd flatten her into the ground with this pudden pan," she said looking at the frying pan.

"How old is she?"

"Evelyn no reach 16 yet you know? But a hear dat Man-Man a come to de yard every day when mi not there."

"But you're here most of the time."

"Yes, but Evelyn is the oldest child and have to take care of the rest."

"How many children do you have Matty?"

"Nine! And all of them for Marse Jasper," she said, jutting out her chest with pride. Not a man ever put him hand on me except for him. And thank the Lard, we is all free." Matty switched topics. "Lard Miss Nessa how the peenie gown last night?"

"Very different."

"Lard, now that de Lady leaving for England, a have to find another job. But Marse Jasper will have to hire himself out more while a find something else then a can keep mi eye on Evelyn. But is a whole heap of things Lady Barclay have to pack. I wonder if she going to take every—." Matty ducked her head under the cupboard to retrieve a stock pot for the evening stew.

"I'll be outside Matty." Nessa took a brief minute to collect a mug of hot tea, added plantains to her plate and escaped.

She sat on the swing chair tied between two orange trees. While she ate she thought of her predicament.

Lady Barclay was leaving in two weeks. What an opportunity to start clean somewhere far away. The baby kicked. With every thud in her belly, she knew she would not leave this place. She had to figure out a way she could stay and support herself. She dismissed the thought of being near Jeremiah from her mind. She had to focus on the present and future. She devoured the last bit of johnny cake from her plate.

She sat back and rocked in the swing but her stomach felt queasy from the coconut oil Matty used to saturate the food. Reaching up her arms to a nearby branch, she picked one of the big navel oranges overhead. She sunk her finger nails at the base and the skin peeled away to reveal the succulent sections. She sucked on the sweet, refreshing juice. An idea hit her at the same time the juice squirted in her mouth.

She had a reputation throughout the Cherokee clan for fine needlework. Gentle Dove used to look at her work in awe and declared the stitches invisible. She made the wedding gown for Rani last year. Indeed, she could look at a person's body and make pantaloons or any garment to fit. She even knew how to use the chain-stitch sewing machine. That's what she'd do. Make clothes. Excitement coursed through her veins.

She had saved most of her generous wages, only spending a small amount on the frequent lunches she had with Jeremiah. Sometimes she had even packed lunches from Lady Barclay's overflowing pantry. She would have enough to live on until business picked up. Plus, another thought occurred to her, she could sell salves and hire out herself as midwife.

After eating her fill of the orange she piled the saps back onto the plate.

Who would she aim her business at? She wondered. She would find out how many of the gentry were left in this area. She knew from the ball last night, lots of mulattoes could more than afford her service. And they weren't going anywhere. In time, they would be the new gentry.

She recoiled from the thought of making coarse, homespun dresses for the ex-slave women and felt guilty. She pacified herself by thinking business was business. She had to go where the coin was.

She hugged her mid-section, rocking back and forth in the swing, her eyes dreamy with possibilities.

"Dysaethesia Aethiopica," a disease causing "rascality" in black people . . . It is much more prevalent among free negroes living in clusters by themselves."

Excerpt from "Diseases and
Peculiarities of the Negro Race,"
Dr. Samuel Cartwright, Debow's Review, Vol. XI

CHAPTER 18

In the stark light of day, Jeremiah gained new perspective. He spent the entire Sunday plagued with remorse. He sat under the banyan tree where he'd last had lunch with Nessa. He knew in his heart she told the truth last night. But why didn't she tell him about the baby before? Now he'd gotten himself in one jar of pickle and didn't know how to get out.

He kept reliving the wounded look in her eyes. What made him respond so? Blinding, gut-wrenching jealousy, his conscience told him. Now he had to stew for a whole week until she returned from Milk River Bath. The mulatto will even have more chances to win her. Anger flared again, sliding through his body like stale grease. Did he throw her to the mulatto by his own cagey actions? He was only biding his time, when everything lined up like the dominoes his co-workers played after work. He didn't foresee this threat. He felt unsure, uneasy. He didn't even notice the unmistakable sashaying figure approaching.

"C'mon handsome, you trying to mess up that face?"

Portia stood before him, arms akimbo, waiting to be noticed. Canary red parrots and enormous coco leaves splashed all over her turquoise dress. She sidled closer to him, adjusting the matching head wrap over her ears.

Despite himself, he smiled at her. "How did you come by that get-up?"

"Bought it from the Jew man down the street. You like it?"

He rolled his eyes to the sky in exasperation.

"She not worth worrying over you know."

"Yes, she is." He rejoined.

"I can make you forget her easy." Portia stuck out her full lips and fidgeted her body to get even closer.

He leaned back against the tree and laughed out loud at her antics. "You are funny, you know that Portia?"

She grabbed his hand and entwined their fingers. "I make up my mind when I first bless my eyes on you that you're the only man for me." She batted her eyelashes and stuck out her chin.

His gaze flickered over her. If he didn't love Nessa so much, maybe he would have given Portia a chance. He didn't know about her character though, but her ebony skin was smooth and supple, her body buxom and well-proportioned. She was a temptress and she knew it.

"Don't get any ideas, Portia." He rose and brushed off his pants. Portia craned her neck, interested in a carriage coming down the street. He turned to leave her when she all but threw herself in his arms. He grabbed her to steady her. "What's gotten into you woman?" He wanted to shake some sense in her. He was getting tired of her already.

The Barclay carriage rumbled by and his eyes collided with Nessa's stricken gaze. He looked at Portia in time to see a calculated gleam in her eye.

He stared after the carriage. Nessa never looked back. His heart sank to his shoes. Now his goose was surely cooked, he thought.

Portia circled him. "So that's what got you in a dither?"

He decided he may as well sit back down and get some information out of Portia. "Who was the white man sitting next to Kendrick?"

"That's Lord Barclay. His ship come in last night. Kendrick told me that he's not taking Lady Barclay to Milk River again. Plans change. They're gone over to the Downs to pack. Kendrick will own all that land and rum factory after them leave. Me brother going be rich," she prattled on.

Jeremiah felt another arrow shoot through his heart. As the day waned he felt his and Nessa's love slipping through his fingers.

Portia filled him in. "Me brother is just as determined as me." She confided. "Anything we want we make sure we get it, whether by fair or by foul," she whispered. Her eyes widened into his. He saw a faint grey ring around the black of her eyes. A chill ran up his spine.

He had to find a way to see Nessa, maybe he could enlist Portia's help. "Do you live at the Downs?"

"Not exactly, me live with me mother nearby in the old overseer's house. You want to come out for dinner?"

He pondered for a second, maybe he should. Afterward he could pretend to leave and scout the main house for some sign of Nessa. He had to speak with her. His need overwhelmed him.

"Mama cooking rice and peas, cooked-down chicken and callaloo. Then we wash it all down with some carrot juice." Portia flashed a big smile to entice him further.

He studied the gap between her two front teeth. "Yes, I'll come."

"Good. Come when it's dusk-dusk. Just follow that road there," she said. "Take it straight until you see a big, white house with a wrap-around verandah. Don't go all the way to the big house. Stop at the first house around the corner. You can't miss it," she said, her eyes dancing the way he imagined the devil's mistress would look.

He started to walk back to his little room he rented over the blacksmith shop near to *The Foundry*.

"I'll be waiting for you at the beginning of the path. Lord Barclay got some bad dogs but once they sniff you and you're with me you'll be alright. They won't bother you again." She talked over her shoulder and walked off in the opposite direction.

When he returned to his room. He took out the new pantaloons the tailor made for him along with a crisp white shirt. Clothes he had bought for his wedding day. But, he thought, this is the right time to wear them because if he didn't do something about his situation, there would be no wedding day.

He opened the windows to let in some of the sea breeze and relieve some of the room's stuffiness. He lay back on his single, lumpy cot and closed his eyes.

Soon dusk arrived and he made his way to Portia's house. The desolate road, flanked on both sides with tall stalks of sugar cane, felt like he walked through an endless cornfield back in Georgia. Way off in the middle of the canefield stood the sugar works, but no gray smoke swirled from its chimneys. Above him, stretched the vast azure sky flecked with white, puffy clouds. Not a bird flew by. Not an animal darted across his path. Not even a slight breeze stirred the air.

Carriage wheels echoed through the vast expanse of canefields. He didn't know whether the sound came from behind or in front. From sheer habit, he jumped over the dune-like embankment and crouched between the cane stalks. Soon the carriage rumbled by with Kendrick at the reins and the Barclays sitting next to each other. He noted Nessa's absence with satisfaction.

Once the carriage disappeared, he jumped back on the road, hopping from one foot to the other. Big, copper-red ants raced into his shoes, knocking themselves over to get under his pantaloons. He brushed them off before they had a chance to bite. Stomping his feet several times, he hurried on down the road.

He sighed in relief when he spotted Portia's house. The dogs came around and sniffed him. Sure enough they went away after, just as Portia had predicted. She sat on the verandah waiting for him. He spoke to her from the front stoop.

"Portia, I'll be back but I have to see Nessa," he said, holding his hands up in front of his chest as if pushing her away.

She gave him a thunderous gaze. "You're just going to walk up to the front door and ask for her?"

"Exactly what I'll do." He turned on his heel and sauntered up to the main house. Changing his mind, he walked to the back entrance.

A formidable looking woman opened the door and eyed him without speaking.

"I'd like to speak with Miss Nessa please," Jeremiah said. She grunted and closed the door.

Soon after, Nessa appeared at the door. Her body looked voluptuous and he wanted to hold her close. Her bronze skin glowed in the twilight. Her eyes large and misty awakened all his senses. He longed to touch her dewy skin or run his fingers through her braid. Jasmine emanated from her pores. So beautiful, he thought. He swallowed hard to overcome the lump in his throat. He couldn't speak.

She fixed him with a cold stare."So you've just come to look at me?" Her voice sounded remote.

"No, Ness . . ." He rubbed the back of his neck."I just want to say . . . I'm . . . I'm truly sorry."

"You needn't have bothered to come. I don't want you in my life."

"But the baby . . ."

"Is mine! I don't need you." She looked at him stony faced." She continued in a whisper, "Furthermore, Jeremiah Browne, I don't love you anymore."

He looked at her stunned, at a loss for words again. Icy chills spread through his body.

"So, if that's all you came to say . . ." She started to close the door.

"No, no. Ness please . . ." he said, knowing his voice deteriorated to a pleading sound. "Give me a chance. More than anything, Ness I—"

She slammed the door in his face.

He stood there blinded with tears, for the first time in his life. He couldn't believe his Nessa would treat him this way. He raised his hand to knock again but decided he wouldn't beg and grovel like a sniffling idiot. Her behavior was uncalled for. Anger coursed through him. "She will have to come to me next time," he mumbled under his breath. If he didn't beg and grovel in slavery, he would be damned if he would start now as a free man.

He stalked away from the house with a profound sense of loss. Wanting to go home and lick his wounds, he took the road away from Portia's house hoping it would lead back to the main road. He reached a clearing, despondency washed over him and he sat on a rock, staring out unseeing into the evening shadows.

It was a glorious sunset. A kaleidoscope of golds, orange and deep blue streaked low in the sky. A gentle breeze grazed his cheek. Jeremiah could not register the natural beauty of his surroundings. His insides churned when he felt a female hand snaking up his back. He knew without looking it wasn't the hand he wished for. Portia sat next to him and cradled his head on her breast. Sorely in need of comfort, he relaxed in her arms.

"You can't starve yourself to death you know. Nobody is worth it."

His stomach growled in response. He didn't realize he was ravenous. Food was the last thing on his mind.

"Come, let's eat." She led him by the hand.

He followed her into the house and walked across the planked floor to the wooden table surrounded by four chairs. Portia called out, "Mama bring the dinner." She seated him at the table. She sat next to him. Close.

Soon after, a petite woman walked in with heaps of plates on a bamboo tray. The food smelled delicious. Portia smiled, he smiled back. "This is me mother, she name Miss Hortense."

"How do you do Miss Hortense?"

The woman set down the tray and extended her hand to greet him. Her right eye had a mind of its own as it directed itself to the ceiling. The left eye did double duty and gazed into his very soul. Chills crept up his back. She broke eye contact and removed the dish cloth covering the food. His mouth watered when he saw the fricasseed chicken swimming in the orange colored, annatto gravy.

"Thank you moomaw. I'll serve now." Her mother left the room with quick, mincing steps. Portia served him mounds of rice and beans, spoons of cabbage and carrots mixed together with some plantains on the side. She ate sparing amounts, devouring him with her eyes.

At last he sat back satisfied, now glad he decided to eat with Portia. Took his mind off his problems, plus the cured herring and stale bread in his room did not appeal to him.

Portia grilled him about his life where he came from. He spoke more of the customs, the food and description of the places he'd been. He didn't speak of the bad times—he didn't want memories to blight this wonderful dinner.

Miss Hortense returned and poured a sweet, strange brew in his goblet. She lit the lamp. Jeremiah sat back, sipped the drink and relaxed. Portia droned on about her life on the island. He became mesmerized with the orbs in her eyes. The faint circle around the iris got wider by the minute. He noticed the anxious glances at her mother who lit two fat, red candles.

He knew he'd better be going back. But he stayed. He felt good, in a buoyant space between sleeping and waking, like he floated outside of his body. The lamp and candle light cast an unholy glow in the room. Everything looked golden. Even Portia's face looked chiseled and void of emotion. He was drifting down … down into a cloud. His eyes fixated on the flickering shadows on the wall. His limbs turned to jelly, his jaw went slack. Hazy bits of conversation wafted in an out of his mind.

"Oh God Moomaw, what did you do to him?"

"Nutten dat I can't remedy chile, tan tuddy!"

Portia's mouth snapped shut at her mother's directive. Jeremiah wondered if he was drowning again. His head felt like it was going under water with bells ringing in his ears.

"It wasn't supposed to happen like this at all!" Portia wailed.

"Get the—"

Jeremiah's mind faded, went blank and new images emerged. Miss Hortense appeared with two heads, one on the back and one at the front of her body. Portia's braids stood up and twisted from side-to-side as if they had lives of their own. Soon faces faded in and out, turning into shadows. He felt transported into another world—a dark, faceless world.

Figures draped in white sheets, their heads wrapped in white turbans glided into the house without feet. Hands clawed and groped, carrying him outside. He sucked in gusts of fresh air, reviving him. They sat him on the grass and leaned him against a tree trunk in front of an open fire. As if on the count of three they all began to chant.

Bodies spasmed and writhed to the chants. Plaintive wails seeped up from the depth of their souls. They danced on in the night with their arms outstretched, flailing wild.

The tempo of the moaning, drumming and chanting increased to a frenzy. Some collapsed prostrate, trashing the ground.

The chants unfurled coils of sorrow and pain deep within his core, pulsating through his veins and pumping his blood. He struggled to stand.

But they pulled him down . . . down.

"Tie him . . ." someone shrieked.

More hands clawed his arms and chest, binding him with a rope. Something inside him snapped. A clear thought came through.

I shall not be bound again.

He shook off hands clutching at him and burst his bonds. He leaped to his feet, swaying like a newborn colt. Gathering his strength, he hurled himself out into the cool night.

Dodging trees and shrubbery, he ran and ran forever until the chants faded and his blood calmed. He floated off from the top of his head like mist from the Smoky Mountain peak. His eyes danced round and round in their sockets. The ground slanted, moved toward him and straightened.

Images from his former life flitted across the landscape of his mind. Between the trees, his father's rotting corpse slithered towards him on his belly. His father stretched out a bone for a hand.

"Husani, wait . . ."

Jeremiah didn't wait. He ran in terror, only to bump up against Janie who Massa George had beaten to a pulp. Her bare mutilated breasts oozed milk and dark blood caked her chemise. She advanced on him with her fingers poised in the air like an eagle's talon.

He changed direction only to meet Jacob with no ears and blood running down the side of his face. Jeremiah turned in the one direction he could. Finally free, he saw an entire army of Indians crowding in on him. Most of them had sockets for eyes. They raised a hair splitting war cry from their skeletal frames. Jeremiah's fog thickened brain filtered one message.

Run!

He ran, and all along the path where he ran white flowers sprang up at his feet. He came to the ocean, its foamy waves crested with blood. He stopped.

In the distance where the sea meets the sky, the silhouette of a ship faded away. A steady hum behind him made him turn around to face his pursuers. But a blinding white light streaked across his eyes. Before he passed out, he felt a multitude of hands seize his arms and legs, raising him high off the ground.

In a horizontal position they carried him away.

CHAPTER 19

Wild exhilaration tingled through Nessa as she strolled the grounds at Barclay Downs. Her plans were beginning to take shape, like little dumplings from dough. She thanked the Great Spirit her brief stint with morning sickness had left. Miss Ilda had found the right remedy.

After an early breakfast, she trudged along the path leading to the house. She stopped to marvel at the poinciana tree with its brilliant orange blossoms. The tree made a glorious entrance to the handsome, white, clapboard plantation house. She paused by a tamarind tree with its hanging pod-like fruits. Those sour things were food for her and Jeremiah when they first landed.

Thinking of Jeremiah made her flinch, a dark pain washed over her. She had to banish her tormenting thoughts. If she could wipe away the memories she would. The hurt. The pain and longing she saw in his face. But something inside her compelled her to seek revenge; the same feeling moved her to avenge Etu's death. She couldn't believe she had killed one of Etu's murderers, but she would not focus on the past. The future had infinite possibilities.

Regret and longing for Jeremiah washed over her but she summoned the hurt which nestled just below the surface of her mind. He spurned her and their baby. He took up with another woman. She could ride on her anger for a long time and let him suffer. An insistent call, like a patoo owl, broke into her reverie. "Yoo-hoo... Yoo-hoo... Nessooo."

"I'm coming ma'am."

Lady Barclay waited for her on the veranda, a bemused expression on her face.

"My word, Nessa, this island food is certainly fattening you up."

Nessa smiled in answer. She was out of breath by the time she got to Lady Barclay's side. The woman never had a child, so she was oblivious to the signs and symptoms.

"This is so overwhelming. So much to pack. And Lord Barclay says, I'm to leave almost everything but my precious items. He doesn't know everything is precious," she said, her tone petulant. Nessa followed her into the master bedroom with its huge four-poster bed. Clothes scattered on the bed and in the half-opened trunks.

"Shall I get Matty and Clothilde to help ma'am?"

"Those dim-witted, lazy twits? No! I don't want them handling my things."

"They've been handling your things all this time."

Lady Barclay shot a furtive glance toward the door then leaned in to Nessa. "Now that I'm leaving, they'll be stealing what they can." She walked over to the window, rattled the shutters and flung it wide open.

Nessa assessed the disarray and decided she'd start with the items on the bed.

"Are you sure you don't want to come with us my dear?"

Nessa shook her head from side-to-side.

"I don't know what I'm going to do without you. You've become my right hand," Lady Barclay said, sniffing the cool morning air wafting through the window. "Who's going to pen my letters and rub those miracle salves all over my joints?"

"Oh ma'am, I'll write you."

"And who's going to read it for me?"

"I'm sure you'll find someone suitable ma'am." Nessa said, saddened by Lady Barclay's impending departure. Despite her earlier exhilaration at a future of possibilities, she now felt alone and adrift. She shook off the feeling. She was already missing her employer that's all.

Lady Barclay placed two fingers at her temple. "God, my head aches. Did you hear that confounded chanting last night?"

"I couldn't sleep either." Nessa said. "I heard the chants too but I thought I dreamed it."

"No, every Sunday night, a group of ex-slaves gather somewhere on the edge of our property and wail as if Lucifer himself ran after them with a pitch fork."

"Maybe it's some kind of religion then?"

"Yes, something called *Kumina*. Banning them from practicing doesn't help in the least."

"But why would the law ban it?"

"Devil worship if you ask me. Bloody hypocrites they are too. Every Sunday they sit up in the regular church, pretending that they are God-fearing." Lady Barclay tossed a few items of clothing in the trunk.

"Next thing you know, decent people cannot sleep at night because of their caterwauling. Oh! I'll be so glad to get away from this place," she said with a sigh. "See all these fabrics? I'm taking the silk Lord Barclay brought back for me from the Orient. All the rest you can keep. My gift to help you start your business my dear."

A stunned Nessa ran into Lady Barclay's arms and hugged her.

"You dear, dear lady. Thank you so much."

Lady Barclay extricated herself from the embrace with an embarrassing, "tut, tut. . . let's get busy."

Nessa wiped the free flowing tears with the back of her hand. She dried her hands in her apron and ran her fingers over the yards of bright, colored fabric.

Lady Barclay tossed a few more items into the trunk. "I'm going to get all new clothes custom-made. These thin fabrics, suitable for the tropics, will not do in chilly Bedfordshire at all." She waved her hand in the air. "You can also have all of my gowns too. I understand from Lady Piccole, who recently returned from London, that the empire waist style is quite out of fashion with the Ton."

Nessa had no idea what the Ton was but whoever it was she was grateful. She scanned the mound of maybe two dozen day and evening gowns. She could start her store with this inventory right away. Nessa spent the rest of the day, humming as she put the room in order. She called Delroy and Man-Man, the two resident groundsmen, so they could stack the trunks on the verandah.

By the end of the day, exhaustion seeped to her bones. Between the Barclays' departure and the excitement of opening her store, she didn't have time to dwell on Jeremiah.

Kendrick popped in whenever he could to help. She gave him a wide berth as much as she could. By the end of the day though he caught on she was avoiding him.

"Nessa," he said in an urgent voice. "Why are you setting up shop? As mistress of Barclay Downs you won't have to work you know?"

She rounded on him. "Kendrick if I told you once I must have told you a thousand times. Apparently you've gotten deaf, so read my lips, "I—am—not—going—to marry—you.""

"We are perfect for each other, can't you see?"

She sighed, exasperated with him. "It's not going to happen Kendrick."

"Well, even if I have to go to the Carolinas, I must find someone like you," he said with a resigned sigh.

She suppressed a laugh. "You don't want to do that, trust me. There is no more of my kind there." She left him on the verandah with a baffled expression on his face. She joined Lady Barclay to remove the last items. She had to see if she could escape tomorrow to secure a place in town to set up shop as well as safe living quarters. The Barclays were not going away on Wednesday and leave her at Kendrick's mercy.

Lord Barclay entered the room and handed Nessa a letter. "Here you are, deliver this missive to Mr. Winthrop that owns the goldsmith shop. He'll see to situating you as is proper."

She scanned the contents. Her eyes filmed. "Thank you both, you are very kind and generous."

"Well, we don't want to see you on the streets now. Do we milord?" Lady Barclay piped in beaming at her.

"No, no not at all." He looked down the length of his nose, tapping his pipe against the window sill.

"If you don't need me anymore I shall retire." Nessa said, automatically mirroring the way they talked. She did a little curtsy and walked out, clutching the precious letter of reference.

"Kendrick will take you in to town tomorrow morning after he takes us to the ship," Lady Barclay said over her shoulder.

Nessa sat on her bed, her chest heaving with excitement. The Barclays had given her a full month's severance pay and a letter of reference so she could rent a place. She dressed for the night and blew out the light. Before she fell asleep, she visualized the store and what it would look like. Visions of gowns, hats, lace and a crawling baby filled her dreams.

* * *

The ship had sailed and the house felt empty without the Barclays. Nessa missed Lady Barclay. She would not forget her.

Matty came up behind her. "De lady and de Massa gone now. Ah don't know why you don't stay here with Mr. Kendrick. You know the man turn to coconut jelly when him see you." Matty said in a teasing voice.

Nessa ignored her comment. "Are you and Clothilde going to help me down at the store?"

"But of course. Me can sew real good too you know and if you ever see the stitches that Clothilde make your belly hurt you!"

Nessa laughed at Matty's expressions and pulled out an old trunk. She called out to Clothilde. "Here are some things you both can use that Lady told me to distribute amongst you."

They pounced into the trunk with glee, trying on hats and scarves. Nessa slipped away to her room to make sure she didn't forget anything. She walked out to the verandah. Clifton brought his wagon plus his friend's wagon. The amount of things she acquired surprised her. Lady Barclay had given her the bed from the Lodge, and even her chain-stitch sewing machine.

"You ready Miss Nessa?" Clifton said, hopping on to the verandah. She had enlisted his aid before Kendrick returned from the pier. Clifton whistled when he saw her belongings. "You came here with just your two long arms and look what you got now?"

She gave him a warm smile. "Thank you so much Clifton for helping me out."

"Miss Ilda would kill me if I didn't."

She laughed. The past two days had been hectic, getting the reference letter to Mr. Winthrop, securing the shop and numerous other details. Mr. Winthrop was so kind, he directed her to a Scotsman who made signs. Delroy and Man-Man, assisted her in lugging the sign back to the shop.

"Brammy," Clifton called to the waiting young man. "Put the bed in first then pile the rest on top. Where's Delroy and Man-Man?"

"They went with Kendrick and the Barclays down to the ship," Brammy replied.

"So them really gone eh?" Without waiting for an answer, Clifton hoisted a table and two chairs into one wagon. He loaded the other wagon with various odds and ends, a cheval mirror, her personal wash basin and stand, clothing and more.

She watched over the loading, not wanting anything to happen to her precious fabrics. She kissed Matty on the cheek, Clothilde bent to kiss her. Matty dabbed at her eyes. "Matty, no need for tears."

"Is just that you're going off on your own, lonely-like."

"All set?" Clifton asked.

"Yes, I'm ready. I'll see you on Saturday," she shouted over the stomping mules to the women. She sat next to Clifton and placed a wrapped present for Miss Ilda in her lap.

Clifton pulled the reins, let out a wild, "Giddyap!" Brammy followed with his wagon in tow down the path. The women waved until the wagons turned the corner out of sight. Portia came out on her verandah, her arms akimbo to investigate, but Nessa looked the other way.

After about two miles, they pulled up in front of Nessa's store. As they entered, both Clifton and Brammy whistled at the glass case doubling as a counter. Another counter ran the width of the back dividing her sewing area from the customer area.

Clifton stepped up to her living quarters and whistled again at the spacious area. She beamed at him. The month's rent did not make a dent in her savings.

"One last thing before you leave, Cliff, hang up my sign please."

"How the devil did you get this big ole thing down here?"

"If it weren't for Delroy and Man-Man, I don't know what I'd do," she said, missing them. They were always eager to do favors for her. After much adjusting, she stood back a distance and admired the new sign.

Carolina Dress Shop and Haberdashery.

Tears filled her eyes and Clifton hugged her.

"Have to bring Miss Ilda and the gals to see this wondrous sight." He said with emotion in his voice.

Nessa rushed back inside. "Please give her these." She had lengthened one of Lady Barclay's gowns to fit Miss Ilda's tall frame. "Here's the bonnet to match. And tell her I expect her to wear them to my grand opening on Saturday."

He took her to the side. "How you feeling?" he said with concern in his voice.

"You mean the baby? Couldn't be better."

"Give him a chance to explain himself Nessa," he implored. He really—

She cut him off with a wave of her hand. "He explained it all to me last Saturday night," she told him with forced brightness.

A heavy sigh escaped him and he gave one last hug. He hopped into the wagon with Brammy trailing behind him. Inside the shop, Nessa locked the door. She stood in the middle of the room, looking around. She couldn't believe her good fortune. It was time to get busy.

She hung lace curtains at the front window and proceeded to hang the almost new dresses in the customer area. The bolts of fabric went in to the glass display case. She included tape measures, spools of thread, needles and the like. She also bought some gloves to match the dresses. And she wondered who she could commission to make ladies' hats. She would hold off on the hats for a while.

She surveyed her sparse living quarters with only a wash basin, a bed but no chifforobe. An old tub, looking like the half of a wooden barrel, stood in one corner. The kitchen was right next to the privy. It was a bit too close to the house for her liking but it would have to do. She was exhausted. Without even changing her clothes, she tumbled into bed for a nap.

Later she woke up to the baby's kicking. She sat up in the dim light, fumbling to light the lamp. Her exhilaration had waned and an empty loneliness crept over her. She took the lamp, wandering into the shop and spotted a bulky object through the window on the verandah. When she went outside she saw not one, but two items wrapped in newspaper. She removed the attached envelope. Her vision blurred. She looked across the street where two little boys played marbles. "Can you help me?" She yelled down at them.

They scampered up on the verandah and struggled to move the furniture into the back room. Afterwards, she gave them each a sixpence. With trembling fingers she ripped off the paper and gasped at the sheer beauty of the chifforobe. Excited, she opened each drawer back and forth to test the smoothness. It was impeccable. She ripped off the paper on the smaller package and stopped short, her knees weak.

A beautiful mahogany cradle.

She swayed and plopped down on the bed sobbing in the pillow. After awhile, she sat up, hugging her knees, then it dawned on her. Jeremiah must have been working on the chifforobe for weeks. It was supposed to be a surprise. Maybe he intended it for her wedding present. Her heart lurched. Oh what a fool she'd been. She rose from the bed to gently rock the cradle back and forth in contemplation. She had to go to him.

Wrapping a shawl around her shoulders, she slipped out into the late evening air. A light breeze carried a rank, fishy odor. A group of men huddled close, under a shop piazza, playing dominoes by lamplight. Their boisterous slamming of the dominoes, accompanied loud laughter and joking. Couples passed her, holding hands. A lady of the evening strutted by, glancing hopefully at any male in sight. Several stray dogs lounged at one corner and Nessa quickly crossed to the other side.

After walking up and down several streets she finally found Jeremiah's quarters. He lived above the blacksmith shop so she had to inquire downstairs. She rapped hard on the door a number of times. Not a glimmer of light shone from the room upstairs. Maybe he's sleeping, she thought. She lifted her hand to rap again but the door cracked open. A dark, dome-shaped head appeared.

"What you want?

"Sorry to disturb you, but I'm looking for the tenant upstairs, Jeremiah Browne?"

"Him gone."

"Gone?" she echoed in shock. "Where?"

He opened the door a little wider and stuck half his body out."He don't talk much so a don't rightly know." When she stood at the door in stunned silence, he scratched his head. "Let me see. He paid some little boys to deliver two pieces of furniture to somebody." A triumphant grin broke his somber face as he recalled more. "Then he left with Miss Portia. She come back later and settle his bill with me, take his clothes and said he won't be needing the room no more."

She hugged her shawl around her shoulders and mumbled a hasty thank you. She had almost made a fool of herself over Jeremiah again. She almost ran all the way back to her home, her eyes blinded by tears.

For the next two days she descended into despair and fits of weeping. By Friday night, when Matty and

Clothilde came to help prepare for the grand opening, she had come to terms with her loss. Her despondency had settled into a kind of anger, simmering below the surface of her mind like a low-grade fever.

* * *

Carolina Dress Shop & Haberdashery opened to the public on Saturday.

Women waited in line to enter the store. Nessa threw herself into the preparations. She didn't have time to think about her broken heart or her fatherless baby. Matty and Clothilde helped earlier with decorating the shop and baking. And now they were in the back, making mint tea to serve the ladies when they arrive.

"My word," a woman said to no one in particular as she stepped inside the shop fanning herself with a paper fan. Her gaze flitted over the dresses, a half smile playing on her lips.

Nessa counted nine women who entered her shop, one after the other.

"I want that blue one Mummy," a young lady said, pointing to the brand new gown.

"Now, Griselda you know there's no way that dress can fit you."

Nessa clapped her hands to gain attention. "Ladies, thank you for coming this morning. What you see here displayed are just samples. If there are any styles you like I can custom-make it to fit you. I also have gloves and can order matching bonnets. Please have some tea and slices of toetoe or tie-a-leaf. If you have any questions or need to order, please let me know."

Soon the customer area shrunk with the number of women who chatted and inspected the gowns. So,

Nessa lifted the hinged counter allowing the growing group of women to spill through to her work area.

"Lizbeth, did you ever taste such delicious tie-a-leaf?" The mulatto woman asked her companion who in turn bit into the cornmeal delicacy, packed with raisins and laced with rum.

"This toe-toe is divine too," an elderly white woman said, brushing away the yellow cake-like crumbs from the corners of her mouth. "Hopefully, this is an example of the exemplary service we can expect from your shop Miss Carolina?"

Nessa didn't bother to correct her patrons she wasn't Miss Carolina. She tried, but they continued to call her by the name anyway.

Throughout the day, Clothilde, Miss Ilda and Matty continued to serve the shoppers. Meanwhile, Nessa stood behind a makeshift curtain, measuring women and taking orders.

"Do you have anyone to help you Miss Carolina?"

Nessa removed the pencil from behind her ears and wrote down the measurements. "Yes maam I do." She saw the orders piling up and knew she had to find people to help her fast.

"Am I finished?" the woman asked.

"Yes ma'am, you're all set. I'm going to need a deposit now for me to cut the fabric. Then I'll need another substantial deposit when you come for your fitting and the final when I deliver." Nessa was glad she'd be so busy. She'd work night and day to fulfill these orders.

Miss Ilda rested her hand at the base of Nessa's back. "Come, you must sit down and eat."

"Lord, she work so hard today. Miss Nessa you have to take care of yourself you know," Matty said, putting up the 'closed' sign at the door.

"I couldn't have done it without all of you," Nessa said, sitting back in the chair and putting her feet up on the stool.

Miss Ilda harumphed. "In your condition, A don't know how you going to manage all them orders." She turned to Matty. "Who you know can sew good?"

"Miss T-T, Clothilde and Jenny are the best and let me see who else."

"Me can send the pickneys to school and come down and help too." Miss Ilda said.

Clothilde brought in a tray with four steaming bowls of red bean soup. Each bowl was packed with yellow yam, sweet potato, cured pig tails and dumplings.

"Come now, drink the soup and give your baby some nourishment, Miss Ilda chided, clucking her tongue. They ate in silence with only the long, loud slurps from the women drinking their soup.

Nessa relished the quiet. Her friends didn't judge nor did they pry into her business. After they had their fill they stacked the bowls and cleaned up the shop.

"You're not doing anything else for the day Miss Nessa. You just sit right there and ponder on your success today," said Miss Matty.

While the women worked, Nessa counted the order slips with elation. If only she could get some good help. At last, the women completed their tasks and all but tucked Nessa in the bed before they left.

Nessa fell asleep, dreaming of Jeremiah and Portia getting married. She heard herself whimper in her sleep when Jeremiah said, "I do." Finally she settled down and slept until the next day.

Sunday mornings everyone went to church. Nessa thought she'd try a different church each Sunday. Last week she visited the William Knibb Baptist Church.

Knibb played a major role in emancipating the slaves, even going to London to eloquently plead their case. She listened to him preach, touched by his fervor. After the service she couldn't get near him. The ex-slaves surrounded him, some just wanting to touch his black, frock coat in reverence.

This Sunday, she visited St. Peter's Anglican. She had a strong desire to mingle and become part of this mixed community of people. She didn't want to spend all day and night by herself. However, when her pregnancy became visible, she knew she shouldn't be attending in her condition without a husband.

After services she stepped out on the curb, one hand holding down her bonnet from the teasing breeze. Kendrick pulled up in his carriage. He too had attended church but she hadn't seen him.

"Miss Nessa I was hoping to catch you," he said and jumped to help her up. He wore one of Lord Barclay's morning suits.

"Why Kendrick, what a surprise," she said, feigning enthusiasm. She had noticed only mulattoes and whites attended St. Peters.

"Mon, I was so busy getting the estate together that I missed your grand opening." He settled her in the seat.

"That's ok, Kendrick." She looked at him with an impish grin. "My shop is for women only."

He chuckled, his amber eyes gleaming with pleasure. "So you had success then?"

"Oh, wonderful," she said, nattering on about all the women who came to her grand opening and the orders she received.

He interrupted her. "Would you like to come out to the Downs for lunch with me?"

"Thank you, but I really have to get back and start working on these orders."

He grabbed her hand. "Nessa I want you to know that my offer still stands. I'd like to marry you." He said in a poor imitation of his father's voice.

She tried to extricate her hands. "Don't—"

His mouth twisted in a harsh line. "Mon, you're wasting your time on that no good bastard you know. He deserves to be where he is."

Images of Jeremiah and Portia together floated before her. Her heart ached. When the carriage pulled up to her shop, he went around the other side to help her out and walked with her up to the front stoop.

"Thank you for the ride ," she said, turning to open the door.

He lifted her chin with one finger and tilted her face to him. "You might as well forget him. He is done for. They'll probably ship him back to America to try him for his crimes or hang him here."

Her eyes flew wide open. "What do you mean?" She started to quiver from head to toe.

"You mean you didn't know you are free from him for good? Mon, he's wallowing in prison a few days now," he said, almost crowing with glee.

Nessa let out a short gasp, clawed the air and slumped to the ground in a dead faint.

CHAPTER 20

Rats scurried back and forth across the cell's floor. The smell of the prison's rusted iron bars permeated Jeremiah's nostrils and lodged at the base. It was no comparison though to the cold, heavy knot in his chest.

He had no idea how many days he had been in jail. And it didn't matter to him anymore. He had two frequent visitors, Portia and the kind Reverend Kersey. The Reverend was doing everything in his power to get him good representation.

After the weird night at Portia's dinner he was wary of her. He had made inquiries from Benjie, one of the few friendly faces down at *The Foundry*. Benjie had peered in his face and said, "Marse Jeremiah you don't look well today, what happen you sick?"

When Benjie heard what happened the night before, he let out a low whistle. "You have to be careful who you nyam food from you know? From what I can pick up, that Portia's been after you. And her mother? hmm."

Alarm crept up Jeremiah's spine. "What about her mother?"

"Nobody mess with her. Look at her eye real good, she a devil."

"What do you mean?"

"She came from Haiti with Annie Palmer, you know who that is? Hmm."

"No, tell me who is Annie Palmer and what does she have to do with anything?"

Benjie removed his pipe, knocking out the ash on an old newspaper. "Well." He licked his lips. "Annie Palmer dead since '32. We call her *The White Witch of Rose Hall*. No black man or woman will go near that place. Hmm."

"What did she do, cast spells on people?"

"Voodoo man, worse than obeah. Kill off every man she come across."

"What! Do you think that's what Portia and her mother were trying to do to me?"

"Not rightly so. Hmm. But she did a love potion to catch you for Portia—more like it."

Jeremiah chuckled to himself without humor. "Well that love potion sure went bad."

In his cell, another rat scooted across the floor. He shook off Portia's shenanigans from his mind. He couldn't stand this unending wait. So he got up and walked around, cracking his knuckles. Feelings of despair seeped through him, the same feeling he had when he left his room that fateful day.

He had felt trapped in his room all day, yearning to be with Nessa and wanting to help her any way he could. Cliff and Miss Ilda had gushed about Nessa's grand opening. He smiled at her gutsiness. He knew she didn't want anything to do with him so he stayed put.

After feeling like one of Miss Ilda's caged rabbits, he had decided to walk by the store and check whether she had accepted the cradle and chifforobe. Maybe she would be more receptive to talking. As he went out into the crisp evening air he heard a familiar voice.

"What you up to handsome?" Portia appeared out of nowhere.

She took his arm and fell into step with him. He racked his brains figuring out how to get rid of her. It would not do to walk by Nessa with Portia by his side, so he sauntered in the opposite direction.

"Was just getting a little fresh air, that's all," he said pushing his hands deep in his pockets.

"Me too." She said, cooing like a dove.

"C'mon Portia all this way in town to get fresh air?"

"The air is fresher down here."

Jeremiah decided he had to confront Portia head on. He stopped in the road and said, "I want you to quit stalking me."

"Stalk?" she repeated. "You're now a corn stalk?" She tossed her head back and let out a laugh from her belly.

Jeremiah's jaw tightened. He said in a low ominous tone. "Want no part of you or your shenanigans. Do you understand me?"

She rolled her eyes upwards, and made a tsk sound through her teeth.

Jeremiah set his face in a pained expression. "Your low-down games are disgusting!"

"What's disgusting or poison to one man is sweet honey in the pot to the odder."

"Well let me tell you something woman, all my life I've been taking bitter and now have found some sweet honey and a pot for the honey." He rubbed the back of his neck. "And nothing, do you hear me? Nothing is going to stop me from licking the spoon!" He stopped himself. He enjoyed word plays only with Nessa.

Portia startled by his vehemence, jumped back, arms akimbo and said, "Coo you! Who tell you that me want you!" She turned up the left corner of her mouth and tossed her head in disdain. "Me can get any damn man that me want. What me a henker after you for." Her eyes flashed and her lips turned up even more in scorn. "All you have is a good job but you don't even have a pot to piss in or a window to throw it out of."

Jeremiah witnessed another of her silly antics. Portia looked him dead in the eyes. She stuck out her neck, closed her eyes and slowly turned her head in the opposite direction. She let out a loud, slow choops through her teeth as she turned her head. She opened her eyes wide, staring off in the distance. Laughter bubbled inside him, escaping in small chuckles.

Her mouth twitched at his response before slackening, eyes widening in alarm.

"Jeremiah Browne?" A stout policeman asked from behind.

Jeremiah spun on his heels. "Yes sir what's wrong?"

"Him no do nothing!" Portia yelled, sounding anxious.

"You are under arrest sir for committing murder in the State of Georgia of the United States of America and running away to this Island."

"I did no such thing!—murder that is."

"Come with us, we want no trouble from you," said another officer getting out the handcuffs.

"Who issue the summons?" Portia asked, her face troubled, hands on her hips.

"George Sylvester Browne." He answered in a terse tone while securing the handcuffs.

As they led him off, he yelled over his shoulder to Portia. "Tell Clifton and Reverend Kersey . . ."

She bit her lip and nodded, tears swimming in her eyes.

Early the next day, Clifton, Reverend Kersey and Portia gathered in his cell. In a turn-a-round, Portia had become a staunch ally. He guessed she felt guilty for trying to obeah him, do black magic or work voodoo on him. He didn't trust her but he needed all the friends he could get right now.

Jeremiah couldn't believe what he heard. Massa George was here to press charges and claim him as his legal property.

"You must be very valuable to him that he'd come all this way." Reverend Kersey scratched his chin.

"You ever seen the quality furniture dis man make?" Clifton looked at the Reverend wide-eyed. "Nothing in any big plantation house look like it Rev."

"Massa George built an entire factory based on my skills alone," Jeremiah said.

"Oh, so that's it then," Reverend Kersey said with dawning understanding.

Jeremiah had no doubt the *Serpentine's* captain had gone back to the Carolinas and somehow located Massa George. He remembered, like yesterday, when the captain said, "It is my moral duty" to report them to the authorities when the ship returned to Wilmington. The captain knew they were fugitives. Perhaps the captain even posted bans, he had knowledge of Jeremiah's whereabouts and Massa George responded to it. Jeremiah shrugged. It didn't matter. The thorn was here. In his side, again.

Jeremiah's friends promised to do all they could to get him representation. "It's not the barrister so much . . ." Reverend Kersey had shaken his head.

"Then what is it then?" Portia grabbed the reverend's arm.

He turned pink, looked deep into her eyes and turned to the others. "We're ruled by the laws of England, different from any other foreign country."

"So what you saying then?" Portia tightened her grip on his arm.

Clifton chimed in, "You mean say, this other country still have slavery but England abolish it? So for the books then, Jeremiah free as long as him on this soil."

"It would seem so." Reverend Kersey covered Portia's hands with his as if tending to his flock. "The murder charge is another thing though." He patted Portia's hand and repeated, "another thing entirely."

"So when do I get this barrister?" Jeremiah asked, cracking the knuckles on each finger.

"We didn't like the ones we talked to, they would be too glad to ship off one less black off the island," Reverend Kersey said.

"No they can't do that," Portia cried in protest.

"So, I'm going to talk to this young Scotsman," the reverend said. "McLaren was very outspoken with his views last year, that he loathed slavery and restricting the freedom of any human being. He'll probably do it pro bono, that's free."

Jeremiah's pulse quickened. The others leaned closer. "Yes, that's the one." Portia beamed at the Reverend who looked down in her bosom. Sweat beaded his brow.

Jeremiah reached out through the bars and clasped each of their hands. He was overcome by their support.

Portia left with the reverend. Clifton remained.

"You're getting outta here old man." Clifton told him trying to raise his spirits.

Jeremiah didn't think this island or any English law was any match for the laws where he came from, but he nodded. He had to hold on to something.

Clifton tapped him on the shoulder. "I'm going to have that house ready for you by the time you get outta here."

"How is that going?" Jeremiah tried to muster up interest in a future he was not sure would happen.

"The money you gave me, I used it to get the supplies and pay off the men. Them very happy to get the work. So we going to put in the doors now. I used pine for the floor."

"And all the trim for the window and the doorways you used the light blue paint?" He asked, knowing it was Nessa's favorite color.

Jeremiah grabbed the bars and said in a low voice, "Clifton, if anything should happen to me, you know where the rest of the money is. Pay off everything, and yourself, and give the rest to Nessa, along with the deed for the house and land."

"Cho man you a talk foolishness. Wait till we hear what this McLaren have to say."

"Alright, alright, time's up," a booming voice interrupted. The guard came down the aisle slapping a baton in his palm.

Clifton had reached through the bars and clasped Jeremiah. Without a word he had turned and left.

Jeremiah paused in his reverie to look down at his present company. The rat didn't find what it searched for because it scurried back again in the opposite direction. It stopped, looked at Jeremiah and sniffed the air. Jeremiah felt a special kinship with this rat. He sniffed too. Nessa had abandoned him.

CHAPTER 21

A day later, Massa George strolled into the jail demanding to see Jeremiah. As Jeremiah watched him approach, the old hatred rose in his chest and bile gathered in the back of his throat.

"Open this gate," Massa George said to the guard who escorted him.

"It's not safe to go in there sir."

"Tut. Just open it." The guard proceeded to turn the lock. "That boy is an idiot but not such an idiot as to try any tricks here," Massa George reassured the guard who walked away leaving the keys dangling from the lock.

Jeremiah leaned on the wall in the shadowy corner, his hands folded across his chest.

"So you think you're smart eh boy?"

Jeremiah stared in his eyes without flinching.

"You know what happens to uppity niggers like you?"

Jeremiah's eyes shot shards of malevolent hate. No point in saying anything, he thought.

"I'm here to look you in the face my boy and tell you. Maiming is too good for you. Hanging you is too easy. Your death is too unsatisfying an end for me."

"Well that's nothing new, suh! And if that's all you came here to say, you may as well turn right back out."

Massa George pretended not to hear him. "No, I shall dig out every one of your nails from your fingers and from all ten of your toes. He taunted Jeremiah. "You'll only have one socket left for an eye and four fingers left on each hand. And your tongue—" He laughed a mirthless laugh. "Your tongue? Sliced and thrown to the hogs. And then you'll work from before sun-up to after sundown." Jeremiah continued to stare, unflinching, listening to the man's rant.

Massa George leaned closer, his blue eyes looking translucent in the dim cell. "I own the finest furniture company in the Southeast. My name is known throughout the land, from North to South, and as far as England." His hot breath fanned Jeremiah's face. In an ominous tone, he continued: "Boy, I'm not going to let you destroy my reputation. I have orders piling up that you're coming back to fill. You're my property. But before you start working again, I will break your legs and see how far you'll run next time."

"Mr. Browne, Mr. Browne." The guard called. I have a message from the Governor 'bout the murder . . ."

Massa George got flustered, "show me where to go."

As Massa George and the guard half-ran back to the office, Jeremiah eased out of his cell. He tossed the bunch of keys to the outstretched, grasping hands of the other prisoners.

Jeremiah skulked to the opposite corridor until he came to an outside door. He pushed it hard and the cool evening breeze slapped his face with an eagerness that echoed through his soul. At the back of the jail, he looked left and right and dashed in the direction of the hills. Soon after, he switched directions just to confuse any pursuers.

Massa George's threats fired his imagination and gave wings to his feet. He would not rest until he felt safe. Stones cut into his soles but he didn't care. He ripped his pants while sliding down a hill but it didn't matter.

Thick jungle-like plants impeded his progress. He passed through a grove where low-lying orange trees flanked him for miles. He didn't stop, but reached out and stuffed every pocket he had with the fruit.

He did not know how long he ran through the night. His steps slowed and his stomach growled. He shuffled along, his feet dragged and he knew he should find somewhere safe before he collapsed.

He trudged through ankle-high grass. One foot stepped on something soft. It croaked! The sound echoed into the still night, sending goosebumps up his arms. By instinct he moved forward, picking out the shapes of bushes, trees and giant rocks in the shadowy moonlight.

At last, a huge rock jutted out of the mountain, forming a canopy. He entered; amazed the further he went in, the more the cave opened up. Finally, he stood straight to his full height.

Cool air blew in from the opposite direction. An exit must be there, he guessed. A torch would be a boon right now to light the way. He went in a little deeper until it was safe to stretch out and rest.

Something sharp and pointy blocked his path like a tree trunk. Solid rock with icicles hung upside down. He would not go any further. The icicle would drip down on him all through the night. He found a dry corner. Despite the screeching bats and mites nipping into his skin, he passed out from sheer exhaustion.

After a day or so, Jeremiah felt caved-in. Even though he had ample, clear water he soon grew tired of eating oranges and those invisible mites biting his skin. Dying was not an option in this cave. He would set off to find his way to Brownsville soon. He hoped he was already going in the right direction.

With nothing to do, Jeremiah washed his clothes in the stream as best as he could. He laid them out to dry while he stretched out naked on the rock. The clothes took forever to dry inside the cool cave. While still damp, he put them on and continued his journey.

About mid-day, the sun nearly blinded him. His head pounded from the sun's frontal assault. Salty air filled his nose and he realized he didn't make as much progress as he thought. Even though high on a hill, he could still see the ocean. Brownsville must be more inland. Disoriented and dejected, he continued to move forward.

Hunger gnawed his stomach. He had to find food soon or else he would not make it. Without Clifton as his guide, he felt lost, as if in a jungle all by himself. Apart from a mongoose, doctor birds and monarch butterflies, he didn't see any other forms of life. The villages must be near the road, but it was dangerous to get closer.

His stomach growled again. At least back home he could snare a rabbit or a possum. But here, nothing. Fruits grew in abundance though, mangoes, bananas, and apples looking like pears. He picked and ate anything growing. Nothing was poisonous on this island.

At last he came to a busy town, much like Falmouth. He stopped a young man. "What town is this?"

"It's St. Ann's Bay." The young man gave him a curious look.

"Do you know where I can get a bite to eat?"

The young man looked him up and down. "Me take you over to me grandmother's shop. Follow me."

"Gang-Gang," the young man cupped his hands to his mouth calling out for his grandmother. When he found her, she sat, her head wrapped in several layers of cloth and tied with a knot over her left shoulder. A stone mortar nestled on the ground between her legs. She used a wooden pestle to grind some kind of brown nuts. "Any more soup left? This man come from far and him hungry."

Gang-Gang looked up and sniffed. "And him dutty too and him clothes tear-up, tear up." She peered up in Jeremiah's face, her eyes hard. "You must be just a come out of slavery. Is which part you come from?"

Jeremiah only knew Falmouth but he didn't want to mention it so "Brownsville" popped out of his mouth.

"Cho! Is back-o-wall that—nobody even hear bout that place, is not even on the map." She got up and spooned a milky-looking broth into a bowl filled with white dumplings and those rooty vegetables again.

The young man left on an errand and Jeremiah spooned down thick chicken soup. At the bottom of the bowl, a chicken foot appeared with its claws intact, the scales on the toes flapped back and forth in the dregs of soup. Jeremiah's stomach retched several times but he swallowed, keeping the food down.

Gang-Gang came out of the shack with a pair of plaid pants, shoes and a blue calico shirt. "Me husband dead but me keep him clothes; see if they can fit you."

Glad to change from his threadbare clothing, Jeremiah put on the dead-left clothes. And the shoes fit over his blistered heel like a glove. "Very grateful for your kindness ma'am. Is there anything you'd like me to help you with, chop some wood?"

"Bwoy you sound like some a de sailor dem dat just come off de ship. No, gwaan now because me don't harbor strangers 'round me."

The woman returned to her mortar and pestle, humming a tuneless hymn. Jeremiah left the old woman's house. He felt a surprising sense of well-being now he had something hot in his stomach and decent clothes on his back. He could take on Massa George and the entire world.

Walking down the dusty road, he held his head down. It wasn't long after before he turned around and looked right into Kendrick's face.

Kendrick smiled slow and wide. "My sister and your sweetheart sent me to bring you home," he said.

"Leave Nessa out of this you hear?"

"Murder, kidnapping a woman, stowing away on a ship, breaking out of jail—you'll surely hang. And I'll be the one to pull the noose."

Kendrick beckoned the militia over before Jeremiah could make a dash for it. The St. Ann's Bay militia handcuffed him and threw him in the back of a buckboard.

* * *

Back in his cell, Jeremiah consulted with McLaren. From what Jeremiah could make of it, English law would protect him from escaping to the island, seeking asylum, McLaren had put it. Apparently, he had only complicated matters by breaking out of jail. Anyway, McLaren was fighting for a trial just for the murder charges. He also planned to go to the Governor's office in the capital on Monday to plead his case. With all McLaren's efforts, Jeremiah had a last ditch idea in mind. He stashed the thought in the back of his mind when a soft voice floated through to his cell.

"Hello, Jeremiah."

He allowed her voice to wash over him, settling to his soul, before he turned. He swallowed and their eyes locked. She looked more radiant than ever. Her eyes held a glint of moisture as she walked up to the bars. He reached out his hand, resting it on her small rounded belly. "How are you?" His voice had a slight tremor.

"I'm so s-s-sorry." She said on a sob.

"Shh-shh. No need for that."

"Yes, there is," she sniffed. "I would have come before but I wasn't well."

"What's wrong . . . the baby?"

"When I heard what happened, I slipped off the verandah and knocked my head."

"Oh my God!" Jeremiah clutched the bars tight, his blood ebbed. He took a deep breath to steady himself.

"No, no everything's fine . . . the doctor made me stay in bed for a week just to make sure the baby was well." She saw his eyes widen again so she grabbed his hands. "I'm ok now though, truly. No harm's done. The doctor said the baby is fine."

"Do you have anyone to help you?" His eyes bored into her.

"Yes, Clothilde stayed with me the entire time."

"Ness, I'm so glad to see you, but I don't want you in here." He gestured to encompass his cell. "Seeing me like this, the foul air for the baby. . ." His hands paused in mid-air and dropped heavy at his sides.

"You just try to stop me Jeremiah Browne. I've seen you in worse situations." She stepped closer.

"Come closer," he whispered.

They touched their lips through the bars and the coldness jolted him back to reality. He yearned to take her in his arms.

"J, I know everything. Clifton, Miss Ilda, Portia and the Reverend came to my shop."

"Congratulations on your shop by the way." He smiled into her eyes. "I'm so proud of you."

Even though pleased, she poked him in the chest. "Look, be serious, I—"

"Did you say Portia came to your shop?"

"Yes, I think her and the reverend are sweet on each other."

Jeremiah tilted his head back. "Thank God!"

"Yes, she apologized for causing problems and we'll all work together to get you free."

"I wondered how Kendrick could hunt me down so easily."

"He's her brother and she probably thought she was helping you. We all thought it was a good idea too. That two-faced bastard."

Jeremiah chuckled without mirth. "She really has been a big help. Maybe it's her guilt. If her brother could find someone else to court . . ."

She poked him harder in the chest. "Let me ease your mind. I have no interest in Kendrick. Do you hear me? You're the only man I've ever loved Jeremiah."

He drank in the sight of her for a long time, allowing those precious words to sink and seep into his bones. "I love you Ness."

She closed her eyes and a tear escaped from the corner of her eye. "And I swear when I get out of here I'll spend the rest of my life proving it to you," he whispered. There he said it. Much good it would do her now. A light feeling swept across his chest as he laid down the burden of his love at her feet.

"You love me?" Her voice quavered. She patted her stomach and bit her lip.

"No matter what happens, know this . . . that I always will." He closed his eyes, a pained expression flicked across his face. "And when the baby comes and if I'm not here—"

"You will get out." She said in a fierce tone. "I'm determined you're getting out. My baby needs his father."

"Only the baby?"

"And me too, J, I love you and I need you."

"Hey Robby, come look at these two lovebirds here trying to make out through the bars." The guard yelled out to his friend.

"Cozy, isn't it, but sweet thing your time's up," the other guard said.

Jeremiah applied slight pressure to her arm. "Go my love, go, and be careful."

She took off before the guards could say anything else to her. Jeremiah's eyes never left her until she disappeared from sight. He turned and faced the guards.

CHAPTER 22

Falmouth buzzed with the news of Jeremiah's breakout from jail and recapture. Nessa did not know how she didn't have a miscarriage. With all they've been through, this was by far the most difficult part to bear. When Jeremiah broke out jail, Clifton had reassured her he knew where to find him. And he and Man-Man went up to a place called Brownsville to search. But Jeremiah must have gotten lost because they never found him there. She didn't waste precious time discussing it with Jeremiah when she visited him a few days ago. She understood why he broke out. Her heart ached for him and all they could be. The prospect of his getting a fair trial looked dim.

On the day of Jeremiah's trial, Nessa dressed in a cool, white, muslin dress. She brushed her hair until it shimmered and collected it at the nape of her neck into a relaxed bun. When he looked over at her in court she wanted to look her best for him. She had to get going so she could get a good seat. She stretched on a pair of blue gloves over her hands, tied on a straw bonnet with matching blue ribbon and walked briskly to the courthouse.

Even though Jeremiah knew only a handful people, his case gained attention all across the coast by the sheer novelty of it. An American black crossing the vast seas, with his Indian lover and chased by his white, slave master. The questions titillated everyone, whites, mulattoes and blacks alike. How did they escape? What was going to happen next? Which law would stand—the English law or the American? Wild stories sprang up about Jeremiah murdering everyone on the plantation in America before he left. He was a prince from Africa and on and on. Nessa heard all the rumors.

She edged her way inside the courthouse. People bumped up against her from every direction. Some sat on long, narrow benches. Even though it was not yet mid-day, sweat shone on their faces and women fanned with colorful paper fans. Nessa sat with Clifton, Portia, Reverend Kersey and Miss Ilda.

Portia leaned across Reverend Kersey's lap to speak with Nessa. Even in this jam-packed courtroom, Portia stood out. She wore a multicolored turban with bright splotches of yellow. Her dress fitted close to her high bosom and ever so often she'd fan her cleavage with a paper fan. Nessa, still a bit wary of Portia, did not look her fully in the eyes while they talked. Instead, her gaze locked on to Portia's fan with the *Lord's Supper* imprinted on one side.

The noise in the courtroom rose to a high pitch. Portia leaned even closer, spreading the fan across her lips and whispered over *Judas Iscariot's* head. "You see the stiff-backed, blue-eyed, white man over there?"

Nessa peered to the right. "Yes, that's Massa George," she answered in a choked voice. The air felt heavy and she could hardly breathe.

Portia just had time to nod when a booming voice intruded. "All rise . . ."

During the proceedings, Jeremiah looked straight ahead, his face inscrutable. Massa George threw him a baleful stare. Jeremiah acted as if he didn't exist.

From the arguments on the prosecution side, Nessa realized they emphasized murder charges more than Jeremiah's running away. They also played down the fact Jeremiah was a slave. Massa George took the stand. After many minutes of cross-examinations, McLaren stopped pacing and got to the crux of the case.

"You are charging this man with murder?"

"Yes, he murdered one of my most valuable hands."

McLaren looked him dead in the eye. "You mean the slave catcher that almost beat Jeremiah to death?"

"Look, that's my property there!" He pointed at Jeremiah. His outburst caused a murmur of dissent in the courtroom.

The judge rapped his gavel and his white wig shook. "Order!" He turned to Massa George. "Please answer the barrister, yes or no."

McLaren repeated his question.

After more close questioning, Nessa wondered why McLaren just didn't get back to the main point of his argument.

Massa George spoke in eloquent tones, giving graphic descriptions of the brutal murder Jeremiah had allegedly committed. Nessa's heart sank into her shoes. She had begged McLaren to let her testify she had killed the man. He refused to let her take the stand. He told her it wouldn't make sense for both her and Jeremiah to go to jail.

"It is evident," McLaren had said. "It's not about you; it's about getting Jeremiah back as property." Jeremiah was adamant she should not testify. Guilt washed over her, draining her.

McLaren continued with the proceedings. "The defendant would possess super human strength to kill your slave catcher while being beaten by the men and dogs biting into his flesh. Wouldn't he Mr. Browne?"

"Yes, he does—he is a brute. Who said he killed him at the same time?"

McLaren steepled his fingers. "Yet the defendant, your slave, was badly beaten. So even if he killed your man it must have been self-defense."

"We caught him soon after he killed my man and inflicted wounds on the others. He is a murdering brute who needs to be punished I say!" Massa George drummed up other horrific charges to bolster his case. But when he said Jeremiah also raped women on the plantation, a murmur went through the court.

By the time they broke for lunch, Massa George had painted Jeremiah as a cold-blooded killer, a rapist and a thief. Nessa could sense a shift in the crowds' sympathies.

Outside, Miss Ilda and Portia spread a checkered tablecloth under the wide-spreading guango tree. Afterwards, all of Jeremiah's friends convened over a basket filled with bammies and fried, red snapper fish. They ate in silence, no one wanted to mention their worst fears.

Clifton uncorked the earthenware jug with Miss Ilda's beberidge and filled each calabash. "How things look for Jeremiah?"

Reverend Kersey smacked his lips. "Not good." He shook his head. "Not good at all for our friend."

Nessa's heart sank even lower. She didn't need the Reverend to voice her fears. Massa George brought his clergy as witness and death papers of the man whom they said Jeremiah had slain. The way the prosecution slanted things, Jeremiah would hang or be carted back to Georgia.

"Kendrick come over here." Portia yelled out to her brother.

Kendrick bounded over and his face lit up when he saw Nessa. "I was looking for you all day. But with this crowd, mon, it's like trying to find a grain of sugar in a canefield."

Portia rolled her eyes at him. "Me didn't call you over here to make monkey eyes at somebody else's woman."

Clifton chuckled out loud.

Portia continued. "You a traitor! Me send you to find Jeremiah and you set the militia on him in St. Ann's Bay."

"And you even find the lawyer for Massa George. Fool, you don't even realize that to Massa George you nothing but a nigga too," Clifton accused him.

Kendrick didn't deny it. He reached for Nessa's hand and she pulled it away like she was being bitten by Miss Ilda's dog.

"Look, the man's a murderer and Nessa shouldn't mix with him." Kendrick looked at all the suspicious faces. "Mon, he could have killed Nessa too!"

Nessa shook with rage. Miss Ilda exclaimed, "Don't upset the baby!"

Portia rounded out Nessa's stomach with her hands soothing the baby's gyrations.

Kendrick eyes popped, his face a mottled shade of eggplant. "All this time . . ." he sputtered. He looked askance at Portia for confirmation. "She's been breeding?"

"Please don't speak as if I'm not here. If you have something to say to me, please speak to me directly," Nessa pursed her lips to contain her anger, her eyes flashing daggers at him.

Kendrick rested his hands on his knees and glared into Nessa's eyes. "And for that no good, poor-assed sonofabitch? I— I—." He swallowed hard and looked at the dirt. "I . . . offered you the world." His chest heaved and his eyes narrowed into slits. His lips curled into a sneer. Looking dead in her eyes, he said, "you've got nothing mon, nothing but a flat mind." He straightened, turned and stalked away before Clifton and the Rev could do anything.

"Don't pay him no mind," Portia said. "Him have 'more nerve than a brass monkey' as me mother would say. Imagine, you who work for everything you have. If anyone got the flat mind is him. All him do is sit down and henker after his father's legacy."

Nessa's entire body trembled now, her breaths coming in short. "He set up Jeremiah to get caught."

"Well what do you expect? The man wanted you." Miss Ilda mumbled.

Clifton wiped his forehead. "That's just the devil's work."

"The Lord's word will prevail." Reverend Kersey said, trying to soothe everyone.

"It won't prevail unless you help it prevail," piped in Portia.

Reverend Kersey clasped his hand over Portia's and beamed, "Quite right my dear. The Lord helps those that help themselves."

A buzz started in the direction of the courthouse signaling the start of the afternoon session. The crowd grew even thicker. Miss Ilda and Portia packed the basket of leftovers. Miss Ilda left to get the children from school. The others traipsed in for the rest of the proceedings.

McLaren called on Reverend Kersey and Jeremiah's employer at *the Foundry* to attest to Jeremiah's good character. Jeremiah was adamant Nessa shouldn't take the stand but by the end of the day it wouldn't have mattered anyway. The signs were there. One woman on the jury, her thin lips flattened into a straight line like Lady Barclay's when she had decided on something. Furthermore, the jury avoided looking at Jeremiah. The judge looked grim and by the veiled looks, even the people had begun to sway for the prosecutor.

After the court adjourned for the day, Nessa and her friends ambled back to her shop wrapped in the silence of doom—except for Portia. "Cheer up, Nessa, everything going to work out for the best, mark my words." Portia wagged her finger and gave a gamine like grin. When Nessa didn't respond, Portia hugged each person and told them she wouldn't be at court the next day.

"It's my day to work up at Vale Royal but I have to go in from this evening."

"Isn't that where Massa George is staying with his friend?" Reverend Kersey asked.

"Really?" said Portia. "I just cook the food. I don't know."

They bade each other goodbye. Reverend Kersey said he would say a special prayer for Jeremiah. As Nessa entered her little shop, she noticed Clothilde had already lit the lamps and had cooked beef soup. Clothilde kept the food warm on smoldering embers.

Later in the evening, Nessa worked on one of her orders. She worked to the point of exhaustion and decided to go to bed. She wanted to be at Court first thing and get a better seat where Jeremiah could see her. She made up her mind what she had to do. Without anyone's permission she was going to stand up for her man in court. She was going to tell the truth and that's that.

* * *

Nessa trudged back to Court in the relentless heat. She had to rest underneath the shady, banyan trees just to catch her breath. Now and then a cooling breeze wafted in from the sea, making the heat bearable.

Even though Court didn't start until 10 a.m., the mosquitoes swarmed around delighting in fresh blood amongst the lolling crowd. People fanned their faces and necks in swift motions, swatting the mosquitoes and resuming their fanning.

Nessa felt saddened at the spectacle awaiting at the courthouse. People arrived in donkey carts and carriages, hitched at odd angles alongside the cobblestone street. But most people traipsed in on foot, dressed in their Sunday clothes.

Barefoot boys clad only in ripped-off trousers at the knees shouted, "coco . . . coco . . . coconut water" as they sold both the water and jelly from makeshift wooden carts. Women strapped baskets around their waists handing out potato pudding, coconut drops and other bake-bakes to buyers. Sweaty onlookers milled with smoke swirling around. They purchased roasted yam, roasted corn-on-the-cob, and roasted breadfruit slices while speaking words like *murder, hang, gallows* in hushed tones.

This was a man's life at stake yet it had the air of a festival. A strong waft of steaming peanuts from a nearby vendor threatened to empty Nessa's stomach. She covered her mouth with her handkerchief and pushed through the throng. People made room for her on the steps of the courthouse. She couldn't wait for the bailiff to open the door so she could sit. Her gaze shifted to the arriving carriage. A tall, familiar figure alighted. Her heart leaped to her throat. She couldn't move.

Devlin strode up to the courthouse.

She flayed her arms wild above her head, jumping in the air. "Devlin, wait, Devlin!" He glanced up the steps and saw her. A wide smile broke out on his face, crinkling his light blue eyes. She ran to him and he swept her up in his arms. She caught her breath when he set her down. "What are you doing here?"

"I followed my father here. I hope I'm not too late."

"You've heard what happened?" She asked, sniffing back the tears.

"Ever since I landed last night. It's the talk of the town. I can't believe my father went to such lengths." He chewed his lower lip for a moment. "Yes of course my father would. He has a lot riding on Jeremiah. His coffers are nearly empty as no furniture has been made for months now.

"I don't know what you can do at this point Devlin, they are about ready to give the verdict this morning."

"I'm sorry, I tried to get here quicker but the gales turned on me."

"It's time to go in now." Nessa said, noticing the jam at the entrance. The bailiff tried to get people through the door in single file.

"I don't think we should sit together, but I'll see you after court," he said, applying quick pressure to her hand.

Barreling her way through the throng, she ducked under several musty-smelling armpits and nearly swooned. She spotted Reverend Kersey and Portia sitting together, fanning with her 'Jesus and his disciples' fan. "I thought you had to work today," Nessa whispered as she tried to retie her bun gone askew. She could still smell the armpits.

Portia fanned herself so fast, the two loaves and fish had multiplied on her fan. Reverend Kersey was enjoying the cool whiff of air from the fan too.

"Me work is done." Portia said with a smug look.

Before Nessa could wonder at her remark the bailiff said, "All rise . . ."

She caught Jeremiah's eye and held it for a long time. His eyes warm and tender gazed back at her, speaking volumes to her of all the love he stored inside. For a second his face slipped into regret. She could not hold it much longer. Her tears started to pool. He broke the gaze, straightened in his chair and put on his mask again.

Throughout the morning the proceedings continued, McLaren pleaded Jeremiah's case. Nessa bided her time. She'd find the right moment to state her case. At one point during McLaren's argument, Massa George popped out of his seat with a slack-jawed grin on his face. The prosecutor looked at Massa George in consternation. A hush descended on the packed courtroom. All eyes locked on Massa George.

The judge rapped his gavel. "Order in my court!"

Massa George plopped down in his chair. He sucked his thumb like a toddler!

A murmur of bewilderment went through the courtroom when Massa George started to rake through his hair, backward then changed his mind, pulling it forward. He scrunched up his face, closed one eye and peered through the other.

Nessa didn't think anyone heard McLaren's defense. She even forgot she was going to testify. Massa George's peculiar antics were so fascinating, completely opposite to the deliberate, powerful man of the day before or the Lord of the Manor back in Georgia.

The courtroom became a bizarre scene afterwards. Massa George jumped up on the bench, crouching and eyeing everyone like a hunted animal. Giggles erupted from his mouth. He pointed to the judge and giggled harder. The judge's mouth dropped open in shock and his pendulous jowls reached near the top of his chest. He continued to rap his gavel. No one paid any attention.

Massa George hopped up and down on the bench. "Wheee, wheee," he said and giggled louder. His eyes looked like the clear part of the sea with only a hint of forgotten blue.

"Order! Order!" The judge shouted. Guards grabbed Massa George's arms and subdued him. A red tint crept up both sides of the judge's cheeks, suffusing his entire face. He turned to the prosecutor. "Is this some kind of joke being played out in this court of law?"

"I beg your pardon Your Honor." Devlin strode up the aisle.

"And who the hell are you?"

"My name is Devlin Browne, this man here is my father. I followed him here from the United States Your Honor because my father is not in his right mind."

A roar went up in the courtroom. All the blood drained from the prosecutor's face. He looked as pinched as the breadfruit Nessa and company had for breakfast. Massa George giggled, drool running down his chin. Nessa's heart flew in all directions before settling back in her chest.

Jeremiah's mask fell and his eyes took on an unholy gleam.

The judge rapped his gavel. "This man was in sound mind yesterday, now he's a lunatic!"

Devlin bent his head to hide the look of pain flitting across his face. "Yes, Your Honor, that's the nature of his illness. Some days he's back to his old self. During that time he makes irresponsible decisions and wild claims. But most of the time . . ." He looked over at Massa George who now had one leg hugging the back of his neck. "Most of the time Your Honor he is like that."

"Mr. Browne, you should have had your father committed and not have him wreaking havoc on innocent people." He pointed to Massa George while looking at Devlin.

Nessa's eyes flew to Jeremiah who had half-risen out of his seat, his shimmering eyes on fire.

Massa George swayed from side-to-side with one leg still locked around his neck.

"As his son, you should have taken better precautions. I'm charging you £20 for irresponsible conduct! And I want this imbecile off the island within 24 hours." The judge continued.

"Yes, Your Honor I will secure him on my ship until we leave." Devlin inclined his head to two of his sailors who appeared at Massa George's side as if Devlin had waved a magic wand.

Massa George shook his fist at the sailors and his eyes bulged, his cheeks puffed in and out. Nessa felt sure he would turn into a toad any minute. He sprang in the air just like toads in the mangrove swamps.

He turned to the judge and shouted at the top of his voice. "When the Lord comes he's going to poom in your heart, poom in your soul, poom in . . ."

The judge stood up. "For what is holy, get Poom out of here now! He sat down and straightened his robe. He glowered at the audience from under shaggy brows. "I would like to make it clear, the fiasco in this courtroom has no bearing on the decision here today." Fans whirred and hovered. "This is unusual procedure. The defendant . . ." he glanced briefly at Jeremiah who stared straight ahead unblinking. "Jeremiah Browne wrote a direct letter of appeal about his circumstances which I shared with the jurors."

McLaren looked at Jeremiah in shock.

"Yes, I believe it was without leave of his counsel. It was a great risk, but it paid off. This court is convinced Jeremiah Browne met with foul play and is now free to go. The Court is adjourned."

The crowd remained speechless while Massa George ranted. "Poom in your heart . . ." He shook his fist at the crowd. "Poom in your soul . . ." He shook his fist at Devlin. "Poom . . ." he flailed both arms over his head and foamed at the mouth while the bailiff and Devlin's crew managed to subdue him.

A low rumble roiled through the courtroom. Everyone absorbed the unexpected turn of events.

Nessa didn't recall moving but found herself in Jeremiah's arms sobbing. He held her and their tears mingled while a big commotion erupted all around them when everyone started to talk at once.

Chapter 23

Later in Nessa's shop, Clothilde and Matty prepared a big lunch.

"Where did you get all this food and when did you get it all prepared?" Nessa asked.

"Looks like someone knew there was going to be a celebration?" Devlin looked around at the faces, doubt sharpening his features.

"Miss Portia plan it all Miss Nessa. She wake me up soon this—"

"Hush your mouth Matty. Whether they convict Marse Jeremiah or not we would have to eat."

"That's true," Jeremiah responded.

Nessa's eyes filled with gratitude. "You've become such a dear friend Portia."

"Well, let's all sit down and eat," Jeremiah said. Matty gave him a plate filled with ackee, saltfish, salt pork, fried johnny cakes and plantains.

As soon as Portia rested her plate on the table, Jeremiah switched his plate with hers. She caught him in the act. Portia sucked in her cheeks, her eyes dancing with merriment. She took up the plate and she brushed past him.

Sitting close to Reverend Kersey, Portia hummed, spooning ackee on his plate.

Nessa had watched the byplay between Jeremiah and Portia and wondered what it was all about. But she soon forgot when Jeremiah kissed her on the lips.

She snuggled closer. She could not get enough of him. "What do you think about my shop J?"

He patted her hand. "I'll tell you about it later." He winked at her.

He turned to Devlin. "Devlin, thank you so much for everything."

"Well you decided your own fate my good man."

"I was about to get up to testify that I'm the one who killed the slave catcher," Nessa said.

"You wouldn't!" Portia said, looking stunned. Everyone else had incredulous expressions on their faces.

Devlin touched her arm. "But you didn't Nessa dear. I killed him,"

Now all eyes lanced into Devlin, their faces slack-jawed.

"B—bbut you weren't even there." Nessa tried to follow his train of thought.

"But I was. You let two arrows fly and they were enough to wound them but I made sure the ringleader was done for."

"So why didn't you show yourself?"

"General Scott had sent me on an urgent mission to New Echota to try to persuade your people to go West peacefully.

Nessa shook her head. "It wouldn't have worked anyway."

"On the way to New Echota," Devlin continued. "I stopped home in Athens to see my mother. I heard about the 'hunt' for Jeremiah. They were going in my direction anyway so I decided to follow them."

"You were always a tracker, Devlin." Jeremiah grinned and slapped him on the back.

"Yup all those times we hunted with those Indians on the other side of the river paid off."

Jeremiah chuckled. "Massa George thought you were somewhere else learning how to shoot."

"Nah, I never liked guns. Even though I have to carry them in the militia I always have my bow and arrows close.

"Well thank God for that. Now that explains the different arrows." She smiled at him. "But you still didn't answer my question, "Why didn't you show yourself to me."

"Can you imagine if the other men saw me and reported back to my father or any white man in Georgia, I'd be hung as an example. Jeremiah was in good hands with you and Rides-With-Winds so I kept going."

Nessa's knees all but buckled. Relief washed over her. Her oppressive burden had lifted. She leaned into Jeremiah for support. He held her close.

Devlin scratched his head. "This is all so darn strange though. What the hell happened to my father? I was wondering all along how to help Jeremiah out of this mess when I noticed my father acting quite bizarre."

"It must be island fever." Portia piped in, her eyes bright.

Devlin shook his head puzzled.

Portia reached over and covered his hand. "The fever will break in the by-and-by, maybe a week. Plenty people get it here all the time but it will go away." She gave Jeremiah a surreptitious glance. "Remember you had it Jeremiah?"

Jeremiah stared at her stunned. The magnitude of what Portia had done to Massa George made him reel but he kept silent.

Devlin's face cleared. "Good, I don't look forward to having a lunatic father. He won't cause anymore trouble after this for sure. He's a very proud man."

"After lunch we need to talk about some business..." Jeremiah said.

"What about Tyanita?" Nessa cut in. "This morning was so chaotic I haven't had a chance to ask."

"Tyanita is now Mrs. Devlin Browne."

"Oh my word." Nessa's hand fluttered to her throat, her eyes wide with surprise and delight.

"I have to leave tomorrow morning. I don't want to be arrested by that judge. Plus, my wife's expecting too." He said with a proud smile, his gaze sweeping Awanessa's belly.

Jeremiah slapped his back. The Reverend and Clifton offered their congratulations.

"I wish so that I could see her again." Nessa said in a wistful tone.

"You will. I'll bring her next year." He glanced down at her rising stomach. "Congratulations to both of you too."

"It's a pity you can't stay for our wedding Devlin," Jeremiah said. Nessa's heart quickened with gladness.

"Devlin, what about my people?"

He reached over and patted her hand. "You're so much better off here Awanessa. This is the best thing that could ever happen to you."

After everyone cleaned their plates, Devlin, Clifton and Jeremiah adjourned to the verandah. Matty ran out there with chairs for them.

Portia and the Reverend were in their own world.

Nessa, Miss Ilda and Matty talking at once began to plan the wedding. Nessa wanted to get married right away. She wouldn't have time to make a dress. She decided to add a small train to the ivory dress hanging in the shop. She would add some of Lady Barclay's fake pearls to the front too.

Later on, everyone convened on the verandah. Miss Ilda served sweet potato pudding with currants, egg custard and cornmeal pone sweetened with cane sugar, currants, and rum. Clothilde served peppermint tea.

No one felt the sweltering heat today. By the time it turned unbearable, a tangy breeze wafted across the verandah. Nessa tucked herself under the crook of Jeremiah's arms but bolted upright when a figure dashed toward the verandah.

It was Delroy. She hadn't seen him since she left Barclay Downs. "Miss Portia! Miss Portia!"

Delroy ran up the steps panting. "Him gone." He threw up his hands in the air.

"Who, who you're talking about bwoy?" Portia said, grabbing him by the collar.

"Marse Kendrick, mum."

"What happened to Kendrick?"

Delroy by now had caught his breath. "Him gone pon de ship."

"Say what!" Portia exclaimed.

"Why don't you slow down and explain exactly what happened." Devlin said.

Delroy puckered his lips over his buck teeth to look more poised but only made his eyes pop more. His rapid breathing subsided a little. He swallowed and stared at the floor as if he was on a high cliff, ready to dive in murky waters. "Well, this is how it go:

Me and Marse Kendrick went to the ship. Marse Kendrick went to the cap'n and say, "I would like to purchase passage on this ship."

The cap'n said, "do you know where this ship is going?"

Marse Kendrick say, "Wilmington, North Carolina."

The odder sailors start to smile.

The cap'n say, "And why would you want to go to North Carolina?

Marse Kendrick say, "I'm looking for a particular type of girl to marry."

The sailors dem start to laugh but the cap'n still serious say: "And what that might be?"

Marse Kendrick say, "she's Cherokee, skin like mine, long, straight, black hair."

The Cap'n looked at the sailors and say, "Dis nigga is crazy!"

The other sailor laugh so hard he hold his side and say, "De nigga is outta his cotton-pickin' mind."

Den the cap'n hold his side and start to laugh too. One a dem laugh so hard the eye water run down his face."

"So what happened?" Portia asked in an imperious, impatient voice, her arms akimbo.

"Well mum," Delroy continued. "Me and him go back to the Downs. Me and Man-Man had to carry some barrels a rum to put on the ship. But me couldn't believe me eyes. Marse Kendrick come back with a bag under his arm fill with food and him pocket bulge out with money and him step into the barrel."

"Say what?" Portia knitted her brow, her gaze flew to Reverend Kersey.

"Yes mum, him tell me and Man-Man dat him going to America for a little while and him soon come back. Since the Cap'n don't want to give him passage. Him is going at all costs."

"Lawd Gawd!" Portia cried, throwing her hands to the sky. Reverend Kersey stroked her arm and made soothing sounds.

Delroy continued. "So we cover up the barrel and punch two hole in a de bottom and me roll him onto the ship."

"De ship gone?" Portia asked, her eyes wide and frightened.

"Yes mum. Him give me the key for the big house to give you and say for you to mind everything for him until him come back." A stunned Portia fell back in Reverend Kersey's arms. He fanned her with two pages from *The Gleaner.*

After Delroy left, everyone looked at each other. Kendrick's unspoken fate lingered in the air.

"I'll see what I can do when I get back." Devlin said.

"Him might not come back. Right?" Portia sniffed. "What me going to say to my mother bout her turn-color pickney?"

Nessa's eyes misted. "Poor Kendrick."

Jeremiah looked at her sharp and she gave a tremulous smile. "He doesn't deserve what is waiting for him when he lands there J, nobody does."

Jeremiah nodded in agreement. "He's a damn fool for you, just like I am." He whispered in her ear.

Portia turned to Reverend Kersey. "That's a big ole house for me one."

"That it is my dear" the Reverend agreed.

"Hold up there, Nessa, lengthen one of those dresses you have in there for me and add a train. We having a double wedding next week."

Reverend Kersey's face broke out into a wreath of happiness. He embraced her and gave her a resounding kiss. Everyone laughed and cheered.

* * *

Later in the night, Nessa and Jeremiah were all alone. "Come here," he said. He peeled away all her clothing to reveal her blossoming belly. He kneeled at her feet. His fingers shook and trailed across the width of her smooth, tender skin. The baby decided to do a somersault. Jeremiah's mouth popped open in shock. His eyes lifted in wonder to hers. He followed the movements of his baby in her stomach. He kissed each protrusion the baby's limbs made.

Tears snaked down Nessa's cheeks. She savored the moment as the most precious of her life. He lifted her to the bed, removed his clothing and they lay side-by-side. After a few seconds of adjusting his big frame on her small bed, he started to rain kisses all over her. "I don't want to hurt you."

"You can never hurt me, J."

"Nothing can ever hurt us anymore." He whispered. They made tender love until they passed out from exhaustion.

The next day, Devlin sailed away from the island with Massa George on board. Nessa and Jeremiah walked hand-in-hand along the beach barefoot. The water lapped between their toes and caressed their heels. Devlin's ship melded into the horizon.

Nessa scooped up some water in her hands and trickled it down the back of Jeremiah's neck. He yelped in mock outrage. He caught her to him and kissed her for a long time.

"I'm just so happy, J."

"Words can't tell how I feel," he murmured. They walked on in silent contentment. "Ness, let's talk about our future."

"My future is with you." She whispered.

"We know that." He said with a satisfied chuckle. I've bought a large piece of land up in the hills."

"Go on . . ." she said

"Before I knew what your ambitions were. So, I built a house on it for us to live."

"A house? Oh my God, J why didn't you tell me?"

"Well it was supposed to be a surprise for you." He shrugged. "Then things took a turn for the worse. And there was no opportunity to tell you."

"That's yesterday's spoiled milk," she said.

He grinned. "Sure would like to take you up there first before we come back and get married here."

"What is this place, J?" Her eyes were shining.

"I'll take you up there today. Man-Man is bringing around Kendrick's carriage and he'll take us."

Soon they were on their way with a picnic basket at their feet. They had left the coast a while now. Huge trees stood on both sides of the road. Their branches overlapped to form a canopy but the sun's rays still managed to filter through.

At last they reached the beginning of his land. He had carved a sign in mahogany wood and painted the grooves with white paint. The name "Brownsville" stood out in stark contrast to the black wood.

"That's the name of our land?" She clutched his arm in excitement and part laughter.

No darling it's the name of our village. Brownsville. It's going to be a village where colored people can live together in peace.

"A colored village?" She asked in disbelief. "Named Brownsville after George Browne?" She said, hooting with laughter.

"Yes," he chuckled. "Clifton and his family are moving here. Plus he has four other families who I'm going to lease property to. Two of them are tradesmen and the other two are farmers."

Pride swelled her chest. "I knew all along you had the makings of a bigwig." She pummeled his chest.

He threw his head back and laughed with unbridled joy. "There's our house," he pointed.

Her eyes opened in wonder. She looked at him and back at the house. She was silent for a long moment. Quiet tears trickled down her cheeks. He pulled her closer and kissed her lips. Salt tingled her tongue. She raised trembling fingers to wipe his wet cheek.

Nessa sat back in her seat with a contented sigh, the rumbling carriage wheels the only sounds. Jeremiah's hands rested on her belly. Her eyes traveled over the mountainous terrain and back to their house on top of the hill. A peace settled in her bones.

"This is so beautiful J . . . and so right."It reminds me of the Smokies back home," she said in a quiet tone.

"Without all that mist," he said, his voice husky.

"Oh there's some," she said with a radiant smile. "But the sun is shining, breaking through the mist."

EPILOGUE

One year later, Brownsville bustled with activity. Clifton and his workers built homes. Vendors from the nearby villages hawked their produce in the makeshift open-air market at the square. Reverend Kersey and Portia had donated a two-room school house which was almost finished. They were even sending a new missionary to run it and teach the children. On Sundays the schoolhouse would double as a church.

Jeremiah looked around his workshop in satisfaction. He had three pieces of furniture left standing in the middle of the floor. These were his gift to Devlin.

All during the week, Jeremiah had sent cart loads of furniture down to Falmouth. This was the final trip for a while. Nessa came running out of the house with a package.

"Wait," she shouted, stopping him. "I have some dresses for the store and a wedding gown for Mrs. Parson's daughter. They can't get soiled."

"Now you tell me?"

"You just have to make room that's all." She said, raising her chin and scanning the packed wagon.

Jeremiah gave a mock sigh of resignation. Man-Man perched at the reins laughed. "Put them up here beside me Mr. Mayor." He turned to Nessa, "I'll take good care of them mum."

"Thanks Man-Man. Make sure you put all the furniture in the empty room of the store. Don't leave them in the front. Ok?"

"Yes, mam." He turned to Jeremiah "Where you say all this furniture going Mr. Mayor. On a ship to foreign?"

"Yes, Man-Man, they're going to America to furnish some wealthy homes in the South."

"Oh," Man-Man said in understanding. He cracked his whip and started down the hill.

Nessa turned to Jeremiah, "Clothilde needs all that stuff to open up on Friday, because the stock is going down," she offered as explanation.

He patted her on her backside and she ran back to the house.

Any day now, Devlin, Tyanita and their baby daughter, Tyan, would arrive. Nessa and Jeremiah were preparing a Brownsville welcome. Jeremiah sniffed the air, smelling the curry goat stewing in the large vats Miss Ilda and the other women tended.

Ben and Chichi-Bud tuned up their banjos in plaintive notes. Marse Josiah's African drums grew louder, pulsating the air. Jeremiah closed the window. He remembered the signals of those talking drums, and Absalom flitted across his mind. "I didn't get kill't Abs" he muttered, his eyes misty.

In the special area of his workshop, Jeremiah glanced over at the divan and watched his wife cradle baby Etu at her breast. His heart swelled with love and elation. During their busy days, she'd find the time to share special moments with Jeremiah and their beautiful infant son. Jeremiah ached to cradle them both on his chest. But he had to make sure he did one last thing before Devlin arrived.

He turned the gleaming, mahogany chifforobe on its side and just as he did with the other pieces; he carved out the words, "H-u-s-a-n-i. 1840."

Dear Reader,

I hope you enjoyed reading Jeremiah's and Awanessa's **Escape to Falmouth** *as much as I enjoyed writing it.*

Even though the story is a work of fiction, the historical background is real, including all public figures as well as the plight of marginalized people in early 19th Century Americas.

The characters in the book are imbued with qualities so they act according to the mores of the time. Awanessa represents the Cherokee maiden, educated at a Mission school, who was strongly connected to her ancestral home. Jeremiah's character reflects the fact some slaves could read, had a trade and were extremely resourceful. The character of Massa George is a prototype of a diabolical southern gentleman planter (of which they were many). On the other hand, Devlin, Doc and his wife, and the Moravian minister represent the numerous white advocates for justice who championed the eradication of slavery throughout the South and the Caribbean.

While some plantation names, places, towns and villages are real, I've taken fictitious liberties with others. The Falmouth Foundry's main function at the time was to repair ship machinery, sugar manufacturing equipment and even manufacture bedsteads for the British army. The latter functionality made it a perfect venue for Jeremiah to practice his trade as a furniture maker. I transformed the Foundry into a bevy of activity for furniture making.

Also, in 1838, Falmouth harbor would have been the logical port of entry for Jeremiah and Awanessa to arrive in Jamaica as it could accommodate big ships like The Serpentine. I chose to have the couple enter from Montego Bay (a shallow port at the time) so they could walk the distance to Falmouth and get acclimatized with the island.

I want to thank you for embarking on this journey with me and would love to hear from you. Please email me at lena@minnapress.com with any comments and sign up for my email updates at www.escapetofalmouth.com.

Until next time,

Lena Joy Rose

Historical Background

The Cherokees

The Cherokee Indians, originally from the Southeast United States settled in Georgia, Tennessee and Western North Carolina. In 1838, they lived in cabins or homes (like any other settler) not in tepees nor were they nomadic, they were mostly farmers and dressed like white settlers. Many spoke English. Sequoyah developed a written language so they had their own newspaper. They also had their own government patterned after the United States. Some Cherokees were wealthy and even owned slaves. During the Trail of Tears, poor and wealthy alike were uprooted from their homeland and made to march on foot or by sea, thousands of miles out West to relocate in Oklahoma. However, some escaped the arduous journey and joined a group of Cherokees who were allowed to remain in the Southeast by a former treaty with the U.S. government. This group is known today as the Eastern band of Cherokees and the ones who were forced out are called the Western Band of Cherokees who still reside in the Oklahoma region.

Chief John Ross, (October 3, 1790 - August 1, 1866) was the principal chief of the Cherokees at the time of removal. He was one-eighth Cherokee and white. His wife Quatie died on the journey.

General Winfield Scott, of the US army, administered the removal of the Cherokees.

The Trail of Tears, is commonly called the "trail where we cried". Some Cherokees were sent by boat but the majority walked the thousands of miles, with little food, and with little more than the clothes on their backs from Georgia, Tennessee and Western North Carolina to Oklahoma. Many died and were buried along the trail. This was part of President Andrew Jackson's grand plan to remove all Native Americas from the Southeast.

* * *

The Seminoles

The Seminole Indians resided mostly in lower Georgia and Florida. A percentage of its members consisted of runaway slaves who sought refuge with the Seminole Indians. Many interbred, hence the term "Black Indians". Of all the tribes of the Southeast, the Seminoles gave the United States the most trouble, staging lengthy, bloody wars. The Seminoles were always on the run as they were hunted by the US army in order to relocate them out West.

John Horse. The Black Seminole warrior, John Horse's (1812-1882) accomplishments were amazing, despite his obscurity. In Florida, he rose to lead the holdouts in the country's largest slave uprising. For forty years afterwards he led his people, the African allies of Seminole Indians, on an epic quest from Florida to Mexico to secure a free homeland. Over a long life he defeated leading US generals, met two

Presidents, served as an adviser to Seminole chiefs, a Scout for the US Army, and a decorated officer in the Mexican military. He defended free black settlements on three frontiers, and was said to love children, whiskey, and his noble white horse, "American." In 1882, he fulfilled his quest for a free homeland with the final act of his life, securing a land grant in Northern Mexico. His descendants live on the land grant to this day. Source: *John Horse and the Black Seminoles:* http://www.johnhorse.com/black-seminoles/faq-black-seminoles.htm*Black

Chief Osceola was born in 1804 of mixed heritage. He led the Seminole people to resist the U.S. Government in relocating them to a territory west of the Mississippi. The Seminole Wars were the longest and costliest Indian wars as the Seminoles wouldn't give up. They fought the U.S. military and thousands of soldiers died. Osceola eventually was treacherously captured by the military under a truce flag and he died in prison.

* * *

Falmouth Jamaica

Falmouth, capital of the parish of Trelawny, Jamaica, is steeped in history. As a boom town in the early 19th Century, it was one of the busiest ports in Jamaica and had running water before New York City. The town was built in the 1700s by the great-grandfather of Elizabeth Barrett Browning – the renowned English poet of

How Do I Love Thee? Let Me Count The Ways fame. She opposed slavery and published two poems (among numerous other themes) supporting the abolitionist cause: *The Runaway Slave at Pilgrim's Point* and *A Curse for a Nation.*

Despite its famous Barrett-Browning link, Falmouth was a wealthy town with a diverse mix of people. It was populated with merchants, masons, mariners, tavern owners, and many types of tradesmen. Planters, manufacturing sugar and rum for export to England, provided the foundation for the town's thriving economy. At a time when sugar was the 'jewel in England's crown', the town had more plantations than any other on the island.

Plantations also went hand-in-hand with slavery. Falmouth was at the forefront of the emancipation struggle in Jamaica where William Knibb emerged as one the great abolitionist who advocated for freedom of the slaves. The church where he preached is restored and still an integral part of the town. Slavery formally ended in 1838 after a period of apprenticeship.

Falmouth is like a living museum of 19th Century Georgian architecture and boasts the largest collection of such structures in the Caribbean.

Some relics of the past that remain today include:

(i) **The Moulton Barrett Townhouse** where Edward Barrett the great-grandfather of Elizabeth Barrett Browning lived. He was a wealthy planter who owned many slaves and was responsible for developing the town.

(ii) **Tharp House** was owned by John Tharp, one of the island's wealthiest planters. It is now the tax collector's office.

(iii) **St. Peter's Parish Church**, built in 1796, is a landmark structure with a graveyard that holds centuries-old tombstones.

(iv) **William Knibb's Home**, otherwise known as the Baptist Manse was where the abolitionist resided.

(v) **The Courthouse** is an imposing Georgian replica of the 1817 building which was destroyed in a fire in 1926.

(vi) **The Foundry**, also known as The Dome, still stands and was a busy place during the early 19th Century mainly for manufacturing ship parts and bedsteads.

Today the streets of Falmouth are dotted with many small houses and commercial buildings echoing the Georgian structures of unique fretwork and sash or dormer windows, dating from 1790 to 1840.

REFERENCES

"A Walk Through Falmouth" *Skywritings,* p. 25-29, No. 20, Air Jamaica's Inflight magazine. January 1979. Kingston Creative Communications

"Boom Town Of The 19th Century" Pieces of the Past, Jamaica Gleaner: http://www.jamaica- gleaner. com/pages/history/story0051.htm

Fanny Kemble's Journals (1809-1893), Harvard University Press. 2000

Howe, Daniel Walker. *What Hath God Wrought: The Transformation of America 1815-1848,* Oxford University Press. P. 414. October 2007.

Jamaica National Heritage Trust: http://www.jnht. com/

Johnson, Samuel. *The Works of the English Poets from Chaucer to Cowper,* Elibron Classics, Vol. 13. 2005

"Map of Falmouth Town" http://ww.silver-sands.com/falmouth-more.html

Narrative of the Life of Frederick Douglass. Yale University Press. February 8, 2001

Private John G. Burnett's Story of the Removal of the Cherokees. Captain McClellan's Company, 2nd Regiment, 2nd Brigade, Mounted Infantry. 1838-1839

Porter, Kenneth W. *The Black Seminoles.* 1996. University Press of Florida

Quotes from Public Figures
http://www.pbs.org
http://www.ourdocuments.gov

Seminole Tribe Website: http://www.seminoletribe.com/culture/storyteller.shtml

"The Poet and the Preacher, Falmouth's Curious Heritage" *A Tapestry of Jamaica: The Best of Skywritings,* Air Jamaica's inflight magazine. Kingston. pp.115-117

Twelve Years a Slave. Dover Publications. 1970

Wallace, Anthony F.C. *The Long Bitter Trail: Andrew Jackson and the Indians.* New York. Hill and Wang. 1993.

ACKNOWLEDGEMENTS

A book may be conceived in a vacuum but it definitely needs the assistance of many hands to bring it to fruition. I want to give special thanks to my friend, Alison Woo, my very first reader, who has encouraged me throughout the process. To my son, Andre R. Claxton, who believed in the book from day one and has offered out-of-the-box insights. To my friend, Naomi Skarzinksi, how can I thank you? What an incredible support, actually reading the book twice! Her contributions have been invaluable in every facet of the book's production. I also want to thank my friend, Jenifa Laidlaw, for reading the serialized version via e-mail and offering feedback. When this book was only a tiny seed, my friend, Mary Ann Shive read it as a short story so many moons ago and encouraged me to create a larger work. I am blessed to have such wonderful and supportive people in my life.

I'm also deeply grateful to Mark Steven Weinberger, of Photocaribe (Kingston) for sharing his knowledge, enthusiasm and his contacts. And to my illustrator extraordinaire, Aeron Cargill (Kingston) you rock! You're a consummate professional. Thank you for instantly capturing my vision.

Special thanks to the following institutions/staff: (i) The National Library of Jamaica for having rare information readily available, (ii) The Charlotte-Mecklenburg research librarian in North Carolina for giving me access to a wide variety of resources, (iii) The Museum of the Cherokee Indians – an interactive, state of the art museum, and last but not least, (iv) The friendly, knowledgeable staff at the New Echota State Historic Site in Calhoun, Georgia, where I toured original, and reconstructed historic structures and learned about the lives of the Cherokee Indians.

Coming Soon!
Escape From Falmouth

1865

Each year since Emancipation, bitter disputes rage between planters and laborers. The religious revival stirs up people's emotions. Unemployment, social injustices and grievances escalate. The colony suffers from a severe drought and the government inflicts unjust taxes. It's the perfect cauldron for a rebellion – *The Morant Bay Rebellion*.

A promising young man, Etu, is the people's champion, marching through the streets whipping up fervor with eloquent speeches of human rights and justice. But Governor Eyre has other plans and is hell-bent in silencing this rabble rouser—by fair means or foul. The main leaders, Bogle and Gordon, are being hung but Etu manages to escape with his head intact. Now, the Governor enlists the Maroons to track Etu and bring him back for a reckoning. Meanwhile, Etu's father, Jeremiah, launches a desperate search for his son and must find a way to spirit him far away.

Escape from Falmouth, a tale of struggle and redemption, straddles two different worlds: Rebellious Jamaica and Reconstruction America where the Civil War has just ended. But Etu's troubles have only just begun. Did he jump from the proverbial frying pan into a raging fire?

8146214R0

Made in the USA
Lexington, KY
10 January 2011